THE CONDEMNED

Novelization by **ROB HEDDEN**
Story by **ROB HEDDEN**
& ANDY HEDDEN and **SCOTT WIPER**
Screenplay by **SCOTT WIPER**
and **ROB HEDDEN**

POCKET BOOKS
New York   London   Toronto   Sydney

Pocket Books
A Division of Simon & Schuster, Inc.
1230 Avenue of the Americas
New York, NY 10020

This book is a work of fiction. Names, characters, places, and incidents either are products of the author's imagination or are used fictitiously. Any resemblance to actual events or locales or persons, living or dead, is entirely coincidental.

First Pocket Books paperback edition April 2007

POCKET and colophon are registered trademarks of Simon & Schuster, Inc.

For information about special discounts for bulk purchases, please contact Simon & Schuster Special Sales at 1-800-456-6798 or business@simonandschuster.com

Manufactured in the United States of America

10 9 8 7 6 5 4 3 2 1

ISBN-13: 978-1-4165-4803-4
ISBN-10: 1-4165-4803-3

The mud-crusted SUV had already seen six countries in fewer than three days, with every border the gateway into a new version of hell. So far its occupants had made stops in Bulgaria, Romania, Hungary, Slovakia, Poland, and Lithuania, in that order. They had just entered the outskirts of Belarus, and their particular route brought the same dismal Eastern European scenery. Smoke-spewing factories. Potholed streets with shattered storefront windows. Cheap Russian sedans, stripped and rotting. It looked like a war zone, which certainly factored in, but the enemy was mostly poverty.

So far they had not found what they were looking for. Their employer was very particular. He would settle for only the worst.

The black SUV passed a decrepit housing project with a canine carcass on the side of the road. It had likely starved to death. The man riding shotgun lifted his high-definition video camera and grabbed a shot of the dog. He didn't bother to remove his sunglasses as he peered through his viewfinder.

"How much farther?" asked the driver as he finished

off a cold fast-food burger that had been sitting on the dash. The vehicle was littered with wrappers spanning the seventy-two hours they had been on the road. He also wore sunglasses, a necessity. The sun was blazing hot with heat waves rippling off the battered road.

The driver's name was James, but everybody called him the "Scout." He had earned his nickname the hard way. In his late thirties, the Scout was an American who had worked many freelance jobs over the last two decades. Most of them involved tracking down hard-to-find items, which had taken him all over the world. The procurement of these curios sometimes involved bending and occasionally breaking the law. Lately, the objects he sought were of the human variety. In a way, he was like a baseball scout looking for the next Babe Ruth, only baseball was a much tamer game than the competition his employer was devising.

The cameraman grabbed one of several maps crammed into the door pocket and unfolded it. His finger traced a lone road that cut through an empty brown patch and passed through a tiny town called Polatsk. One inch later, his dirty fingernail arrived at an intersection.

"Take a left in about ten klicks."

The cameraman went by the name of Donaldson. He was Australian, in his late twenties, also a free-lancer. Up until now, Donaldson had mainly worked shooting news footage for Australian television. The thought of trekking through the worst parts of Eastern Europe held little appeal, but there was a big carrot dangling if his footage was good.

The Scout wadded his burger wrapper and attempted to dial in some music. Every station brought scratchy Belarusian music with vaguely Russian lyrics. Finally he landed on an English-language oldies station playing Aretha Franklin's "Chain of Fools." It gave them a moment of respite, though the fatigue, boredom, and depressing landscape could not be blotted out.

Fifteen minutes later, they passed through the deteriorating town of Polatsk, made the left turn, and entered a barren no-man's-land. A stone fortress appeared through their streaked windshield like a mirage in the dust and heat. The foreboding compound, lined with two layers of razor wire and gun turrets, was more than enough to expel their weariness.

The Scout wordlessly handed paperwork to the machine gun–armed guard manning the entrance. The humorless guard, of Russian descent, looked it over carefully. He eyed the satellite dish attached to the roof of their SUV but said nothing, handing back the paperwork as he motioned to his comrades. The massive arched gate swung open. The Scout drove in, watching the gates close behind him in his rearview. Donaldson was already videotaping.

"Save it for the audition," advised the Scout.

"Breckel wanted B roll if we end up buying this guy, mate."

He continued to shoot.

They parked in the dirt beside the rock walls that housed the prisoners. The Scout climbed out and stretched his back, his spine cracking. They had reached their final destination, and it wasn't pretty. The aroma of death was palpable. The sooner they finished their business here, the better.

Two more guards appeared and opened a thick steel gate in the wall of the fortress, ushering the visitors inside. As ominous as the exterior was, the prison's belly was a hellhole not fit for animals, much less people. It smelled of sweat, defecation, and decomposition. Red-brown bloodstains blotted the concrete floor. Gaunt, shadowy faces gazed back through rusty steel-meshed cages that functioned as cells. Survival of the fittest was only one criterion for staying alive in here.

A large, bearded Belarusian in a khaki military uniform with red lapels approached the Scout, flanked by two more guards. He was the warden. The official smiled broadly as he offered his handshake. The Scout sensed he was about as honest as a nine-dollar bill, which confirmed his research. He'd also heard that the warden ruled his prison with an iron fist. The warm grin didn't fool him—this was a man who personally shot misbehaving prisoners. If the deal soured, both he and Donaldson would end up spending the rest of their days inside this shithouse, if they lived at all.

Donaldson lifted his camera to grab a shot of the warden. A guard instantly shoved his lens down. Words were exchanged that Donaldson didn't understand, but the Scout did. He was fluent in Russian, among several other languages.

"No shots of the warden," he sternly told Donaldson, apologizing to his host in his native tongue.

The warden's gracious smile returned, along with a

steely gaze as he briskly strode away. The Scout motioned for Donaldson to follow.

The group scaled a wooden ladder to a second-floor balcony that overlooked the cells. Donaldson tapped the Scout on his shoulder, motioning at the cells. He nodded back his approval and Donaldson began to videotape them, quickly falling behind the group. When he caught up, the procession was passing into the warden's cluttered office, its cement walls tacked with Russian military decorations. Donaldson noticed an antique mahogany liquor cabinet in the corner and other expensive furniture. An original Chagall hung opposite his desk. Since Belarusian wardens generally were not well paid, their host evidently had plenty of side deals going. Donaldson resisted the urge to videotape anything in here.

The group breezed through another door that led to a caged balcony overlooking the prison yard.

The Scout followed the warden's gaze downward.

There were no tables, chairs, or recreational equipment, just broiling concrete. And one man, if you could call him that. More like a beast.

He's as big as a horse, thought the Scout, though he said nothing out loud. It would be foolish to tip his hand this early. Still, it was hard to hide his excitement. The prisoner, Petr Raudsep, had muscles befitting a lion and was pouring with sweat as he ate stale bread and gray slop from a wooden bowl. His shaved head was lumpy and oblong. His heavily scarred face was as pretty as a piece of roadkill.

The Scout had already seen a mug shot of Petr

Raudsep and his impressive rap sheet. Raudsep was one hundred percent Russian and two hundred percent mean. In his thirty years on the planet, the giant had managed to kill fifteen men, five of them right here in this prison, and had also dabbled in rape. Most of the time he had murdered with his bare hands. Raudsep was a threat to the prison population at large, hence his isolation in the yard. He was currently on death row.

On paper, the Russian had looked great. Raudsep was a magnificent specimen in the flesh as well. The Scout's hopes were nearly confirmed.

The final decision, as always, would be based on the audition.

"Looks good. Big. Can he fight?" he asked in fluent Russian.

The warden grinned widely. He banged his baton on the metal cage. "Bring them in!" he bellowed in Russian.

A steel mesh door opened in the prison yard. Three prisoners marched onto the concrete, all massive Eastern Europeans. The door slammed shut and was bolted behind them. Each had the requisite muscles, body ink, and scars. All were murderers who enjoyed their vocation. The Russian had slighted them in various ways during their incarceration, which accounted for some of their scars. They were especially hungry to shed his blood and add a big new stain to the yard.

The Scout's eyebrows rose. Individually, the convicts were formidable competition for Raudsep, but all three combined? If he survived this, they had their man.

"Start shooting," he told Donaldson.

Donaldson raised his HD camera and swung up the twelve-inch antenna attached to it. The Scout lifted his digital phone and speed-dialed a number.

"It's the Scout. We're transmitting."

The Russian rose to his feet. The behemoth looked at least seven feet standing, easily a half foot taller than his competition, all of whom were massive in their own right. They surrounded him like Indians circling a wagon. He would need eyes in the back of his bald head to fend off his attackers.

Donaldson zoomed in as the first aggressor lunged from behind. For such a goliath, the Russian spun with surprising dexterity, but it wasn't quick enough to avoid a headlock. His attacker instantly gouged his eyes with his dirty, gnarled fingers, but this only angered the beast. The Russian hooked his gorillalike arm between the convict's legs, hoisted him, and threw him against the prison wall like a sack of fertilizer. Bones audibly crunched as he collapsed on the ground, unconscious.

He would end up being the luckiest of the three.

The second and third prisoners attacked simultaneously, drilling Raudsep with sledgehammerlike punches. The smaller of the two, who was still linebacker big, shoved his knee into the bottom of the Russian's chin. Blood spewed from his mouth like water from a garden hose. The Russian had bit off the end of his tongue.

The Scout's face sank. He knew that Ian Breckel, his employer, needed a star, someone who could fend off ten attackers, let alone three. The audition was shaping up to be another rejection. Even worse, the warden wouldn't be happy if they decided to back out of the deal. He might take the money anyway and kill them both.

The Russian spit out the bloody chunk of flesh and shoved his gorillalike arm between the linebacker's legs. Far from defeated, Raudsep effortlessly hoisted him, gripped him in a headlock, and snapped his neck like it was a twig. The Russian flung the dead body on top of his first victim as if he were stacking kindling and then turned his attention to the final survivor, who had been pummeling him the entire time. The brute was nearly his size, but his body language was now on the defensive as the Russian lunged into him.

While revolted by the brutality, the Scout was nonetheless smiling. He had done his homework to find this animal, and he had struck gold. He imagined his boss's expression on the other side of the video transmission. How could the man not be pleased? Keeping Ian Breckel happy was a very good thing. The gig was bizarre, to be sure, but the pay was top dollar. If Breckel's new venture took off, the Scout would be making a lot of money in commission.

Donaldson, like many cameramen, was distancing himself from the reality through his viewfinder, which helped fictionalize what he was seeing. It was all about the framing, when to push in, what to push in on, and not about the content. He was thrilled that he had caught the blood spraying from the Russian's mouth in all its backlit glory. It was a beautiful shot by any cinematographer's yardstick, even more so because it hadn't been staged.

The sick barbarity of what he had deftly captured wouldn't hit him until a day later, when he was back home in Melbourne tucking in his eighteen-month-old daughter. Up until that moment, Donaldson had been more than ready to accept a position as a live cameraman on Ian Breckel's new reality show, which paid extremely well and was being produced on a lush tropical island. But the graphic images of the Russian's bare-handed killing began to haunt him. The prison in Belarus was simply a warm-up for the job to come. He would not be documenting the war in Iraq or the violence of Hezbollah for Australian television. This killing would be in the name of entertainment. At home, cradling his innocent daughter, he felt like he was selling his soul.

The fight continued in the prison yard, though annihilation would be a better description. The Russian charged his final adversary like a runaway train plowing into a truck. Both men went down hard with Raudsep on top. His anvillike fists rammed the convict like dual jackhammers, turning the man's face into ground meat.

Thousands of miles away, the battle was being splashed across a flat-panel screen. The colors seemed too vivid, a heightened reality. The image suddenly went grainy, and then choppy. It disappeared for a few seconds and then returned in all its vividness.

Ian Breckel watched the live feed on one of the

many large displays that surrounded him. He was sitting in a specially made leather lounge chair, comfortably dressed in jeans and a crisp white cotton shirt with the sleeves rolled up, no socks under his tan sneakers. A Rolex worth fifteen grand adorned his right wrist, though he rarely checked the time—he had a staff that did that for him.

Contrary to the Scout's assumption, Breckel wasn't smiling, or frowning for that matter. His reaction was intensely analytical, as if he were a producer auditioning his next star.

Which, of course, he was.

Ian Breckel's current surroundings were reminiscent of a state-of-the-art MASH tent. Aluminum struts and heavy-duty green canvas formed the walls, with the interior housing a myriad of flat-panel screens, computerized editing bays, and top-end audio-visual equipment. Breckel had a Bluetooth headset in one ear, which was a fashion statement as much as a practical accessory.

Surrounded by his high-priced toys and beck-and-call underlings, Ian Breckel was clearly in his element. Like the Belarusian warden, he was the king of his domain, but the comparison ended there. A Los Angeles native with sandy hair, blue eyes, and a Malibu tan, Breckel carried himself like the hip CEO of a Fortune 500 company. He had made millions producing reality television shows.

At thirty-five, Breckel was handsome and charismatic enough to attract any woman he desired, even without his wealth. He had already been married three times and divorced three times, usually within a year. Wives were fun but bad financial investments, like cars. While diverting at the beginning, they depreciated almost immediately, required constant maintenance, and broke down if you drove them hard, which he always did. He also became bored easily and essentially traded in his wives for newer models, literally—one was on the cover of *Sports Illustrated*—though the early termination penalties had taught him never to marry again. Breckel looked at every lemon for its juice and hardly considered them failures—his marriages spawned a highly successful reality show called *Lease a Wife*.

What made him stand out was his innovation. A Stanford graduate with an MBA in business, he had begun his career as an apprentice on a controversial talk show. It was Ian Breckel who came up with the idea to pit husbands against cheating wives and to reunite abuse victims with their abusers. He soon pitched a show to a cable network that put six strangers under one roof and documented their every move. The executives passed on the idea, saying that no one would watch it. Three months later, a nearly identical show popped up on the same network and became a national phenomenon.

Rather than offering a diatribe for stealing his idea, Breckel wrote the network a congratulatory letter. He actually admired the theft. In their shoes, he would have done the same thing. The network execs liked the young Turk's attitude and hired him to "write" for the show, which was supposed to be unscripted. Breckel

11

introduced inner conflicts and unsavory backstories that sent the ratings sky-high. He was quickly given a commitment to create his own show, and he never looked back. Ian Breckel knew what most of America wanted to see, and he delivered it. He was the P. T. Barnum of reality television.

The fight continued on the plasma. Raudsep was beating his unconscious opponent to death and no one was intervening. The Russian rose to his feet and let his boots finish the job, ramming his heel over and over into the lifeless convict's face. Breckel viewed it dispassionately. It was as if he were watching a fictional network TV drama. He lifted his remote and brought up a mug shot of the Russian on an adjacent monitor. Petr Raudsep's rap sheet scrolled down on yet another, displaying his litany of transgressions against humanity. The final note read: *Awaiting execution by lethal injection.*

Breckel took a final look at the Russian on the screen as he crushed his opponent's face with his boot, then spoke into his headset. "I want him."

The Scout smiled. "You got it, Breck."

Five minutes later, the Scout set a duffel bag containing twenty thousand euros onto the warden's desk. The big Belarusian carefully counted it and shook the Scout's hand with a crooked grin.

Breckel's tenth and final contestant had just been purchased.

2

The huge control room tent was bustling with energy. A dozen technicians were manning several editing bays under a big plasma display suspended overhead. The big screen was filled with ten boxes reminiscent of *Hollywood Squares*. Each box contained a mug shot. Seven men and two women were on display, with one box still empty. Along with their names, flags sat beneath their faces denoting each criminal's nationality, not unlike the Olympics.

The Russian's face abruptly filled the empty space, rounding out Breckel's "cast." There was an Arab al-Qaeda terrorist. A middle-aged Nazi. A black man with dreadlocks. Two Mexicans, a male and a female. A wiry Japanese martial arts expert. An incredibly alluring young black woman. An Italian with a ponytail. An Englishman with a psychopath's eyes.

Like Raudsep, all of them had been carefully handpicked. They were the most ruthless killers on the planet.

Breckel admired his contestants, smiling for the first time as Julie walked up behind him.

"Hey, babe. Good-looking cast, don't you think?"

"You're amazing." She smiled, rubbing his shoulders. "I didn't think you could pull this off."

Julie had a distinctive British accent that made her even sexier.

"You doubted me?"

"I didn't think anyone could," she defended. "It was impossible to imagine."

"Well, babe, that's what I do. I imagine the impossible and make it happen."

"Maybe that's why I keep you around." She grinned, letting her long blonde hair spill onto her shoulders.

Julie Weston was Breckel's latest. She had all the prerequisites for a long relationship, which to him meant a year. High cheekbones. Thick lips. Hotel-room eyes. With a body to match. Not only that, Julie was intelligent, a quality he enjoyed in a woman . . . just as long as they were on the same page.

He rose from his leather lounger and kissed her. The exhilaration of his enterprise had raised his testosterone, but the sex would have to wait. He observed his dedicated crew as they made his vision come to life. Graphics were spinning on one display, promos were being cut on another, blogs were being tracked and web ads placed.

"How are we coming with promos two and three?" chirped Bella, who was in charge of the editors and graphics team. Bella was twenty-two, dressed in funky camos out of a Milan boutique and hip black-framed glasses that matched the color of her short-cropped hair.

"We just put 'em to bed," answered a techie on her team.

Breckel circled the room, kicking into gear. The sex wouldn't have to wait. This *was* the sex.

"Talk to me, Bella."

"New thirty-second spot's ready to roll," she answered in a caffeinated voice, "along with the YouTube and MySpace promos."

"That's what I wanted to hear." He glanced at the Russian's image. "Cut in a few images of our new guy. His mug is priceless."

"You got it, Breck."

Breckel moved to a team exclusively working on the internet.

"Eddie C, how we tracking?"

"We're hot," answered Eddie, a young redheaded dude with a month-old goatee that was just now starting to show.

"How hot?"

"White-hot. I got the A team blitzing chat rooms and blogs, B team's buyin' ads 'n' placing the spots. Site's gettin' seven hundred hits a minute. Awareness on porn and fight blogs is ninety-two percent," he said with a twenty-year-old's energy.

Eddie C, which stood for Carson, was Breckel's web guru. A former hacker who avoided jail because he was a minor at the time, Eddie C knew the Internet highway like a Porsche knew the Autobahn.

"Bella has a new thirty," said Breckel, "and I want that spot running across every sex, fight, and gamer site within the hour. Hit the gamers hard."

"Done."

Eddie spun around and let his fingers do the talking. Breckel marched past him, pumping with adrenaline and never losing stride. He addressed his troops like a general preparing for war.

"Push it, people—push it! Somewhere, someone on this planet does not know about this show. Asia, Africa, Antarctica, there's a fucking Eskimo sitting in his igloo who does not know we go live in twenty-two hours. Find 'm. Get to them."

He spun back to Eddie C. "Eddie, ninety-two? I want *one hundred*. One hundred percent awareness across the Internet. You got it?"

"Got it."

Eddie C kept typing, not skipping a beat. He had been working twenty-one hours straight, just like everyone else inside these hot canvas walls.

Breckel strode up to a technician who was downing a foam cup of coffee, obviously having trouble staying awake. He wanted to slap the kid, but he knew that pushing his minions too hard would be counterproductive.

"C'mon, wakey, wakey, soldier!" he yelled in a joking tone. "It's battle time, not nap time!" He squeezed the kid's shoulders and roused him playfully, but firmly enough to convey his message: *I won't tolerate anything less than total commitment.*

"Bella, stay on them," he delegated as he marched toward the door. "Tell your people for every million viewers we get beyond our target, everyone gets a bonus of ten grand."

The room immediately perked up. Breckel's crew was young and hungry. He took in their eager faces as he left the control room tent. Money always talked louder than anything.

Julie watched him go with a look of admiration, as well as concern. She had known Ian Breckel for only six months, and naturally he had wowed her. A confident woman herself, his intellect and power turned her on more than his wealth. She had grown up in the tony Kensington neighborhood of London with servants and a Cambridge education under her designer belt and tropical wardrobe. Money was something she already had, along with a promising career as a fashion designer. What she didn't have was excitement in her life, at least not until Ian had turned up at a London fashion show. When they met, he told her he was there to see the clothes, but she knew better. Men loved models and she called him on it. "Guilty as charged," he confessed instead of denying it. A few glasses of champagne later and she'd given him her number. It had not been hard to fall in love with him.

He had told her about his new project called *The Condemned* and invited her to consult on the contestants' wardrobe. At its root, the idea had seemed crazy, but the way he'd pitched it made it sound like cutting-edge entertainment and beyond exciting. There was no doubting it was an outrageous concept, but he promised he would be handling it tastefully. *It's all in the execution*, he had told her.

Standing in the room, with real faces up on the

screen, the reality began to sink in. Sure, these were murderers already condemned to death, but they were going to brutally fight and possibly kill each other. Ian couldn't have been more excited about it, which made her feel uneasy.

Breckel exited his control center into a makeshift village consisting of tents, canopy shelters, multiple satellite dishes, and camouflaged vehicles. The entire compound was surrounded by a ten-foot fence topped with razor wire. Befitting his militarylike speech, it was more like a wartime command post than a video production center.

Not so ironically, their present location had a history of warfare. In yet another shady side deal, Breckel had leased the abandoned island off the coast of New Guinea from corrupt officials running Papua. The island had served as a Japanese command post during World War II. The American military had fought here before, specifically the Third Battalion, 124th Infantry, and its victims were posthumously cited for outstanding performance of duty. The ghosts of many soldiers on both sides supposedly haunted the lush tropical island, at least according to Breckel's press releases, though he carefully kept its exact location a secret. Furthermore, they were smack-dab in the middle of Oceania, miles from intervention should anyone wish to prematurely shut down his production.

The compound was built around a rickety weather tower left over from the war, which served Breckel in much the same way. The latest weather-tracking equipment and satellite communications had been installed, along with a qualified tech to run them. The structure poked above the thick rain forest, allowing a view of the island in all directions.

Breckel strutted past a group of audiovisual techs beneath the tower setting up camera rigs as if they were prepping for a rock concert. There were more than a hundred cameras on view, in all shapes and sizes. Many were camouflaged with sticks and leaves. A jeep drove off with a pile of them, security guards allowing it through a gate into the jungle. Everything beyond the razor wire was known as the "playing field."

Breckel gave them a cursory glance, knowing better than to micromanage. He had his right-hand man for that, Lee Goldman. Goldman was his longtime technical director and camera whiz extraordinaire. His relationship with Goldy had lasted longer than all three of his marriages combined. Goldy liked to complain, but he always got the shot.

"Okay, okay, *Rochi?* Were you the one who left this orange here by the HVX200? This jungle's got ants the size of Cadillacs, you want them crawling all over our equipment? No more oranges out here, man, that's it with the oranges!"

Goldman was stressed, as usual. Anxiety was his middle name. Breckel secretly believed he thrived on it—Goldy was actually more neurotic when he was bored. Still hanging on to his thirties, Goldman had a puffy face, hefty luggage under his eyes, and a rapidly spreading bald spot. He hadn't changed his T-shirt in days, which was white with long red sleeves like a baseball player would wear. Goldman didn't play baseball, or any sport. He had no time for exercise, even when he did have time. He didn't enjoy doing anything except playing with cameras and video switchers.

Breckel stepped into Goldman's view.

"Oh, hey, pal," sighed Goldman, walking toward one of the satellite dishes. Breckel smiled and followed, waiting for the inevitable. He didn't have to wait long.

"Just so you know . . . um, we're fucked," he declared. "Oh, yeah, we're screwed. This show ain't happening."

Breckel said nothing, remaining cucumber cool as Goldman marched up to a heavyset kid slowly working on the big dish with his iPod blasting.

"*Rochi, Rochi!* Out! Music out! No more music! Work on satellite, right? Told you that an hour and a half ago!"

Goldman pulled out an amber-tinted prescription bottle and popped a pill dry.

"Want some water with that?" Breckel calmly offered.

"Nope."

"Red Bull?" He grinned. Goldy was already as wired as a triple espresso.

"No thanks," he retorted. "I don't have time for water, I don't have time for Red Bull, I don't have time to piss or take a dump. Breck, here's the hard truth, okay? This show is not going off. Trust me, I know. Remember that event I used to do? The small one where they throw the football around, kick field goals?"

"The Super Bowl."

"Right. Did that twice for ABC. What's the other one where they kick the soccer ball that I did?"

"World Cup," he answered, continuing to play along.

"That's right. Did that twice for ESPN. Then there was that lil' small bicycle race that goes for twenty-four days called the Tour de France that I did, right? So we got the Super Bowl, World Cup, Tour de France—I've done 'em all. All at least a forty-cam operation, so you'd think I know a thing or two about live TV, right?" He paused dramatically, as serious as a heart attack. "News flash: we're fucked."

Breckel knew this was the most ambitious project he had ever created. It was rife with possibilities for failure. Goldy had given him a speech like this before, but never quite as adamantly. The show *would* go on, but it would require Goldman's expertise to pull it off. He needed to keep him on board.

"Goldy, c'mon. Talk to me," he said, revealing just the right amount of concern. "Where are we?"

"Where are we? I've got eighty-seven cluster cams ready and rigged. I got a hundred and forty-seven solos all with built-in mikes. Okay? I got sixty, seventy all ready to go out in the field. So all together there are four hundred lenses, right? But there are dead spots all over the island. I don't have enough time, I don't have enough equipment, I don't have enough personnel. This show is not going to come off." He was practically foaming at the mouth.

Breckel had heard enough to know that they would

be okay. Four hundred angles, plus a live unit he had neglected to mention, would more than suffice if the cameras were placed strategically. And they would be, with Goldy's expertise.

"We're at war, Goldy. You have to improvise, overcome, adapt."

"This is not war, Breck, this is *television*," he shot back. "It's much more complicated. I do not have enough hardware, and we, in case you haven't noticed, are in the middle of nowhere. I mean, would you like me to do the ten-thousand-mile breaststroke to Radio-Shack? You know I'll do it. I'll do it because I love you, right?"

A satellite dish being adjusted by two techs emitted a hugh spark. Goldman reacted as if the shock had gone up his own spine.

"Hey! Mango! Do not touch the wiring! What did I say before? I told you an hour ago, do NOT touch. Thank you!"

They stared back, understanding not a word.

Goldman turned to Breckel, leveling a finger at his crew like a prosecutor pointing at defendants on trial.

"Here's the really cool thing—I got these all-stars. It's really great because between the lot of them, they all speak like three words of English. So I'm supposed to run an operation that is basically bigger than Farm Aid meets Live Aid and I'm supposed to do it in sign language? Are you out of your mind? Do I look like Quincy Jones?"

Breckel paused long enough to make sure Goldman had finished ranting.

"Do you know why it's going to work out?" he said with enough of a smile to really piss Goldman off. If there was one thing the man hated, it was a positive attitude.

"Why?" he replied, though he really wanted to say: *Fuck you, Breck, you just don't get it.*

"Because you're the best."

He opened his mouth again and then slowly shut it. Breckel had him. He *was* the best. Problems aside, Goldman knew *The Condemned* was going to turn out like no other reality show ever produced.

3

"Donna Sereno just arrived."

It was Julie. Streaks of sunlight through the palms were lighting up her long blonde locks. Once again, Breckel thought of having his way with her, but it would have to wait.

"She knows the score?"

Julie nodded.

There had been definite ground rules in allowing one of network television's top journalists to visit the island. He had taken precautions to keep their location a mystery, but if she still somehow found out, she was not allowed to divulge it under any circumstances. Sereno also had to promise to make it her lead story with round-the-clock promos in exchange for her exclusive interview with him.

"Tomorrow morning, you're her top story," Julie said. "But be ready, she's a tough cookie."

Julie knew of her toughness by reputation; their brief meeting when the reporter arrived via Ian's private helicopter confirmed it. Donna Sereno was no celebrity ass kisser. She was as thick-skinned as any journalist out there. She'd interviewed presidents, world leaders, and billionaire CEOs, never shying away from the tough questions. While she had agreed to the conditions of the interview, Sereno told Julie she would pull no punches during the interview. If Ian Breckel thought he could intimidate her, or charm her, for that matter, he was in for a very big surprise.

Breckel didn't need Julie to tell him this. As always, he had done his homework. Tough questions were exactly what he wanted. Even condemnation. The more controversy, the better.

"She's the big dog," he answered. "If you want the big press, you have to go to the big dog. How do I look?"

Julie ran her hand through his hair, making it perfect.

"I'd do ya," she joked.

"Yeah, but how do I look?" He smirked, then pulled her close and kissed her. She fully returned it, but in truth, sex was not on her mind right now. The upcoming events still made her uneasy.

Ever the showman, Breckel had a makeup artist standing by to make him look perfect for the interview camera. Sweat would look great on his contestants but not on him. He needed to project total confidence.

He had a tent specially set up for Donna Sereno, complete with a gourmet champagne brunch. Per his instructions, Julie had taken her there to wait for him. After changing into a stylish Tommy Bahama silk shirt, he strolled over to greet her.

"Donna, it's a pleasure," Breckel said graciously as he entered the tent.

Breckel was so good at handling journalists that to an untrained eye it was impossible to tell if he really meant it. Donna Sereno's eyes, however, were as trained as Walter Cronkite's. His "pleasure" was not in meeting her but in the publicity this would bring him.

"The pleasure is all mine," she replied, matching his charm to the ounce. Sereno was wearing a cobalt blue silk jacket that was too warm for the tropics but would look great on television. Its color matched her eyes.

"How was your flight?" he asked with concern. Of course he didn't care. She had shown up, which is all that mattered.

"Awful. My crew and I were blindfolded the entire time. Made it a tad difficult to do my crosswords."

"Yeah, sorry about that," he lied. "My whereabouts must remain a mystery, hope you understand."

"Anything for an exclusive," she said self-deprecatingly.

This was partly true, though she would have come with other journalists if necessary. Sereno's agenda was bigger than an exposé on Ian Breckel. It was about reality programming as a whole and the extremes to which it had gone.

Ian Breckel had a reputation for making squirm television, producing reality shows that were not for the faint of heart. He had arguably crossed the moral line with many of them already, though rumors put *The Condemned* in a whole new league. He'd already tried to televise prison executions live on pay-per-view and had been shot down by the FCC. If the promos were true, Breckel was likely breaking international laws with this one, though good lawyers could not be underestimated. By the time the dust settled, he would have collected millions in profit. For these reasons, keeping his location a mystery made total sense.

"Would you like to join me in some champagne?" he offered.

"Of course."

He poured for both of them.

"Here's to entertainment," he said, toasting her.

Neither drank more than three sips before the interview began. Both wanted to be at their sharpest.

"You've left Hollywood. Why?"

One camera was poised on Breckel, another on Sereno for her reactions. He had insisted on using bounce lights to soften his face, having once suffered a hatchet job by reporters who used harsh lighting to make him look unpleasant.

"I want to push the envelope, Donna. I can't do that in Hollywood, New York, Canada, even Europe. Everywhere I produce a show, I'm shackled by rules, regulations, the FCC, gutless executives. I've come to a place where nobody can tell me what I can or can't do."

Julie watched the interview from the sidelines, marveling at his poise and conviction. He wasn't acting. He truly believed this. And it was hard not to appreciate his rebellious attitude. She hated the crap on television. It was all derivative, unoriginal pabulum. No wonder people were abandoning it for entertainment on the Internet and elsewhere.

"Without a major network behind you, how do you plan to broadcast your show?" asked Sereno.

"The Internet. I'm going live across the world wide web, direct to my audience. Anyone with a computer and a credit card can watch my next show—live, uncensored, uncut."

"Really. Tell us about *The Condemned.*"

"I've pulled ten contestants from third-world prisons. Each was on death row. I will free one of them. You see, tomorrow, I'm bringing them here, to this island, where they will have a fighting chance at a new life. A fight to the death. The winner gets a suitcase full of cash and a ride to any port in Southeast Asia. Set free."

Sereno stared at him. She'd heard about the recruitment of ten convicts and knew they would be fighting each other. But to the death? With the winner being set free on society?

Julie's stomach began to churn. Ian had also told her there would be fighting, but this was the first she'd heard about the prisoners being required to kill each other, as well as the winner getting to go free.

"One lives, nine die?" Sereno said incredulously. "You're airing a live snuff film?"

Breckel was thrilled with her judgmental reaction. You couldn't ask for better advertising.

"No, no. Look, Donna, these contestants are already dead. Condemned. I'm allowing one to live. Is that so wrong?"

"It's immoral and illegal," she said with no hesitation. "What are you charging for this live horror film?"

"Forty-nine ninety-five. Unlimited access to the site. And my attorneys will have strong opinions about its legality."

"Why do this? What's driving you?"

Her tone made her sound like she was interviewing a serial killer, which was also fine with him. He'd been in the hot seat before. Controversy meant more subscribers.

"When my first show premiered on network TV, do you remember what the Hollywood trades called me?"

" 'A soulless hack,' " Sereno answered instantly. " 'The Town's Most Affluent Failure.' The *Times* called you the Antichrist. The *Reporter* said—"

"Right, right, you get my point." Breckel cut her off. Her maligning diatribe was beginning to annoy him, but it was worth it. Their site hits would skyrocket once this aired. He figured she was smart enough to know her ratings would soar, too, once the word got out.

The truth was that Donna Sereno was repulsed. Her bosses had sent her there to get a juicy story, which was par for the course. But she was more than a top-notch journalist. She was the mother of two and an ethical human being. Her interview notes fell to the ground.

"You're a multimillionaire who maybe will become a billionaire producing *murder*. Have you no shame at all?"

He forced a smile, keeping his eye on the prize. "I make shows people like to watch."

"Okay, here's a question I'm sure all my viewers will

have running through their minds: When you look at yourself in the mirror, what do you see?"

Her voice had risen in pitch, full of disgust. He had plenty more to tell her about *The Condemned*, titillating facts about the Mexican married couple who were competing against each other and the German they called the Nazi and the psycho Englishman who raped, murdered, and mutilated dozens before being caught, but his trademark composure began to flag.

"You know, I'm tired of being judged and shit on by critics and journalists like you. I'm done with Hollywood. I'm going straight to my audience, worldwide and live, and my numbers will demolish EVERY SHOW and EVERY NETWORK this year. Mark my words."

Sereno could see that she was getting to him.

"And you seriously believe that justifies what you're doing?"

The interview went on like that for another ten minutes, rapidly becoming contentious. He finally stood and yanked off his lapel microphone.

"I'm done," he said with a frosty smile. "A pleasure working with you." He marched from the tent.

Donna Sereno had served her purpose. He was happy to be the bad boy of television—and now the Internet—if it brought in the highest number of viewers.

Julie stood frozen. She had just seen a side of Ian that he had carefully kept hidden from her. Losing one's composure was to be expected of all powerful men, and he was only human. It was also possible he was putting on a show for the cameras . . . but his self-confidence had seemed more like an ego run amok.

She and Sereno exchanged an uncomfortable glance.

"I'm sorry. He's under a lot of stress," Julie apologized.

Sereno studied her. "Did you know what he was going to do here?"

There was no simple answer. She loved Ian. She also believed in capital punishment. These convicts had killed, raped, ruined many lives. They had all been sentenced to death. They deserved to die. In her home country of England, public executions had once been commonplace. Ian *was* giving people what they wanted to see. But the interview had nonetheless shed an ugly new light on his exploitation of it.

Julie said nothing and left the tent.

Outside the control room tent, Breckel's perturbation was about to get some new fuel.

"Umm . . . Breck, we have a problem," Bella said, spotting him. She and Eddie C had just stepped out to find him.

"I like to think of it more as a challenge," chimed in Eddie.

Breckel looked at both of them, in no mood to hear bad news.

Bella cleared her throat and lowered her voice. "We just lost one of our headliners."

He exploded. "What happened?"

Breckel stormed toward the control room without waiting for an answer, his underlings in tow.

"The terrorist dude from the Moroccan prison landed ten minutes ago at the mainland airfield," rattled off Eddie. "He freaked out—"

"—In full chains, he starts choking a guard to death," finished Bella, talking even faster.

"The other guards start beatin' his ass, hittin'm, givin'm the whole Rodney King routine but—"

"But *what?*" interrupted Breckel. He didn't want the novel, he wanted the log line.

"They couldn't stop him," answered Bella.

Eddie C cleared his throat. "They kinda opened fire on the guy."

"Shot him in the head," she finished. "He's dead."

Breckel stared at them. They had absolutely nothing to do with what happened, but he wanted to take it out on somebody. Bella and Eddie C were loyal members of his team—he'd plucked Bella right out of USC as an apprentice. She had given all the right answers during her interview. Bella was high energy. Loved reality television. Thought what was currently on TV was way too tame. She had had no qualms whatsoever about *The Condemned*. Eddie felt likewise, though his degree came from the University of Hard Knocks. They didn't teach Eddie C's brand of computer science in any school. Breckel had found him via an attorney friend who had represented Eddie as a juvenile hacker. *This kid knows more about the web than the guys who invented it*, his friend had said. Like his technical director Goldman, Breckel needed both of them to turn his dream into reality entertainment.

That didn't stop him from yelling at them and

everyone else in the control room as he stampeded inside.

"They shot my Arab? We had him on the mainland and they fuckin' shot my Arab in the head?"

No sooner had he said it than the mug shot of the al-Qaeda terrorist blinked off the plasma, leaving a blank square. They were down to nine contestants again.

"Get on the fucking phone and call the Scout, Eddie. NOW."

"Okay, okay. Relax, relax," said Bella, talking to herself as much as her boss. "We have a replacement."

"Replacement?" he snapped. "Who? What? Where? What do we have?"

As Bella went to her terminal, Julie walked into the control room, watching from the sidelines.

Eddie C lowered his phone and whispered to Julie. "How'd the interview go?"

"Smooth as butter," Breckel said before she could answer. Nothing escaped him.

Bella brought up a mug shot of a bad-ass Hispanic killer on the screen, along with his stats.

"José Havanado. Hard-core Guatemalan. Convicted of thirteen torture killings. He's ready to go."

Breckel barely looked at him. "I don't want a fuckin' Guatemalan. I already have two Mexicans. Demographics, people, demographics. Diversity. I want the United Colors of Benetton."

He stomped toward a mural-sized world map hanging on a canvas wall, his finger aiming at the Middle East region.

"See here! This is the Arab world. They need a man to cheer for or they don't log on. I want an Arab, goddamn it. A child-killing, suicide-bombing, Koran-ranting Arab."

Eddie C lowered his phone with a big grin.

"We're on! The Scout's got a line on a six-seven Islamic fundamentalist in Central America, a real get-things-done kinda guy. Crew's en route to the prison as we speak."

"Where? What country?"

"He's in a joint in El Salvador. Warden's good to go. He's ours if we want 'm."

"Yeah, for a price," Breckel said skeptically.

He stared at the long-haired Arab's photo. He looked menacing enough, but that didn't mean he could survive against the others.

"I wanna see him. Get him online."

4

Thousands of miles away, a dirty SUV with a satellite dish on the roof raced up a wet mountain road. It was not unlike the rig driven by the Scout and Donaldson, nor were its occupants. The Scout couldn't be in ten global spots at the same time, so he'd been forced to delegate and hire local talent for some of his auditions. The El Salvadoran scout and cameraman who were en route to Sonsonate Prison in Acajutla had been a backup if any of the contestants fell through.

The Scout had already negotiated the purchase of the Islamic terrorist incarcerated at Sonsonate. His name was Najeeb ur-Rahman and he was every bit as dangerous as the al-Qaeda terrorist he would be replacing. Rahman had been in El Salvador on a fundamentalist recruitment mission. He had killed several local *policía* who had gotten in his way. Like the others participating in *The Condemned*, Rahman had been sentenced to die.

The prison was a crumbling fortress built high in the mountains overlooking the Pacific coast. It had been built in the 1800s out of stone, sweat, and blood. Due to its altitude, it was constantly shrouded in clouds and miserably damp. The smell of mold drifted down the mossy, narrow turnoff miles before the SUV pulled up to the rotting wooden gates and barbed wire. The guard barely glanced at their paperwork and allowed them through.

The El Salvadoran driver and his cameraman climbed from their vehicle and approached another guard, who was guarding the entrance of the warden's office while talking price with a local prostitute for some after-shift sex. He shouted toward the door. "Jefe!"

The warden revealed himself, a half-smoked cigar clenched in his yellowing teeth. Two teenage girls were visible inside his office wearing skimpy halter tops and minuscule cut-off denims. One had on his general's cap. She giggled as he removed it and placed it on his own sweaty head. His eyes were bloodshot, his face unshaven, his nose alcohol-swollen. The warden's uniform lacked a tie and two buttons, which allowed his ample gut to spill over his belt. He greeted his visitors with a knowing look, motioning for them to follow him into his lair.

Inside, there was no huge foyer lined with cells, no eating area, no prison yard for exercise. It was more like a labyrinth. Moss-covered walls and narrow corridors led in all directions but mostly downward.

The warden's boots echoed off stone steps as he descended into the prison's bowels. The stench of mildew permeated everything. The ceilings were low down here, with dirty brown, sewage-smelling water seeping from rusty pipes that hung overhead.

They came to a dark passageway and followed it

for another twenty yards, arriving at a steel door with two guards posted. Both were armed with shotguns. A stream of light was leaking from a narrow food slot in the door. The warden motioned for them to unlock it.

The rusty door creaked open, exposing a big cell—thirty by thirty feet. A dusty, diffused glow spilled in from a barred window high in one wall. There was a steel cage built in one corner, currently empty. Its occupant was standing in the middle of the room, gazing into space.

"Najeeb!" shouted the warden.

Najeeb ur-Rahman slowly faced him. A steel collar was locked around his neck, attached to a thick chain. The chain was bolted to a steel plate in the ceiling. The hulking Arab could move only about ten feet in any direction.

"Él es un animal," he told his guests.

Shirtless, with filthy black hair that extended to his waist, Rahman did look more animal than human. His torso rippled with muscles and was crisscrossed with scars. The look he gave the warden was that of a caged tiger.

"Deseo probarlo," said the Salvadoran scout, telling the warden he wanted to test him.

The warden puffed out smoke from his stale cigar, annoyed. His attitude was reminiscent of a lazy used car salesman who didn't want to bother with a test drive.

"Vaya consiguen a Saravia y a gringo," he told the guards.

37

The warden had just ordered them to fetch a Latino killer named Saravia and the American he had locked up to fight Rahman.

The guards retreated into the corridor and wound their way down another narrow passageway. They eventually arrived at a dungeonlike cell that was one-tenth the size of Rahman's quarters. The con known as Saravia was its sole occupant. He was sitting in the corner, gazing off pensively.

One guard unlocked the cell door as the other kept his shotgun leveled.

"Saravia! En sus pies! El guarda le desea!" he shouted.

Saravia stared back defiantly and then rose to his feet, just as he'd been ordered. They said that the warden wanted to see him, which only meant bad news. But it might provide an opportunity for escape.

With Saravia covered by his partner, the guard unlocked the adjacent cell. It was the same cracker box size but had a dozen convicts crammed into it.

"Move it, Conrad," one of the guards shouted in passable English. "The warden, he want choo now."

Jack Conrad, the American, was standing opposite a tiny barred window that provided the only light into his stench-filled cell. He was feeding bread crumbs to a trio of rats on the window ledge, facing away from the guards. The back of his stubbly head shined with a thin layer of sweat.

"The warden can go fuck himself," he said matter-of-factly. His accent was one hundred percent Texan.

Conrad had never caused any problems, hence his ability to share a cell with other inmates. But he was causing problems now. The guard cocked his shotgun.

Conrad's cell mates backed against the wall, allowing the guard a clear shot. He wouldn't be the first prisoner to be gunned down in this toilet.

The American set his last crumb of bread down on the sill and then faced him.

The view from the front left no doubt that Jack Conrad was built like a brick shit house. His normally shaved head had a week's growth on it. His slate-blue eyes, like his muscles, were no-nonsense. He had a mustache and goatee framing a mouth that hadn't smiled in a long time.

Like Saravia, Conrad knew nothing good would come from a meeting with the warden. However, he'd been raised on a ranch and had fired a 12-gauge just like this guard's before he had turned ten. Their blast left a mighty big hole.

He slowly stepped out of the cell into the corridor.

Conrad thought about Sarah as the shotgun barrel jabbed into the small of his back. He'd left her without as much as a good-bye. *For her own good*, he reminded himself. *Her and the boys*. His heart was well callused by now, but it still hurt to think about her. Sarah Cavanaugh had grounded him like no other woman. He had never wanted kids, but living with Sarah had come as a package deal. Michael and Scotty, two years apart, were fine boys, but they had had their share of problems when Conrad came into their lives. Although they didn't have his genes, he could see a little of himself in both of them. Michael, the elder, was only seven when Conrad and Sarah met, and the boy was already getting into fights. Conrad had lost his dad when he was close to the same age, so he and Michael had plenty in common. He was proud of the fact that he'd turned the boy around—the fights had ended in a matter of months. At the one-year mark in his relationship with Sarah, he felt the same way about Michael as if he'd been his natural-born son.

Scotty was far more introspective and internalized his feelings. He spoke very little and communicated with his eyes. Some people thought he had developmental problems, but Conrad knew better. Scotty also reminded Conrad of himself. The kid was sharp; he just held it all in. The problem was that Scotty would eventually explode if he didn't let it out, as Conrad knew all too well. As with Michael, it took no time at all for him to fall in love with Scotty.

His thoughts drifted back to Sarah. He missed her something awful. She had a soft, creamy face that was perfect without any makeup and sky-blue eyes that he never got tired of searching. A Texas blonde who looked better in jeans than any other woman he'd ever seen. Conrad cursed himself for leaving her now. He had tried to retire, but they had pulled him back in like they always did. That blissful year with Sarah and the boys should have taught him to walk away once and for all.

His only hope now was that she and the boys knew how much he loved them, because the odds were he'd never get to tell them himself.

Another jab from the shotgun barrel brought his thoughts back to the rotting prison in El Salvador. He'd been fucked over plenty of times in his life, but being stuck here, with a death sentence no less, was a new low. As they walked, the prison's geography told him that it wasn't his turn to die, at least not by hanging. The gallows were in the opposite direction.

He also had company in the form of Saravia. The big Latino beside him had brutally killed two of his cell mates without breaking a sweat. He had a serious reputation as a street fighter.

The warden had something planned for them today other than hanging, though Conrad knew better than to rule out death.

They reached Rahman's huge cell and were shoved inside. Conrad saw the massive Arab chained like a dog. He'd never seen Rahman before now and had no idea of his reputation, but the dog collar, along with the cage in the corner, left little room for interpretation. Conrad looked at the warden, who was already grinning, as well as at the video camera.

"What's this all about?"

"Fight," said the warden in English.

Conrad was in no mood for a dog and pony show, at least not with this dog. "Bullshit," he muttered to himself.

"FIGHT!" shouted the warden.

Saravia needed no encouragement and dived into the Arab, who was at a distinct disadvantage being chained.

It made little difference. Rahman fielded the blow

and shoved his knee into the Latino's chest, knocking the wind out of him. He wrenched Saravia's face upward and repeatedly slammed his fist into his face, pulverizing it.

The warden chomped on his cigar, enjoying the show, which didn't last long. Rahman continued to beat Saravia unconscious for another ten seconds and then snapped his neck. He tossed the huge man aside like a rag doll and then leveled his gaze on Conrad. The big Arab moved toward him as far as his chain would allow, practically growling.

Conrad looked back with zero expression, refusing to engage him.

The warden's patience ran out. He reached into his pocket and tossed the long-haired terrorist a key. Rahman quickly unlocked his collar, released a guttural growl, and launched himself into the American.

The blows were quick and efficient, a mixture of martial arts and good ol' boy street fighting. In the space of three seconds, Rahman had his rib cage shattered, a lung crushed, his jaw broken, and his nose vaporized. He went down like a felled redwood, his weight shaking the room.

Conrad faced the warden, barely panting.

"Can I go now?"

The El Salvadoran scout stared with amazement as the cameraman zoomed in on Conrad's face.

Breckel gazed at Conrad's face, which now filled several monitors. He stepped toward the largest display and scrutinized Conrad, who seemed to be peering back at him. The transmission was going in and out, but he'd seen what he'd seen. The producer was in awe.

"Who the hell is this guy? Where'd he come from?"

"The Arab?" asked Bella.

"Yeah, the bloody Arab lying unconscious on the concrete fuckin' floor!" he shouted. "NO, Bella. *This* guy." He leveled his finger right between Conrad's eyes. "Where the fuck did *he* come from?"

She had no answer.

He impatiently turned to Eddie C. "Eddie, what do you have?"

The young hacker had already anticipated his boss's reaction. He had all sorts of data up on his terminal, with more downloading.

"Aah . . . American. Arrested in San Miguel, El Salvador, one year ago."

A new window popped up. Eddie's eyes lit up as he skimmed it. "Oh . . . *yeah*. He's a nice guy."

"How nice?" asked Breckel, starting to get encouraged.

"*Really* nice. Blasted a building to smithereens with a fifty-pound load of fertilizer. Killed three men. Awaiting death sentence."

Breckel sighed. "Thank you, God."

"What about 'demographics' and 'diversity'?" said Bella, still smarting from his earlier put-down. "I thought you wanted an *Arab*."

"I don't need an Arab, I got this guy," he said as if she were an idiot. "He's perfect. With anti-Americanism rampant all over the globe, people will love to hate this cowboy."

Bella swallowed her humiliation. He was right, as always. Film school had taught her all about rejection and how to rise above it. She was going to have her own reality show someday. She was lucky to be learning from the master.

Breckel moved face-to-face with the plasma, staring at Conrad as if he were a Ferrari he wanted to buy. *Had* to buy.

"I want him."

5

Conrad had never flown in a private jet, though illusions of grandeur were dispelled by his leg irons and wrist shackles. He, the pilot, and a pair of rent-a-guards were the only passengers on the eight-seater craft. He had no idea where he was being taken or why. Just as when he was taken from his cell, Conrad figured very little good would come from it.

He had pieced together enough information to realize he'd been auditioned for some sort of job. Most likely the Arab had been the initial point of interest, but that changed after he won the fight. The video camera he'd seen had an antenna on it; he'd also noticed the van with the satellite dish when they'd taken him to the airport. Somebody had been watching them fight. He had been chosen. For what, he did not yet know.

Conrad was told to clean himself up in the plane's restroom before landing. As one guard kept him covered, another unclasped his right wrist so he could give himself a spit bath and shave. He made his head and face smooth again, leaving his goatee alone.

As he stepped off the plane, he took in the tiny

airstrip and made some mental calculations. Conrad had never been here before, but the climate, topography, and distance traveled told him he was somewhere in Oceania, possibly New Guinea.

His guess was right on the money: the Gulfstream G550 had touched down on a private airstrip near the town of Aitape, on the north coast of Papua New Guinea.

Conrad squinted as a bearded man paced in his direction from a nearby hangar. *American. Civilian*, the Texan deduced. The man was wearing combat fatigues, but the way he carried himself belied any military training. Wiry and less than six feet tall, he carried a holstered automatic pistol and nodded at the rent-a-guards, who both stiffened. Conrad decided the guards worked for this guy. He eyed him again.

Head of security. For whom?

The bearded man's name was Baxter, though Conrad wouldn't find that out until they were inside the hangar. While Baxter was in the thirty-something club like his employer, he and Breckel shared less history than the producer did with his tech director Goldman. Baxter had been a Florida cop with a bad attitude. He'd eventually been discharged for using excessive force and prisoner abuse, as well as the questionable shooting of a suspect. Shortly thereafter, Baxter had opened a private security business that had a reputation of satisfying its clients by any means necessary. Breckel had first hired him for a reality project set in the Florida Keys that involved the Cuban mafia. With Breckel's wealth and controversy on the rise, Baxter's security services gradually became more personal. At least a dozen threats had been made on his life to date, several of which Baxter had dealt with privately and swiftly. In one instance, a fanatic who'd protested every one of his shows was crippled by a mysterious hit-and-run driver. In another, after a visit from Baxter, a rival reality producer backed off on a new series that was vaguely similar to a show Breckel was planning to produce. While the boss remained blissfully ignorant of his operations, Baxter knew he was no dummy. Private security was a necessary component to his personal and professional life, and Baxter was happy to provide it. He knew Breckel didn't consider him a friend like Goldman, which was fine—he wasn't in this business to make friends. Breckel slept easier with him on the payroll, and so did Baxter because the pay was big.

"Welcome, Mr. Conrad. Right this way," Baxter said as he shoved him toward the hangar. Conrad had already decided not to like him, but acting tough against a shackled man who could otherwise kick his ass upped the ante.

Inside the hangar, the fun was already beginning.

Conrad's nine competitors were clustered in the rear of the empty space. All were chained just like him. A half dozen guards were lining them up against a rusty corrugated wall and locking them to large grommets normally used to secure aircraft. None of them were cooperating. A cacophony of international obscenities was being spewed at the guards, who responded with gun butt jabs and gut punches.

The Japanese contestant, Go Saiga, was straining to punch and kick the two guards who were hauling him over to a metal table. Lean, mean, muscular, and intense, Saiga managed to trip one of them and jab his elbow into the other's face. The less than six-foot Asian had been an assassin for the *boryokudan*, which translated as "the violent ones." It was the hot new name that the Japanese National Police Agency had dubbed local crime groups, though the gangs were more commonly known as the *yakuza* worldwide. Go Saiga was a master at kung fu; he also knew his way around swords, knives, and guns. He had personally killed more than thirty people, six of them women.

Even shackled, it took four guards to hold him down so another could clasp the gunmetal-colored gadget around his right ankle. The device looked like a home arrest security bracelet on steroids. LED lights blinked above a series of microchips and a gaggle of wires.

As Conrad joined his fellow competitors inside the hangar, Breckel's private Bell JetRanger set down beside the Gulfstream. It was the 206B-3 model that sat five, but right now it was carrying only the pilot and two passengers—Breckel and Julie.

During the flight over from the island, Breckel had mostly been on the phone putting out brush fires and calming down Goldman. Julie had wanted to talk with him about the issues that Donna Sereno had brought up, but there had been no opportunity. Being truthful to herself, she wasn't sure she really wanted to. Julie was not naïve. Going in, she knew the show would not be PG rated. It was hard-core adult entertainment. Ian had promised he would handle it tastefully, so she decided on a wait-and-see approach. She wanted to believe him.

Julie had convinced herself that she was here to consult on the convicts' wardrobe. Despite the humidity, she felt a chill as they entered the hangar. The faces she'd seen on the plasma were standing there in the flesh. It was like being in the same room with Charles Manson, Jeffrey Dahmer, and every other psychotic, sadistic killer made famous by the media. One was bad enough, but ten together took her breath away.

Raudsep, the Russian, was straining against his chains as Breckel and Julie walked past him. They stayed just out of his reach, Breckel examining him like a horse breeder studying one of his prize studs. Raudsep was wearing a torn, stained, sleeveless shirt and pale green prison pants, though it was his massive size, oblong head, and plethora of scars that drew complete attention. Julie briefly made eye contact; the look he returned made her instantly nauseous.

"What do you think?" asked Breckel, pleased that the Russian creeped her out.

"I wouldn't change a thing," she said, making a note on her steno pad.

Julie would have the same answer in just about every case. This was a reality show and they were the real deal.

Helmut Bruggerman came next. The German was in his fifties, his hair ash gray like his eyes and cropped short. He wore a sleeveless vest that showed off an array of military tattoos, along with biceps and a taut physique that contradicted his age. Bruggerman was his given name, though authorities and the media knew him as the "Nazi" and, occasionally, the "Butcher." He had been a military commander responsible for killing civilian Jews not during Hitler's regime, which was well before his time, but during supposed peaceful times. Men, women, boys, girls—it didn't matter. For that matter, neither did being Jewish. A steadfast believer in ethnic cleansing, any race other than Aryan was fair game. His grandfather had been in charge of a concentration camp and had shared many stories. Bruggerman's big regret in life was that he had been born too late.

The Nazi paid no attention to Breckel or Julie, instead leveling his eyes on the Mexicans and the two blacks.

"Hey, gringo, you think you're a big man, huh?" spat Rosa Pacheco as Breckel slowly passed her. "No, no. You're just a worm. A lil' piece-of-shit worm."

Breckel offered a small grin, eyeing both her and the Hispanic man beside her. He knew all about Rosa and Paco Pacheco, the Mexican equivalent of Bonnie and Clyde. They had robbed and killed their way across Guatemala, showing no mercy. Their competition had been unarmed store clerks and gas station attendants, not hardened, ruthless convicts who had nothing to lose. They were a pair and had fear behind their eyes. If bets were to be placed, and they would, these two would be the first to die.

"Hey, sweetie, you think you're hot?" Rosa went on, gazing at Julie. "You're not so hot. You're the worm's whore, that's all."

"Ignore her," dismissed Breckel, moving along. Julie lingered, wanting to slap the woman. She had despised Rosa and her husband well before the insult; she now held zero pity for their fate.

Breckel was now standing opposite a true beauty. Her name was Yasantwa Adei, and she could've held her ground with international model Iman or Halle Berry. Her coffee-colored skin was creamy smooth, with naturally long eyelashes and gemstone irises. Her short, black, wavy-curly hair, which hadn't seen a stylist in years, still looked amazing. In other circumstances, Breckel might've considered a woman this stunning as a potential conquest, but the woman gazing back at him was a cold-blooded murderess.

Yasantwa came from the poor section of South Africa but was very smart. She knew how to use what God had given her. Yasantwa was a seductress. She had successfully infiltrated the rich neighborhoods and tempted lots of men who should have known better. She'd killed every one of them.

Breckel's eyes left her face and moved to her chest. She was wearing a ratty, baggy prison shirt over a white tank top.

"Get this shirt off her," he told Julie. "We're in show business, not a soup kitchen."

The comment had been callous, but Ian was right. The woman would look better without the shirt. Julie began to unbutton it. Yasantwa put up no resistance, her eyes never leaving Julie's. Julie couldn't help feeling that Yasantwa was trying to seduce *her.*

Breckel moved on, giving the remaining prisoners a cursory glance.

"Hey, where's my new guy? The American?"

"Over there." Baxter, who had just appeared with a clipboard, pointed. "Just got fitted with a bracelet."

Breckel walked away, passing Ewan McStarley, the Englishman. Breckel gave him a polite nod and McStarley grinned back. He looked happy to be here.

The Brit was as rugged as a chunk of granite, with a square jaw to match. He sported a short, military-style haircut. No beard to hide his good looks. Ewan McStarley had star quality like Sean Connery from his Bond days, except his DNA was imprinted with bad genes and his eyes were PCP wild. "Psychopath" was a label that fit him better than any of his competition.

McStarley was chained next to a male African American, K. C. Mack, who had killed his way through Inglewood, California, for a solid decade before being popped. He then escaped to Malaysia and landed on death row for a drug deal gone bad. K.C. was a midsized roller in the illegal substance business, the type who started on the street and never left because he liked staying close to the action. The job required protecting his turf, which meant heads needed to roll now and then. This was a task he preferred to handle personally. A good-looking black man, he wore dreadlocks tied back and carried himself loose.

K.C. eyed the talent on display, looking for angles, as always.

"So where'd they pull you from?" he whispered to McStarley.

The Englishman pierced him with a stare. "Muzzle it, boy, you're already borin' me."

"Who you callin' *boy*?"

McStarley grinned back. He couldn't wait to kill this idiot. Kill all of them.

"Ewan McStarley, London, England," read Baxter, taking it directly off his clipboard. "Four years Special Forces. Three peacekeeping tours through Africa. Set fire to a village in Rwanda. Executed seventeen men. Raped nine women, three of them children. Torture. Mutilation . . ."

Baxter looked up, giving him a final appraisal. "Good stuff. You ladies should get along real good."

K. C. Mack deadpanned McStarley. "What the fuck is wrong with you?"

The psycho smiled back. "All in a day's work, Rasta."

K.C. turned away and met Yasantwa's face. The young woman had heard it all and looked more than a little scared. She had killed people, just like K.C. had, but it had been out of necessity, not for pleasure. The two held each other's gaze, making a momentary connection.

Meanwhile, Conrad had just been fitted with the security bracelet. Unlike the others, he had paid it very close attention.

GPS. Clock. Explosives, he ticked off in his mind.

Indeed, a block of plastic explosive was housed under a thin metal covering. A red metal strip protruded like a pull tab beside it, functioning like the pin on a grenade.

At some point he would have to either disarm it or get it off, and the sooner the better. It looked like state-of-the-art stuff, probably packed with C-4 and an antitampering microchip.

Two guards guided him past the Italian, who looked to be in his forties with a dark brown beard and ponytail.

"Hey, brother, gimme the key, gimme the key," the Italian hissed at the guards leading Conrad. "I give you a deal, you help me out. Jus' between you 'n' me."

They ignored him, walking on.

Dominic Giangrasso had a motor mouth and a hot temper, the latter of which had caused him to shoot his wife, both her parents, and a couple of neighbors who had foolishly tried to intervene. He had sold Fiats before his murderous rampage and subsequent death sentence. Dubbed *Assassino Della Bocca del Motore*, or "Motor-mouth Killer," his case had made national headlines.

The guards guided Conrad to an isolated floor grommet and chained him to it. Within seconds, Breckel was facing him, genial as ever.

"Hi. I'm Ian Breckel. I produce television."

Conrad sized him up. "Well, good for you."

"Maybe you've heard of me?"

"I haven't been watchin' too much TV lately," he drawled.

Conrad carefully considered Breckel, along with the previous twelve hours. The high-tech video camera with the antenna he'd seen back in El Salvador, the fancy jet, the private security all went into the stew. This man had to be the chef.

At first Conrad had suspected some sort of covert military operation, most likely suicidal since everyone here was expendable. His dad had loved a movie called *The Dirty Dozen*, which was about an army major training a dozen convicted murderers to pull off an impossible assassination mission. This wasn't the case here. The slick executive standing opposite him and his half-assed security force were anything but military. They weren't even CIA. If this rich asshole was telling him the truth about making TV shows, then he was involved in something even more twisted.

"Why don't you take a seat," offered Breckel, grabbing a folding chair.

A cameraman abruptly appeared, aiming his lens. Conrad took it in without comment and sat down, his chains rattling against the flimsy metal chair.

Julie walked over, ogling Conrad just like she had all the other murderers. She stood behind Breckel and quietly made notes, which was mostly an excuse to avoid direct eye contact.

"You and the others will be taken to an island where you'll fight against each other," the producer casually explained. "If you are the last one left alive within thirty hours, I will set you free with a pocket full of cash. How's that sound?"

Conrad stared back for quite a while before responding. "What's this got to do with TV?"

"Not TV, the Internet. I'll be streaming the entire event live across the world wide web."

Now Conrad really studied him. *This is some seriously fucked-up shit*, he thought. He was curious what kind of man would put on a freak show like this. Then, on second consideration, he didn't want to know. A man like this wasn't worth knowing.

Breckel shot a look over at Baxter, motioning for his clipboard. The producer flipped through it until Conrad's rap sheet appeared. It was only one-third of a page long. He shook his head.

"Your résumé's a little thin." He read it out loud: " 'Jack Conrad. American. Blew up a building in El Salvador. Killed three men.' " Breckel looked up at him. "Is that it?"

Conrad said nothing.

"We like to do a biography for each contestant. Tell me a little bit about yourself."

"Name's Jack Conrad. I'm American. I blew up a building in El Salvador, killed three men," he recited, mirroring what Breckel had just read.

Now it was Breckel's turn to pause. Conrad was cocky. That was okay. He wanted his cast to have attitude.

"What were you doing down in El Salvador?"

"Workin' on my tan."

Breckel smiled. "Why'd you blow up that building?"

"It was blockin' my sun."

"What do you do for a living, Mr. Conrad?"

"I'm an interior decorator."

The wise-ass routine was wearing out its welcome. Breckel changed his tone, more sincere and less inquisitional.

"Hmm. Okay. Let's forget about your criminal career. Tell me, Jack, where are you from, back in the States?"

Conrad paused, his expression serious. "Alaska."

Breckel nodded. Finally, a straight answer.

"Alaska, huh? I hear it's beautiful up there. Whereabouts?"

" 'Bout eighty miles north of Anchorage. Maybe you've heard of it, a little fishin' town called Fukyermama."

Breckel smiled through his teeth. He glanced back at Julie, still behind him.

"Babe, do me a favor. Write a bio for this redneck. Say he's from somewhere in"—he appraised Conrad unflinchingly—"Arkansas. Arsonist. Racist. Klansman. Blew up a Baptist church. Fugitive from the FBI . . ."

He was firing it off faster than she could scribble it down.

". . . Ran off to Central America where he blew up a clinic for retards and handicaps. The blast killed dozens—women, children, blah, blah, blah."

Julie stopped writing and looked at Ian. Was he serious? She shifted her eyes to Conrad. On the surface, Ian's fake bio fit Conrad to a T—he definitely looked the part of a cold-blooded racist murderer. Everywhere except his eyes.

Conrad was sizing her up as well. She was Breckel's girlfriend along for the ride. He'd given her something to do, probably bullshitted her about what was really going down here. She didn't look stupid, which was why she was hesitating about the bio. It was all in her eyes and body language.

Conrad shifted his gaze back to the producer. "I don't know who you are. Don't care. But I don't play games."

"You don't have to win," Breckel slowly replied. "But *everybody* plays."

Breckel got up and walked away. The ten convicts were now all accounted for and prepped for the show. The showman took center stage, relishing his power as he faced all of them. He had assembled the worst of the worst this planet had to offer, all under one roof. Breckel had always enjoyed public speaking, though the speech he was about to give took "captive audience" to a new level.

"Killers, thieves, racists, and rapists. Your crimes vary, but you all have one thing in common—you are the condemned," he opened dramatically as his cameras rolled.

"Fuck you!" shouted the Nazi, continuing his diatribe in German. A guard nearly shattered his kneecaps with a baton.

"Careful," Breckel scolded the guard. "He needs to be able to walk. At least at the start."

Giangrasso let his gums flap next, obviously learning nothing from the Nazi. "*Amico!* I fuckin' have-a rights! You letta me make-a my call or I no participate in this fuckin' *concórso!* Who the fuck you think you—"

A baton jab to his gut shut him up.

This was a pissing contest now.

"Hey boss? How 'bout somethin' t' eat? I need fuel you wan' me to perform, *ese.*"

"Or some water," chimed in K. C. Mack. "We ain't had shit since yesterday."

Bitching and moaning echoed through the hangar.

Conrad remained silent. He had a pretty good idea of what was in store for him now, so he decided to take inventory. There were lots of loudmouths barking, which generally meant no bite. The only convicts not hollering were the black woman and the crew-cut limey. The woman looked terrified, but the big Brit was scanning the others, just as he was. Their eyes locked at one point. McStarley aimed his finger at Conrad and shot it like a pistol, offering up a friendly wink.

"Once you're on the island, supply bags will be randomly dropped," continued Breckel. "Water, food, weapons. First come, first served."

"Is this shit for real?" K.C. said to McStarley, who simply offered a wide grin back. The black man shook his head and then stole another glance at Yasantwa, the South African beauty. Her eyes flicked at him and then looked away.

"You will have thirty hours to kill or be killed," Breckel pressed on in a booming voice, relishing every word.

"Lil *pequeño pene* . . . you ain't no real *hombre*," shouted Rosa. "You a worm, *jefe*. *Un pequeño gusano* piece a shit!"

She reached out toward Paco and the two clasped hands, straining their chains. Both had matching hearts tattooed on their arms.

Breckel was more amused than offended.

"Ah, yes, husband and wife. Lovers. How touching. You can stick together, but the fact of the matter is that only one of you can make it off the island alive."

Rosa lunged and spat in Breckel's face, hitting her target. She released a flurry of expletives in Spanish, exploding like a fiery volcano. A guard yanked her back by her long black hair and ratcheted his baton around her throat, cutting off her voice.

Breckel wiped his face with his sleeve, keeping his composure.

"Hope you can run your feet as fast as your mouth," he responded as her face turned red from lack of oxygen.

Paco strained to help his wife but couldn't make physical contact. "Let her go!" he screamed.

The guard finally released her and she coughed in fresh oxygen.

Paco's face was just as red now. "You want me to play this game with my wife? Are you fucking crazy?"

"Sorry, friend. Everybody plays." Breckel shrugged. He'd grown tired of talking to them. They were subhuman and didn't deserve his presence.

"Let's get out of here," he quietly told Julie. He nodded at Baxter and then left the hangar. Julie was happy to be away from this lot and followed without a word.

Baxter paced in front of the convicts and took over for his boss.

"Okay, listen up, gang. On your ankle, you've all got a rig packed with twenty ounces of plastic explosives. Twenty ounces. That is enough to incinerate

60

you, your dog, and whatever small house you may be residing in at the time."

Every prisoner shot a stunned gaze down at his or her bracelet save Conrad and McStarley, who were still gauging their competition.

From McStarley's point of view, the Mexican couple was an instant write-off. He'd have some fun with them, to be sure, but they posed no serious threat. Same with the black woman. The Russian was big but he looked stupid, the Nazi was old, the loudmouth Italian had killed only his wife and parents for Chrissakes. The Jap and Rasta-boy were question marks, but he still wasn't concerned. This would be like shooting fish in a barrel.

Except for the American. He was hard to read. A late arrival, his background was a mystery. He'd be keeping an eye out for him.

Conrad was sizing up McStarley as well. From across the room, he had heard only bits and pieces when Baxter recited the Brit's background, but he comprehended the most salient bullet points. *Military, Special Forces.* The haircut, attitude, and the fact that he already knew he had a bomb on his ankle all confirmed that. *No fear. He's enjoying this.* Here was a man who likely found pleasure in the killing and suffering of others. The military sometimes did that to a person if he was crazy to begin with. Either way, this Englishman was a poster boy for sociopaths.

"Thirty hours from now, that plastic explosive will do what it does best," continued Baxter. "If you want that rig removed from your ankle, simply be the sole survivor before your time runs out."

Baxter paused. It was barely visible, but Conrad detected a small smile at the corner of the security chief's lips. He could guess what Baxter was about to tell them, which had something to do with that red tab. Moreover, Baxter was also a closet sadist. Not a big man, he compensated for his lack of physical power with guns and gadgets. Even the beard was all about making him feel more masculine.

"There are two other ways to detonate the ankle rig," he went on. "One: see that red pull tab? Yank it out, and after a ten-second delay, *boom.*"

Again, all eyes darted to the red tab.

"Two: tamper with the rig, mess with the wires, try to pick the lock, and instantly, without delay, BOOM. It's a very simple game. Kill or die."

Conrad digested what he *hadn't* heard. Baxter had neglected to mention the GPS. He, and most likely McStarley, were the only two convicts who knew that their every move would be tracked on a grid. This made turning the tables on their real competition— the operators of this sick game—extremely difficult.

His thoughts were interrupted as the digital LCD panel on his ankle bracelet suddenly beeped and illuminated with a string of digital numbers: *30:00:00.*

Conrad looked up at Baxter just in time to see him nod to one of his guards, who was sitting opposite a laptop. The guard entered a code and then pressed the Enter key. Conrad's bracelet chirped again, along with everyone else's. He glimpsed the numbers rolling backward, beginning with *29:59:59*. The last two digits, indicating seconds, were ticking down like a time bomb.

Not *like* a time bomb. It *was* a time bomb. And everyone there knew it.

The convicts freaked like horses trying to escape from a burning stable. Paco and Rosa were screaming in rapid Spanish. The Nazi was shouting in guttural German, trying to pry off his bracelet. Giangrasso was hopping around, talking so fast that his words were incomprehensible in any language. Raudsep was yelling in Russian, but with a third of his tongue missing from the prison brawl, his words were gibberish. Yasantwa stood frozen like a deer caught in headlights; K. C. Mack tried to distance himself from his own leg, gazing at the device as if it were a living creature about to eat him alive. McStarley was simply laughing.

Conrad stood still, watching the chaos with concern. Tampering with the devices could set them off, and there was plenty of tampering going on.

Somebody's gonna blow himself up 'n' take me with him.

Baxter was thinking the same thing and ordered his men into action. More beatings took place until the group was subdued, but not enough to do serious damage. They all needed to be in tip-top condition when they hit the island and the killing began.

6

Breckel's private helicopter landed on a bluff on the rugged northwest edge of the island. Sheer, treacherous cliffs surrounded three sides of the landing pad. Rough seas slammed into jagged rocks a hundred feet below. The area was inaccessible by sea and extremely difficult by land, with dense jungle, wide rivers, and steep ravines isolating the region from the rest of the island. Breckel planned to scatter the prisoners along the south shore, adding further insurance that the puppeteer and his puppets would remain separate.

His compound was less than a mile away, secluded in the rain forest. He and Julie hiked a hundred yards down the steep bluff to a jeep that awaited them below the landing pad. The driver, one of Baxter's men, whisked them along a bumpy overgrown trail into the jungle.

Julie had said nothing from the moment she had boarded the chopper. Her disquiet had begun to fester, her justifications evaporating in the tropical heat one by one. *These are condemned men and women already sentenced to die*, she told herself. But who gave Ian the authority to expedite their punishment? He wasn't committing the acts with his own hands, but he was certainly the catalyst. *He is giving the audience exactly what they want to see . . .* but did that absolve him of exploiting death for profit?

It wasn't only Ian's culpability that disturbed her. She had begun to see a different side of herself as well, and she didn't like what she saw. Consulting on clothing and creating fictional bios had made her a willing accomplice. "Accomplice" seemed like the appropriate word—it connoted the commission of a crime. Ian had assured her that while rules were being bent, he was not committing a felony by producing this show. Why would he advertise it to millions if that were the case? Ian was a master of spin, she knew that, and his charm was irresistible. She had believed in him, trusted him with her heart, or she never would have joined him. It was only in his silence that she had time to think logically.

Breckel had not spoken the entire way over either. He had sensed Julie's unease, which was to be expected. She needed time to get used to the idea. Like all good salesmen knew, there was a time for the hard sell and a time to back off. He had no doubt that Julie would come around, especially when they went live. Watching it unfold on plasma displays would be much easier to stomach than standing in a room with flesh and blood. The editing, graphics, music—all of it would heighten the experience to an irresistible level. Even people who despised what he was doing would not be able to turn away from the screen. He knew Julie didn't detest what he was doing or she wouldn't have come along. She was in love with him. His daily self-assessment always yielded the same result: he was brilliant, powerful, incredibly handsome, beyond charming, and very rich. How could she not be utterly captivated by him?

The jeep rolled through the opened gate into the compound. Breckel hopped out and turned to one of Baxter's guards. "Lock it down. Showtime."

The razor-wired gate swung shut and was chain-locked. Breckel's adrenaline level was palpable as he marched into his control room, the vibe already at high intensity before he spoke a word.

"The choppers are coming—the cons are on their way, people! Are we ready? Goldy?" He delivered each word like machine gun fire.

"Ah, no," replied Goldman, his voice even more depressing than before. "What, are you kidding me? Absolutely not."

The technical director was sweating as he gazed at a cluster of monitors, some displaying as many as a dozen windows. Live camera angles filled the rectangles—paradiselike beaches, waterfalls, the rusted hull of a crashed military transport plane, even an underwater shot worthy of a Jacques Cousteau documentary. Goldman's assistants were hastily sticking masking tape below each image and labeling them with camera numbers and location abbreviations.

Breckel knew from their history together that Goldman's depression meant they were in good shape. If he had reacted in any other way, there would be cause for concern.

"Bella? You ready?"

"I was born ready," she volleyed back, genuinely pumped.

"Eddie?"

Eddie C offered a thumbs-up between keystrokes. "Good to go."

Breckel felt an erection coming on. This was the most ambitious project he had ever tackled, even better than sex. The foreplay was over and it was showtime.

"Bella, give me some old school. Rock and roll."

She grinned and grabbed a CD, slapping it into one of her machines.

Goldman was starting to melt down, which also was normal just before broadcast.

"JJ, I thought I said camera 142," he whined to a girl manning the console who was twenty but looked fifteen. "At least that's what I thought I said. Christ, I'm losing it. Could you please point the camera away from the palm trees and out to sea?"

Breckel saw intermittent snow on his main monitor.

"Goldy, is our satellite going to hold up?"

"Nope."

The monitor contradicted him a second later, the snow vanishing. A crystal-clear image of the island's lush south shore filled the screen, looking out on a turquoise sea.

Less than fifty feet above the ocean surface, two military choppers were roaring toward the island, five prisoners in each.

Breckel's eyes were riveted on the monitor as the helicopters grew larger, coming right at him.

"Cue the music, Bella."

She punched the Play button. Guns N' Roses's "Welcome to the Jungle" blasted from the control room speakers.

"Eddie, take us live to the web."

7

The contestants had been split into two helicopters, each containing a pilot and two guards. Conrad was in the Alpha chopper, along with the Russian, the Mexican couple, and McStarley. All were chained to a cable running the length of the cargo bay. Baxter was also along for the ride at Breckel's request. The producer wanted nothing left to chance.

The selection had not been random. Breckel wanted one woman in each chopper to torque the men, several of whom had sexual assaults on their résumés. Having Paco and Rosa Pacheco together, with McStarley in the mix, was also strategic—knowing the Englishman's history, Rosa would be an appealing target, and he wanted the dynamics of her husband sensing McStarley's lust. Dropping the Pachecos close together would also facilitate the couple teaming up, adding yet another dimension since only one could ultimately live. Conrad getting to know the Russian seemed like a good pairing as well—he'd also noticed McStarley and Conrad scrutinizing each other in the hangar and wanted to push that envelope. Having seen the video feeds of each one in action, Breckel gave them equal odds, which would make for a nice battle if and when the two intersected.

Conrad ignored his companions for most of the ride, all of which was over water. Forty-five minutes into it, he peered out through the pilot's windscreen and saw the island. Its size was hard to judge at their water-skimming altitude, but he guessed it to be at least eight miles wide and maybe twelve long. It was thick with jungle and extremely hilly, with vertical mountains and deep valleys. Going off the angle of the sun, they were heading west. That meant he was viewing the east side of the island from this approach, which faced open seas with no landmasses or barrier reefs to slow the swells. A strong onshore wind brought whitecaps, confirming that they were facing the eastern windward side. Arriving on this section of the island by boat, or escaping for that matter, appeared to be impossible.

He shifted his look to McStarley, assuming he was making the same mental calculations.

Strangely, he wasn't. McStarley's vision was focused on the Mexican woman, Rosa. His gaze drifted from her legs to her breasts and then back again. Conrad could see he was mentally raping her.

Rosa also became aware of it and stiffened. "You got a problem, *jefe*?" she said in her toughest voice.

McStarley smiled back, flashing his big white teeth. He turned to Paco, who shifted along the cable closer to his wife, as if to protect her. "Your wife is very pretty," he said politely.

"Fuck you." He glared.

70

The Russian, who understood none of the words, understood completely. He too was eyeing Rosa, his size dwarfing her. He grinned at her, his teeth yellowed and rotting, flapping what was left of his tongue at her like a lizard.

As she cowered away from both of them, the chopper abruptly dropped altitude and banked left. Conrad caught a glimpse of the other helicopter swooping right. The water was too rough on the east side, which meant the choppers were circling around each corner of the island into calmer seas. *Gonna spread us out*, he thought. He eyed McStarley again, who was still ogling Rosa. *But not too much*. Conrad was beginning to get into the producer's head. What he saw made him sick.

Baxter slid the side door open and a strong wind rushed in as they rounded the tip of the island. Conrad caught a glimpse of something in the jungle. It looked like an old weather tower . . . with a big, modern antenna on its roof.

He tried to see through the thick foliage, which was passing in a blur. There was movement on the ground beneath the trees, a grouping of large tents, and the white flash of a big round disk pointed skyward—a satellite dish.

A second later, it all disappeared in a wash of green jungle.

Conrad peered over the pilot's shoulder, catching a glimpse of his compass. The needle was now pointing northwest, as he had suspected. Sunlight splashed into the chopper's interior as they continued their bank, bringing a view of tranquil beaches and a less rugged coastline. They were heading into the trades off the island's south shore.

Conrad began to form a plan.

The Bravo chopper was noisier. All because of one man—Giangrasso—who almost managed to drown out the thudding drone of the aircraft blades. He'd been upchucking his random Italian-Sicilian-mixed-with-English fulmination for at least a half hour to no one and everyone.

"Oh! *Amico! Sente*, listen up! *Sono numero uno di Palermo. Ho matsaou sete masculi, Taglia la gola, ha sparanno* and each of you *dead!* You, you, you, *morta!*"

He gazed at the Japanese con, Saiga, who was using his chains to do pull-ups. Siaga was in Zen mode and had dialed him out.

"*Come se dice!* I pound you like a *cotolétta parmigiana.*"

He then leveled a crooked finger at the black man with dreadlocks. "*Uno per uno*, dead, dead, dead!"

K. C. Mack stared at him like he was from the Italian section of Mars. Giangrasso didn't scare him, not like that Nazi fucker Bruggerman, who practically had the word "racist" tattooed on his forehead.

"Yo, spaghetti head, how 'bout you stick your head in a pizza oven and give us some peace?" volleyed K.C.

He saw Yasantwa give him a glance. She didn't quite smile, but he guessed she would have under other circumstances. Her eyes fell to the ground again, afraid to make contact with anyone else—especially the German.

72

Bruggerman had been salivating over her ever since the orientation. She had prayed they wouldn't be on the same chopper, but like every other wish in her life, God hadn't heard her. Or maybe he had and had ignored her. There was no getting around the fact that she had taken several lives, but all of them had deserved it from her viewpoint. Men wanted only one thing, and they always wanted more than they'd paid for. She had been ogled and raped as a young girl, which yielded two valuable lessons: men were animals, and she was very desirable. Poverty eventually led to prostitution. A few men indeed got more than what they'd paid for. Yasantwa usually gave it to them with a knife. She had ended up on death row as a result.

The Nazi drank in her tight tank top and the faint impression of her nipples in the fabric. While he wanted to murder the man who brought him here, right now he was thanking Breckel for putting him on the same chopper with this bar of chocolate. He couldn't wait to get her alone on that island, and sex would just be the starter. The other spade and the Mexicans would be fun to kill, too, but not like her.

Giangrasso was still running his mouth, his round-robin diatribe having returned to Saiga.

"Eh, you! Guess what, *paisan?* I love Chinese. *Mi piace tantissimoi Cinése!*" He raised his fist at the Nazi as he ranted on. "And when I'm done with this, this *pezzo di merda*, this piece of shit, I'm gonna eat you up like a bowl of fried rice. Then spit you out like a bad seed."

No reaction from either one, but K. C. Mack laughed. The whole thing was too absurd for words.

"Hey! Don't know why you laugh, black boy. 'Cause when I'm finished with Dim Sum here, I'm gonna chop up your dark ass into little squares and make the ravioli. *Mangio tutti, tutti!*"

"Man, you is the tutti-frutti. Now shut the fuck up."

Giangrasso stopped talking, but not because of K.C. The chopper had rapidly dropped altitude and was making a hard turn to the right, passing around the southeast corner of the island.

As in the Alpha chopper, Breckel had carefully selected the Bravo passengers for the proper dynamics. Friction, along with sexual tension, would whip them all into the proper frenzy for when they faced off.

Goldman wet his lips. "Gimme a slow push."

JJ, his female tech, pushed a joystick on the console and the image zoomed between the palms, framing the choppers. "Welcome to the Jungle" was heading into the chorus as a flashy graphic superimposed over the oncoming choppers, telling the audience they were watching *The Condemned.* The title exploded off the screen just before the choppers banked in opposite directions, disappearing from view.

"Cameras sixteen and twenty-three, I wanna split screen," ordered Goldman.

The helicopters reappeared on opposite sides of the plasma display. Alpha was directly over the lens, which was mounted on the roof of the weather tower. The Bravo chopper was swooping past a white sand beach, captured by a palm-mounted camera.

Breckel watched it unfold with rapt attention, holding his breath for any mistakes. All showmen knew you had to grab them in the opening seconds or lose them for good—there were too many alternatives a mouse click away. Not only that, electronic word of mouth in the form of instant messaging and blogs would launch or sink the enterprise within minutes. He knew better than to interfere with the technical direction unless things went horribly wrong. Micromanaging Goldman, which he'd tried to do on their first show together, had made the product worse. Goldy knew where every camera on that island was located. It was time to let him do his job.

"Bravo's coming up on the south shore—"

Goldman lifted his finger like a composer conducting his orchestra. "—Switch to thirty-eight . . . NOW."

He waved his finger and the screen image cut to a wide shot of a crescent-shaped bay. A split second later, the Bravo chopper swooped into view, perfectly framed.

Inside Bravo at this same moment, Giangrasso was yammering again as a guard slid Yasantwa along the cable toward the open door. She was first in the string. The guard's hand stroked her thigh as he moved her, but there was nothing she could do about it.

"Open your mouth!" he shouted over the din of the engines.

She refused, trying to back away. The other guard held her from behind.

"Bite this!" he yelled again, showing her a key.

She glanced at her manacles and understood. Yasantwa opened her mouth and let him put it inside, biting down hard. Her hands, while still chained together, were released from the overhead cable by the other guard.

The first guard blew her a kiss as he shoved her out the door. She free-fell about forty feet, end over end, before splashing into the turquoise bay.

Goldman's camera captured all of it on the main screen. He snapped his fingers at the moment of impact: "One eighty-two B."

The screen cut to an underwater shot and the action seamlessly continued with Yasantwa's body whooshing into view. Everyone in the control center was riveted to the screen as she writhed beneath the surface, still locked in chains and sinking fast. Yasantwa pulled the key from her mouth and almost dropped it, gasping away precious oxygen as a twelve-foot tiger shark cruised by.

Breckel was grinning ear to ear. The shark was pure luck, which was a good omen. You couldn't buy production values like this. It would be wonderfully visual if it attacked her, but he hoped it wouldn't happen. It was too soon in the game to waste a contestant, especially this one. Yasantwa smoldered with sex appeal; she was his female lead. He needed to milk the suspense for as long as possible.

The shark paid her no attention and swam on.

Yasantwa fumbled the key into the shackles on her ankles and freed her feet. She kicked to keep from sinking, rapidly running out of air. She couldn't seem to find the keyhole in her wrist clamps.

Breckel's grin vanished. His leading lady was about

to drown and the show hadn't even begun. The shark scenario was beginning to look good now. Nothing would be more boring than a drowning. It had been Baxter's suggestion to drop them in the ocean shackled. Breckel had endorsed the idea for the very reason he was now cursing: the possibility of drowning, right off the bat, created another layer of tension.

Much to his relief, Yasantwa finally found the keyhole. Seconds later, the heavy clasps and chains were sinking to the ocean floor. She swam for the surface with her last breath.

"One eighty-two A," snapped Goldman.

The screen cut to the ocean surface just as Yasantwa exploded from it. Goldman had a camera rigged to a buoy fewer than twenty feet from where she had been dropped. He instinctively grabbed the console joystick himself and did a quick zoom on Yasantwa's face as she choked out water and gasped for air.

There was an audible gasp in the control room, Julie among those captivated by the action.

Breckel was ecstatic. "Genius, Goldy. I'm tellin' ya, you're the best."

Goldman never took his eyes off his monitors. "Say that again."

"You're the best."

"Thanks."

He glanced at Breckel and actually smiled, his first since the project had begun. Breckel wasn't one to fling around compliments, much less call someone a genius. On his shows, there was room for only one genius— himself.

Yasantwa swam to shore, unaware that several cameras were tracking her every move. One was high in a tree, another lodged in driftwood, yet another shooting through beachfront banana palms. The beach itself was stunning, something out of a tropical travel brochure. Gentle blue-green water as clear as an aquarium lapped at the powdery white sand, not a footprint in sight. Coconut palms swayed above her as tropical birds chattered. The only thing missing was a hammock and a mai tai.

Yasantwa staggered along the sand, catching her breath, happy to be alive. She arched her back and closed her eyes, drawing in the scent of plumeria and wild mangoes being carried on the breeze.

A camera lens slowly panned with her.

There in the control room, Yasantwa's lithe figure filled the monitor as she strolled along the beach.

"Dissolve to one thirteen," said Goldman, "and do a slow push."

Yasantwa's wide shot faded into a backlit shot from the waist up. It looked like a tourism ad for Jamaica or the Virgin Islands. Her soaked tank top was clinging to her chest in all the right places as the camera pushed in, ending on a close-up of her incredible face just as her eyes opened, the ocean reflected in them.

"Damn, she's hot," said Eddie, gazing at the monitors, verbalizing what the other men in the room were thinking. Goldman was the lone exception, thinking purely technically. He had gotten the shot and it was time to move on.

"What's Alpha up to?" he said, mostly to himself.

He scanned the myriad of images on his screens and found a shot of the helicopter hovering over an inlet on the southeast shore.

"Cut to two thirty-five."

The image in the small window instantly replaced Yasantwa's close-up on the main monitor. His timing was excellent once again—a beat later, a body was cascading out the open door of the chopper.

It was the Russian, whose sheer mass made a huge splash. Unlike Yasantwa, he had no problem unlocking his restraints and freeing himself. He swam for the beach, which had less foliage and more rocks but was an equally stunning bay.

Raudsep, like the Nazi, understood very little English and had been privately briefed via a translator. He knew what was expected of him. Easily the largest and strongest contestant on the island, the Russian had been hunted through the worst parts of Communist Eastern Europe in alternately blistering and freezing weather conditions, so this island already seemed like a vacation. After his murder spree, he had nearly been caught on four separate occasions, each time taking bullets and/or beatings and still managing to escape.

Raudsep had been a kickboxer in his youth and had always loved to fight. His parents were hardworking Slavs who never understood him—how could they understand a child who broke his brother's neck and felt absolutely nothing about it? He and Yuri had been roughhousing; he hadn't meant to hurt him, he told them. But his parents were wrong—he *had* felt something. And he wanted to feel it again. What eventually made him a serial killer and rapist was anybody's guess; even he didn't know. What he did know was that he had an appetite for violence.

Naturally he wanted to win the contest and be freed, but the competition itself was just as attractive. Raudsep moved between the rocks and disappeared into the jungle, looking for someone to kill rather than hiding.

The Alpha chopper banked around the inlet to a longer stretch of beach. Paco was next in line. Baxter shoved him along the cable and stopped him opposite the open door.

"Open up!"

He reached into a bucket full of keys and shoved one into the Mexican's mouth. Paco took a last look at his wife, his eyes doing all the talking.

"*Te quiero,*" she said back, tears in her own. Her love for him now, on the brink of death, made her heart swell to the point of bursting. She had hated the world before fate brought them together. Paco had been her life preserver in a sea of poverty and abuse. Looking back, their six-month spree of robberies and shootings now seemed like a fuzzy dream. The killings had seemed surreal at the time. The victims had been face-less and interchangeable. She had erased most of them from her memory, the way you blotted out the bad parts of a vacation and clung to the highlights. Paco was the only highlight in her miserable life. Once he was shoved out that door, she feared she would never see him again.

Paco had much the same thoughts, except that he

had erased nothing. Rosa hadn't been the first woman in his life, but she would definitely be his last, even if they somehow survived this bullshit contest. He had been with enough *putas* to know he had found his Mary Magdalene. Rosa's love was pure and loyal. It transcended both their human flaws. He had given her a gun and taught her how to shoot it. She never questioned him. Paco took no enjoyment in killing store clerks and the occasional witness, and neither did she. They did what they had to do to survive. At least that's what he had told himself so he could sleep at night. Now, with fewer than thirty hours until that thing on his leg exploded, his guilt was making a comeback. He hoped God was more forgiving than his Catholic upbringing had taught him.

He looked at Rosa again and forgot about himself. He would gladly give up his life for her if it came down to that. The thought of any harm coming to her . . .

"Don't worry, gringo, I'll look after the wife," McStarley said with a smile, interrupting his thoughts.

Paco peered at the Englishman, his guilt about killing the clerks gone in a heartbeat. As soon as they hit that island, he and Rosa would do what they had to do to survive, including murdering this English gringo.

McStarley's grinning face was the last thing he saw before Baxter shoved him out the door.

Conrad had been continually observing the married couple, along with McStarley. It was clear that Paco's love for his wife would cloud his judgment and hinder his chances for survival. It stirred his own thoughts of

Sarah and her boys, memories that Conrad quickly pushed away. They were a key reason for him to make it through this, but his wits needed to be razor sharp and focused on the present. This would be a thinking man's game as much as a test of brute force. Factoring in those prerequisites, the Brit appeared to be his toughest competition. But there were others, like the huge Russian and the experienced German, who likely had survival experience and equal cunning.

At this same moment, Bruggerman was being pushed from the Bravo chopper on the control room monitor.

The German had been dropped a short way down the pristine beach from where Yasantwa had been delivered, which was no accident. Breckel knew exactly what the Nazi had in mind and wanted them to connect early on. Yasantwa's near demise had given him a start, but now they were back on track.

"He'll be on her in less than five minutes," he predicted. "Gotta grab your audience right up front."

8

The Nazi easily removed his restraints and made it to shore. As Breckel surmised, he was of single-minded purpose. They had made it easy for him to accomplish his goal, dropping him on the same beach as the South African woman but out of her view. She would not see him coming.

The Bravo chopper, which he'd just left, was already two coves down. The rusted and rotting wreckage of an American World War II PT boat protruded from the sea just offshore as the helicopter approached it. Eighty feet long with a wooden hull, the torpedo boat had been built by Elco Naval Division in 1942 and had been crippled by the Japanese before being abandoned. All three officers and fourteen crew members on board had died here, several shot down as they crawled up on the beach. Death was no stranger to this part of the island.

Giangrasso was up next and still fuming, the guards now the target of his wrath.

"*Aspetta—lasciami stare*," he seethed, making no sense to anyone. "I'll be waiting for you dogs in the bush!"

The guards were fully aware of his background as a wife killer who sold crappy Italian cars. He was just a regular asshole, not military trained like some of the others. His threat level was low.

"Whatever you say, pizza man," said one of the guards, sliding him toward the open door and unlocking his cable chain.

"I'll be eating you, you, and you!" he shouted at Saiga, K.C., and the other guard. *"Mangio tutti come prosciutto e melone, mangio tutti or come coniguio cacciatore.* Breakfast, lunch, and dinner!"

The guard shoved a key in his mouth to shut him up.

He tried to push him out the door but underestimated the Italian's volatility. Giangrasso recoiled, diving into the guard. His partner jumped in to help. Fists were flying. Saiga and K.C., still restrained, could only watch.

"We're past the mark!" shouted the pilot.

Giangrasso got to his feet and screamed at them. One of the guards let loose and hit the Italian squarely in the jaw, which sent him backward out the door. He continued to shout as he fell toward the water.

His voice was abruptly cut off as he landed directly on top of the boat wreckage. A crooked three-foot shaft of corroded iron impaled him through his back and out his chest.

Up on the control room monitor, blood gushed from the Italian's mouth in vivid color, his eyes bugged in a hideous death stare. It was something out of a horror flick, too graphic to be real.

"Oops," Goldman quietly said.

"Ooooops?" exclaimed Breckel. "That's no fuckin' oops. That just cost me a hundred fucking Gs!"

Breckel had paid a healthy sum for Dominic Giangrasso. The Italian warden had not been as easily corrupted as his third-world counterparts. Not only that, he had hoped for a suspenseful hunt and possibly some comic relief from the diarrhea-mouthed contestant. Adding insult to injury, the coverage of his fall was only mediocre since it had not been planned.

"Give me that," Breckel snapped at Bella, grabbing her radio mike. She was already talking with one of the guards, trying to figure out what went wrong.

"Hey, idiots, I got a show to put on! Watch where you're throwing these guys!"

A guard's voice came on the line. "He went berserk, Mr. Breckel, there was nothing we could . . ."

Breckel tossed the mike back to Bella and walked away. Excuses were something he had no patience for. Results were all that mattered. He would be having a chat with Baxter and make sure the guards responsible not only were fired but would never work again.

He caught Julie staring at him. He realized she had never before seen him like this. He didn't have the time to assuage her right now, but a few well-placed words would bode well for him when they retreated to his private quarters later.

"Nobody said producing was easy," he said quietly.

She nodded back without comment.

"How'd you like the opening?"

She hesitated to pick the right words. "It was exciting," she finally answered.

Her answer had been truthful. The helicopter arrivals, graphics, stunts, and underwater shots had been as stunning as any big action film. But she couldn't stop her eyes from drifting back to a monitor displaying the impaled Italian. Breckel followed her look.

"He killed his entire family, Julie. He got what he deserved. Besides, he did it to himself—if he hadn't gone crazy, he'd still be alive."

This, too, was correct. Fortunately, Giangrasso's death had mostly been obscured, which also made it easier to stomach.

It's immoral and illegal, she heard in her head.

It was Donna Sereno's voice. The journalist was long gone now, putting together her story back in the real world. But as she watched it unfold on the monitors, the island and the people on it no longer seemed quite real to Julie. Separated from the action by millions of pixels, it was slowly becoming fiction.

Up there in the Bravo chopper, it was one hundred percent reality.

K. C. Mack had heard enough of the guard's radio chat to know that Giangrasso was dead.

"Tutti-frutti is off the books." He grinned at Saiga, who was next in line to be shoved out. The Asian didn't seem to understand or care. K.C. ignored him after that. *Fuck 'm. I'll be turnin' his scrawny lil ass into sushi anyway,* he mused.

In reality, Saiga understood perfectly. He had glimpsed the boat wreckage and had studied the guard's body language as he talked on the radio. The Italian had died thanks to the guards' ineptness. They were amateurs, allowing a prisoner to get the upper hand like that. The Italian was also an idiot, since fighting them had served no purpose. He should have conserved his energy for the island; instead he got himself killed.

Saiga eyed the black man with the funny hair. There was no indication of any martial arts training, so he'd be going down fast. In his mind, only three convicts posed any real competition: the Englishman, the big Russian, and possibly the American—only because of his eyes. While the others were easily readable, there was something lurking in there he couldn't quite define. Something spiritual . . . a will to survive.

"Open up!" shouted the guard as he proffered a key.

Saiga obeyed, staring at his reflection in the guard's mirrored sunglasses. The sun was intense out there, the white sand beaches blinding. Dark glasses would come in handy.

The other guard unlocked him from the cable as the key went into his mouth.

His hands moving in a blur, Saiga snatched the glasses off the guard's face and backflipped out the door, managing to salute the guard with his middle finger as he fell.

"Hey!"

K.C. chuckled at the guard, more than a little amused.

"You think that's funny?" shouted Baxter's man. The Ray-Bans had cost him over two hundred bucks.

"Yeah. I do." He grinned.

The guard slugged him in the gut. K.C. would have doubled over if he hadn't been chained to the cable.

Thirty seconds later, he had a key in his mouth and he was free-falling into the sea.

The prisoners now having all been delivered, the Bravo chopper returned to the mainland.

Over in the Alpha chopper, Conrad and McStarley were the last prisoners remaining. They were taking stock of each other like prizefighters before the bell.

McStarley was the first to break the silence. "Are you enjoying the ride, big fella?"

Conrad stared back. The Brit's accent wasn't upper-crust English. Maybe even had a bit of cockney in it, or blue-collar Liverpool. Conrad guessed he had come from low income with a chip on his shoulder and joined the military to vent it. Or could be he was just plain crazy. Either way, fighting for queen and country was not part of McStarley's agenda. It was purely for himself.

McStarley sensed the cold inspection but was unfazed. "I take that as a no. Don't worry, it'll be over soon enough."

Conrad felt a jab in his side.

"Slide on down, redneck. You're up."

He eyed Baxter and didn't budge.

Baxter gave him another shove, which was like pushing a brick wall.

"You're goin' one way or another," said the security chief as he slapped his baton into his hand.

Conrad could see he was looking for an excuse to crack it over his head. He slid his chain down the cable, stopping at the open door. Baxter pulled out a key.

"Open your fucking mouth."

Conrad kept it closed. Baxter's power trip was beginning to grate on him. He decided he might not get another opportunity to teach the asshole a lesson.

"I said, OPEN YOUR FUCKIN' M—"

Conrad's elbow was in motion as the last syllable left Baxter's mouth. He cracked the side of his head hard enough for him to see stars. Baxter careened backward, falling into the other guard. He had wisely kept Conrad chained to the cable, or the damage would have been worse.

McStarley was bellowing with laughter. "He never saw *that* coming!" he howled.

Baxter got to his feet, unsheathing his black-handled combat knife. He wanted to gut Conrad right then and there and almost did, but he stopped himself. Breckel would be livid. His boss had been thrilled to land the American, especially at the last minute. They had just lost the Italian as well.

But he couldn't let this go unpunished.

Baxter shoved the blade against Conrad's throat, drawing a trickle of blood.

"You're gonna pay for that." He glanced at the pilot. "Turn inland."

The helicopter swooped to the right, the beach coming up fast. They were flying over a stretch of sand dunes.

Baxter nodded to his subordinate, who carefully unlocked Conrad's chain.

"What about his key?" said the other guard.

Baxter said nothing and shoved Conrad out the door.

9

Conrad fell more than fifty feet. The world was spinning from his point of view, alternating among blue, green, and tan. The sky accounted for one-third and the green was jungle. Tan was the predominant color. If he landed on the sand dunes right, he wouldn't break any bones.

The thud knocked the wind out of him and he immediately started to tumble. His shackled arms and legs were restricting his movement so he couldn't slow himself down. He shut his eyes and mouth to keep out the sand, having no sense of direction other than what gravity told him. Eventually he hit bottom and rolled to a stop.

Conrad spat out the powdery sand and opened his lids. The rusted chassis of a World War II jeep was half buried ten feet away at the high-tide mark. He thought again about the weather tower, which had also looked vintage Second World War. This island had some stories to tell, with new ones on the way.

He appraised his shackles and realized he was screwed without a key. Elbowing Baxter had seemed like a good idea at the time, but now it was just plain stupid. He thought of Sarah's older son, Michael, who also had the tendency to act on his aggressions without thinking. *Use your head first and your fists second*, he had told him. It was time to practice what he preached.

His vision went to his ankle bracelet. The digital timer read *26:31:03* and was relentlessly ticking down. With no guards hovering over him, he was now able to carefully examine the wires and the housing containing the plastic explosives. Conrad was a bomb expert, among other things—but on closer inspection, he realized that Baxter had been telling the truth in the hangar. There was no way, even with the right tools, to disarm this bomb or stop the clock. The device could be shut down only wirelessly via the host program, or with a special key. Glancing around, he didn't see any keys or laptops on the beach.

McStarley came to mind. He had sensed the Brit wanted to murder everyone in that chopper while still in the air but had smartly held back from acting on impulse. In his mind's eye he saw McStarley sliding along the cable with no backtalk, taking the key with total cooperation, and allowing himself to be pushed out over water.

That, in fact, is exactly what happened, all of it captured for broadcast. Back in the control room, everyone but Conrad was being featured on the main monitor.

Breckel frowned at the screen. He turned away from it and moved to Goldy. "What happened to my American?"

Goldman eyed the monitor that displayed all of his

camera angles. He found a wide shot of the sand dunes and spotted Conrad by the rusted jeep.

"Got launched over the dunes."

He pressed a console button and Conrad appeared on the main screen. Two seconds later, the shot cut to a much closer angle. A lens was hidden in the rusted jeep.

"Why isn't he unlocking himself?"

"Must've lost his key when he tumbled." Goldman shrugged.

Breckel didn't think so, but that was a conversation he needed to have with Baxter. Even though the odds were now stacked against Conrad, the producer didn't think it would take him out of the game. Breckel always prided himself on good casting. He knew talent when he saw it. Jack Conrad was a definite contender.

He pulled his eyes away from the screen again.

"Eddie, talk to me."

Eddie C had a computer graphic image of the island up on his panel. Nine + signs were scattered across the south shore, shifting positions in real time.

"I've got 'em all in a nice little cluster on the south end of the island. It's only a matter of time."

"Good. Goldy, what's happening with black beauty and the Nazi?"

"On it. Bring up the split screen," he told his tech JJ.

Two images appeared on the main monitor. Yasantwa occupied the right half, the Nazi the left. Their body language made it clear who was the hunter and who was prey. Yasantwa was fearfully looking everywhere, the Nazi focused in one direction. He was stealthily ducking in and out of foliage; she was aimless.

Yasantwa walked past a huge branch of driftwood and continued on. Two seconds later, the same branch appeared on the Nazi's screen and he stalked past it. He was almost within striking distance.

The screen images couldn't capture the tension there on the beach. Gentle waves kissed the shore, an offshore breeze ruffling the palms. It gave Yasantwa a false sense of calm. She let her guard down and began to relax.

Something hummed above her and she stiffened. There was a cable running the length of the cove, strung between two trees. A motorized cluster of three cameras was rolling down the cable and stopped directly overhead, almost like it was waiting.

She looked away and saw the Japanese convict, Saiga, dart behind a rock a hundred yards down the beach. Had he seen her? She didn't want to stick around to find out.

Yasantwa turned to run and stopped dead in her tracks.

The Nazi was staring back at her, not ten feet away.

She gasped and ran.

"Action, action, we have action!" shouted Breckel in the control room.

The split screen was gone. Both convicts now appeared in one shot, Goldman's cluster cam racing along the cable as the Nazi chased her down the beach.

"Get me in there! What have we got?" barked Breckel.

"Twenty-three, twenty-four, thirty-one," answered Goldman. "All good angles. We're on twenty-three now."

The cluster cam zipped down the wire, continuing to follow the action. Yasantwa was a gazelle but the Nazi was fit and determined. He tackled her in a matter of seconds, rolled her over, and slugged her hard in the face.

As Goldman intercut various angles, Bella mouse-clicked a button on her display and brought up tribal chants.

"Okay, great!" exclaimed Breckel. "Get me in tighter, Goldy! GET ME TIGHTER!"

Goldman winced as he tried to focus on the action. "You know what's really awesome? When you yell at me like that it really helps my concentration."

"Bella, layer some jungle music on top of those chants," ordered the producer, ignoring Goldy. "Let's go now! Right away!"

On the beach, Yasantwa scrambled out from under the Nazi and clawed her way through dead branches on the driftwood. Her heart was pounding jackhammer hard. Memories of her childhood were fueling part of it, with momentary flashes of her violent past mingling with the present. She had crawled under a bed in much the same way that she was crawling under these dead limbs. Like then, she also felt the grip on her ankle dragging her back. Yasantwa had been only fourteen, her attacker a boyfriend of her mother's. She remembered her fingers clawing into the throw rug to no avail, just like her fingers were now trying to gain purchase in the sand. The boyfriend had pulled her out, rolled her over, and slapped her. Her cries had been ignored as he tore at her clothes.

It happened in much the same way now, only the Nazi was far more brutal. His age did nothing to slow him down; his slaps were hard-fisted slugs. He got up and kicked her brutally enough to crack ribs. She clawed, kicked, and bit back ferociously—she was tougher than she looked—but she was no match for him. The German clocked her with a roundhouse and she flew backward into the branches, hitting her head hard. Part of her wanted to lose consciousness and let this be over, but she willed herself not to give up.

With the look of a coyote about to eat a wounded rabbit it had snared, Bruggerman gazed down at her. He was salivating and didn't even realize it, his desire to viciously rape and murder her purely instinctual. Like the other non-Aryans he had violated during his military stint, she had lost her identity as a human being and had simply become an object to quench his craving. Bruggerman had used guns and especially knives to achieve his goal in the past, leading to his "Butcher" nickname. In his steely blue eyes, he might as well have been slaughtering a farm animal.

Everyone in the control room watched the main screen, no one speaking. It was as if they were driving by the scene of a horrendous car accident and slowing down to get a glimpse of the gore. Some clearly felt guilty, while others gawked.

"This is hard fuckin' core," said Eddie, who was in awe.

"Gnarly," chimed in Bella, also riveted.

Julie had a completely different reaction. The images were sickening to the point that she had to look away. How far was Ian going to let this go? Was he going to televise a rape in graphic close-up?

Breckel ogled the screen, glimpsing Julie out the corner of his eye. He knew her reaction would not be unique. Of course there would be fallout. The press would hail him as a sick monster. There would be legal challenges, government commissions, new restrictions put on internet content. But in his world—the world of entertainment—the judge and jury were ratings, box office, and subscriber count, not critics and politicians. Watching the screen, he knew he had a hit on his hands. He had no intention of cutting away.

The Nazi climbed on top of Yasantwa and grabbed her tank top, one second away from shredding it off.

Yasantwa again flashed on her childhood attacker. At that age, she had been too terrified and powerless to resist. Older and wiser, she had evened the odds several times over. She felt that same rage now and lunged forward, grabbing his genitals, squeezing them as hard as she could.

The Nazi howled in pain, momentarily paralyzed. Yasantwa tried to extricate herself but he snatched her back with one hand, his other holding his aching groin. He slugged her again, roiling with anger. The desire to rape fell by the wayside. He wanted her to die quickly and brutally. Bruggerman grabbed her throat with both hands and dug his thumbs into her larynx, strangling her.

Yasantwa flailed. She gripped his forearms, futilely trying to pry his hands away, her legs kicking but making no contact. She struggled to breathe like a drowning swimmer searching for air that didn't exist. The beautiful woman stared into his icy eyes and saw the devil. The Nazi was every man who had ever taken advantage of her, every man she had killed. They had come back from death to torture her one last time and then snuff out her life.

Her hands slipped from his arms. Her lids fluttered. The world grayed. She was dying. It wasn't fair.

No, she told herself. *I won't let them win.*

Yasantwa blindly reached around and latched onto a dead branch. She bent it and heard the snap. With her last burst of energy, she swung it toward him.

The Nazi screamed. His hands left her throat. She sucked in air and life flooded down her windpipe, her eyes fluttering open again. The Nazi's neck was gushing with blood, the branch sticking out of it like the bolt in the Frankenstein's monster's neck. He screamed in German, trying to pry out the shaft. Yasantwa got a leg free and kicked him in the face, sending him on his back.

Several people in the control room applauded, caught up in the action. Julie looked back at the screen and felt a wave of relief that the tables had turned.

"Run!" she yelled at Yasantwa on the screen, unable to help herself.

Breckel glanced over at her and beamed. His show,

97

his genius, had won Julie over, just like he knew it would.

Yasantwa didn't hear Julie or any applause. She didn't run either, though she certainly could have. The woman knew she'd put the Nazi out of commission long enough for one of the others to find and kill him, if he didn't bleed to death on his own . . . but her personal survival required more than simply escaping. She wanted him dead, gone, having never existed.

The convicted killer from South Africa crawled toward him and pulled the red tab on his ankle bracelet.

The clock timer numbers abruptly flashed to *00:00:10* and began ticking down, each second beeping. Yasantwa stared into his face as it began to beep.

It was Bruggerman's turn to see the devil.

The Nazi forgot about his blood-gushing neck and frantically tried to pry the device from his leg as she scrambled away.

Bruggerman shouted at her in guttural German as he futilely tried to free himself of the bomb. The timer now had three seconds to go. For the remainder of time he was alive, he howled to the heavens with hateful rage.

The fireball was massive, as Baxter had promised in the hangar. Twenty ounces of C-4 created a house-sized explosion, turning Bruggerman into a vapor that painted the sand red.

There was an audible gasp in the control room.

"Hard fuckin' core," repeated Eddie to himself. He glanced at his computer display just as one of the + signs vanished off the screen.

Above him on the big plasma, a red X crossed out the mug shot of Helmut Bruggerman.

Breckel was enjoying the same display. The contestants had been vividly narrowed to eight and they were only an hour into the show. He had delivered his audience a bang-up opening, with a nice little twist. Still, it was way too early to gloat. He had twenty-nine hours to go and seven more convicts to kill before a winner could be declared. It needed to be carefully orchestrated to maximize subscribers. The longer it lasted, the more paying customers, but not if it got boring. None of his shows had ever been criticized for being dull. He was not about to break that streak now.

10

The blast was heard for miles, and they all knew what it meant.

Saiga, who was the closest, saw the fireball, which was reflected in the sunglasses he had torn off the guard's face. He narrowed down the death to one of two people: the black woman or the German. Both had been shoved out just before him and were in close proximity. The woman was the logical victim, since she could easily be overpowered, but there was a good argument for exactly the opposite. He couldn't picture the Kraut blowing her up right off the bat, if at all. He would want to have his way with her first and then most likely finish her off with his bare hands. Saiga hoped she had somehow gotten the advantage. With the German and the Italian out of the way, his odds of winning would substantially increase.

He glanced in the other direction and saw the distant wreckage of the PT boat that had claimed the Italian's life. The mushrooming fireball and the sunken war boat triggered thoughts of his grandmother, who had been living in a poor village on the outskirts of Nagasaki when the atomic bomb had been dropped. She had survived the initial blast, which was worse than if she'd died instantly. Saiga's mother, who had been spared because she was visiting relatives in Kyoto, told him that the radiation poisoning took its sweet time killing his grandmother. Unable to afford adequate pain medication, she had suffered for two horrible years before dying. Ironically, his own mother succumbed to lymphoma when he was thirteen. Japan had a high rate of cancer, which some chalked up to mercury poisoning and other environmental contamination, but others blamed the remnants of radiation poisoning.

He hated the Americans for dropping the bombs, as well as their current political arrogance in the Middle East. America was a big, stupid, redneck bully. He especially looked forward to killing the one they called Conrad, who was the poster boy for everything he despised.

Two miles away, Conrad heard the blast and saw the smoke, also knowing exactly what it meant. He was still coming to terms with being locked in chains with a bomb ticking on his ankle.

This shit is fucked up, he told himself as the black cloud continued to mushroom.

The smoke was rising due south. Whoever had died had come from the other chopper, which eliminated McStarley, the Mexican couple, and the Russian.

He decided it didn't matter a whole lot. While McStarley and the Russian seemed to be the greatest threats to him, he was fair game for all of them if he didn't get these chains off.

Conrad moved to the jeep, looking for something to pry a chain link or pick the locks. He grabbed the steering shaft and it disintegrated into rusty dust. The jeep would be no help.

He noticed a lens hidden in what was left of the dash and glared. If he hung around here for too much longer, the assholes on the end of that camera would get the show they wanted. Here on the sand dunes, he was fully exposed for an attack.

Conrad looked south. The expanse of sand ended a half mile away and rocks took over. They would provide temporary cover; possibly he could break his restraints with a heavy enough rock.

As Conrad began his trek, the tail end of the Nazi's blast filled the control room monitor. Bruggerman's death had been almost surreal, one of those moments where everyone in the room questioned what they'd actually seen. Action fans replayed scenes like this frame by frame to see where the computer effects kicked in.

Breckel knew his worldwide audience would be doing exactly that, soon discovering it was the real thing. He was pleased with the turn of events even though he hadn't seen it coming. His demographic, which would be predominantly male, would have liked to have seen the Nazi have his way with the sexy murderess, but there were plenty of others standing in line to take over for him. Word would spread like wildfire that the island had a deadly black widow on it.

Eddie C was already on it. "Breck—five million. Five million subscribers have logged on to the site."

"That's a start."

Goldman looked up. "That's a start? What are you after?"

"You know how many households watch the Super Bowl?"

"Forty million."

"That's what I'm after."

Goldman, Eddie, and Bella all stared at him.

"That's impossible," declared Goldman.

Breckel didn't acknowledge the word, never had. His detractors had said half of his shows would be impossible to pull off, yet he'd done it.

"Wait till the blogs and chat rooms hype up the fact that some sadistic Nazi dirtbag just got wasted, *live*, by a hot African chick with a nice rack," Breckel exclaimed. "Trust me, Goldy. The Internet—it's wildfire."

"The posts are already flying," Eddie confirmed as he hopped among sites.

Breckel slapped his old friend Goldy on the shoulder. "Good work."

Goldman smiled weakly as Breckel turned to his entire staff. "Good work, people. Good work!"

He looked around for Julie, but she had left the room.

Paco had splashed down just off a rocky shore with a coral reef. The shallow reef kicked up three-foot waves wrapping around the point to his south, with an expanse of sand dunes beyond. He managed to unlock his leg shackles before his oxygen ran out and he was forced to surface. A wave washed him into the rocks, his knees scraping across the sharp coral and his pants tearing.

With his key tightly held in one fist, he crawled over the coral and boulders, slipping twice and bruising his forearms. He eventually made it onto a flat, rocky terrace filled with tide pools and slumped from exhaustion.

A huge explosion shot fresh adrenaline into his veins. He got to his feet and looked around, but the rocky landmass and high cliff behind him obscured his vision in all directions except out to sea. He glanced at the ticking bomb on his ankle and felt a rush of dread. One of them had died, which was fine with him as long as it wasn't Rosa. He had no way of knowing it was the Nazi, so panic hit him hard—could it have been her? Right now his whole body ached, but not as much as his heart. He had only one mission—to find and protect his wife from the others.

Paco unlocked his wrist restraints and tried to get his bearings. The helicopter had continued south after he'd been dropped, which meant Rosa was in the direction of the dunes. He'd been able to see the mass of sand from the water, so he knew which way to go. The thought of being highly visible on the expansive beach never crossed his mind like it had Conrad's. Paco had never been hunted. He had always had the upper hand in all of his robberies, his victims defenseless.

He started to move and thought again about the explosion. Unless somebody had tried to remove his bracelet or had intentionally killed himself, both of which seemed like a long shot, he had been attacked.

Paco instantly felt naked without a gun, something to protect himself. He went back and grabbed one of his chains. It was better than nothing.

Meanwhile, Conrad crossed the dunes and made it to the edge of the rocks. Climbing them while shackled was no easy task and progress was slow. Fortunately, the sound of crashing waves drowned out the rattling of his restraints; if anybody was waiting for him on the other side of this landmass, at least he wouldn't hear him coming.

He reached an unscalable rock and waded into the breakwater up to his neck, coral crunching under his boots. Once around the boulder, Conrad climbed from the sea, his chains catching in the crags. He was now a sitting duck if an adversary happened by. Conrad held his breath and ducked underwater, using up two lungfuls of oxygen before freeing himself. These chains were becoming a real pain in the ass.

He climbed back onto land and found himself on a huge rock terrace filled with tide pools. While searching his surroundings for a loose rock to break his restraints, he spotted movement reflected in one of the pools. Conrad eased behind a rock as the shape took on human form. The reflection was upside down and rippling from the breeze, which obscured the convict's identity.

The reflection disappeared as a boot stepped into the pool. Conrad crouched. Listened. And sprang.

Paco never saw it coming when Conrad knocked him on his back. The Mexican tried to swing his chain, but Conrad easily ripped it away and dragged him to his feet, slamming him against the rock face. He wrapped his own chains around Paco's neck and began to choke him.

"What're you doin', boy? You trackin' me?" he spoke into Paco's ear.

Paco angrily tried to punch him, but Conrad easily dodged the blows.

"You can move on, or things are gonna get a little rough," he said matter-of-factly, tightening the chains.

The Mexican struggled harder. His anger and pride had been replaced with fear. He knew he was about to die if he didn't do something. Everyone was there to kill or be killed.

Conrad choked him even harder, all business. He spun him around and stared him square in the eyes. "You can live or you can die."

Paco had no choice but to stop struggling. The chain was crushing his Adam's apple and he could barely speak.

"*Esai*, please . . . I'm looking for my wife . . . that's all I want."

Conrad appraised him. He'd seen enough in the hangar and the chopper to believe him. Moreover, he respected what the man needed to do. Criminal or not, he was a human being.

Although the Mexican posed very little threat, Conrad still eased up cautiously. He removed the chains and backed away, allowing the Mexican on his way.

Paco picked up his own chain, digesting Conrad's act of mercy. The rules were last man standing, yet the

American had spared his life. Why? He couldn't win if he left anyone alive.

The only explanation was that he wasn't an animal, like the others. Maybe Conrad had a wife. Maybe he had some compassion.

Paco reached into his pocket. "Gringo. Try this." He pulled out his key and tossed it to Conrad. "*Gracias*," he added.

Conrad slid the key in his wrist shackle. The lock popped open.

The two exchanged a look of mutual respect, and then Paco resumed his search for his wife.

11

Like Paco, Conrad was on a mission, which was to locate the weather tower he had seen from the air. Short of murdering his competitors—not that most of them didn't deserve it—his best hope for survival seemed to be in communicating with the outside world. Jack Conrad was many things, but he wasn't a cold-blooded killer. He also knew that the next twenty-four hours and thirty-one minutes, which is what his timer now displayed, would hardly be a cakewalk. He needed to talk to Sarah one last time.

Approaching the tower from the sea had appeared impossible due to the sheer cliffs. This meant taking an inland route. The sun set in the west but it was nearly straight up now, making an accurate course difficult to plot. The curvature of the island also contributed to directional disorientation. What he needed was a compass.

Besides his extensive training in firearms and explosives, Conrad had been taught basic survival skills as part of his job. Right now, he didn't want to think about the job, which had indirectly put him on this island, but the training he had been given would help keep him alive. He thought about making a simple sundial compass by shoving a stick in the sand, which he had done before. All he had to do was connect the points of its shadows over a period of time and then draw a perpendicular line to indicate north and south.

He abandoned the design for two reasons. It wouldn't be portable, and it relied exclusively on the sun. Since he would need periodically to check his course in the jungle, many areas of which saw very little sunlight, he decided to make a traditional water-cork compass, which solved both problems.

First, he needed to magnetize a needle or sliver of metal. The way to magnetize it was to rub it against another magnet.

Conrad glanced at his ankle bracelet. The device contained an electromagnet as part of its GPS mechanism. Now he just needed the needle and cork equivalents.

Stripping one of the wires on his bracelet would work, but he would likely detonate himself in the process. He thought hard and realized the key to finding it was right there in his hand . . . literally. Paco's key.

He wedged the key into a crevice in the rocks and repeatedly bent it until its head snapped off, leaving only the shaft.

Finding the "cork" was much easier—a puffy seaweed bulb.

When Conrad spotted the clump of seaweed, he instantly thought of his father. As a kid, he and his dad had gone to South Padre Island one summer. It was a six-hour drive south from their house in Granville, Texas, but it had seemed like a trip to a distant planet. Granville was off Farm Road 2497, about eight miles from Lufkin in Angelina County. It was flat, boring, Texas farmland. Not a lot of seaweed was being plowed there. South Padre had miles of sandy beaches and the infinite blue sea. It meant escape from chores and school, but most important of all, it was a chance to spend time alone with his dad, who was frequently overseas. Conrad's father was a military man serving his country, but on that island he served nobody but his son. They had walked on the beach and popped seaweed bulbs during that once-in-a-lifetime visit. His dad shipped off to Grenada a week later, and returned in a coffin. America had victoriously eliminated a Marxist regime and President Reagan awarded his father a posthumous medal. Conrad hung tough at the funeral like his daddy would've wanted. He saluted the coffin and held back his tears. He was prouder than any boy could possibly be, which certainly influenced his career choice.

His thoughts flashed forward. Over the years, Granville hadn't changed much—his mom had passed and now resided in the town's lone cemetery; the podunk downtown with a funky bar and grill and smattering of farmhouses was all that kept it on the map. It had Sarah and her boys as well.

Right now, it seemed like paradise.

He shoved aside all of these recollections. It did no good to think about it under his present circumstances. He set out to make his compass, carefully rubbing the key against the electronics in his bracelet. Two minutes later, he balanced it on top of the seaweed bulb and floated it in the same tide pool that had telegraphed Paco's arrival.

It slowly turned and pointed north, showing him the way.

One minute later, Conrad appeared on a control room monitor as he hiked into the next cove and immediately trekked inland. His seven competitors were similarly featured on screens as they traversed the island's interior. There was no fighting, no interaction at all.

Breckel paced off his frustration. If something didn't happen soon, viewers would drop off. The blogs would kill him.

"Take a look at this," he barked at Baxter as he walked in. "This is no good. Give me a supply drop at the B-25 wreck. Right now."

Baxter nodded and got on his radio.

K. C. Mack made it to shore and removed his restraints with little fanfare. His ribs still ached from the guard's punch, not to mention the crook in his neck from hitting the water wrong. Back home, he would have sicced his posse on the motherfucker or probably just done the job himself. That guard would be lying dead in some alley right about now. But not here. This was not Inglewood. He didn't have a posse or tickets to a Lakers game or a table waiting for him at the Brown Sugar strip club. Couldn't buy off anyone, couldn't trade dope for favors, couldn't cap his way out of this. By his own estimation, he was fucked up the ass.

The bomb on his ankle didn't help matters. Forgetting Baxter's warning speech, he gave it a quick appraisal and decided it needed to be removed. K.C. grabbed a leg shackle he had just removed and banged on the lock.

Lights flashed on the device, followed by a slow, deliberate beeping sound. This couldn't be good. He froze in a stare, waiting to see if he was about to die.

The explosion sent him three feet in the air.

It took him a few seconds to realize he was still alive. The bomb had gone off about a mile away, around where they had dropped off the others. He could see the ball of smoke rising.

He darted his eyes back to his own bomb. The beeping had stopped, along with the blinking lights. He decided not to mess with it again.

The smoke was still mushrooming. Who was dead? He hoped it was the Nazi. The dude had been staring at him the whole ride over like he wanted to lynch him. Whoever it was, it was good news. Two of them were dead now, right off the bat. K.C. bet horses occasionally and found himself recalculating his odds. The women could be handicapped as well if it hadn't been one of them, leaving him with five real competitors. Things were looking up.

He made his way into the jungle with the intention of winning this contest. *Damn, could I use a gun*, he dreamed, but it wasn't like a firearm would be falling from the sky any time soon.

He spotted a dead branch and picked it up. It wasn't a gun, but it would have to do. He put his foot on one end and snapped it down to a manageable six feet, breaking off the side branches to make a spear.

A faint motorized noise drew his attention. He carefully pulled back a palm branch and found a camera lens staring at him, pivoting into a close-up. He stared into the lens.

"Fuck all a ya."

He beat the hell out of it with his spear.

One of the monitor windows went to snow in the control room. Bella was the first to notice. "We lost one twenty-two A."

"Great," moaned Goldman. "As if I didn't have enough problems without the talent smashing my gear."

"Be patient."

It was Breckel. He was ogling the screen, anticipating what was about to come. His care package would be arriving any time now to stir things up.

K.C. continued on in relative obscurity, arriving at a clearing overgrown with tall grass. He halted at the sight of a massive rusted airplane, or what was left of it. It looked like one of those World War II jobs he'd seen in the movies. The body, wings, and engines were spread everywhere like body parts.

It gave him the creeps. There were dead bodies here, dust and bones by now, but dead all the same. Not only that, if somebody wanted to spring out of a hiding place and kill his ass, this was the place.

K.C. cautiously raised his homemade weapon and stepped forward, unaware that a half dozen cameras mounted inside and out of the rotting B-52 were capturing his every move.

He was just about to enter when the sound of an approaching helicopter drew his gaze.

McStarley had been on a permanent adrenaline rush from the hangar briefing on. He fantasized about the order of his kills and what he would do to the women before ending their lives. There were lots of possibilities, and all had their merits. The married Mexicans held plenty of appeal because they would undoubtedly try to team up. He could make the husband watch while he took care of his wife. The Russian was big but brainless, like hunting down a wild rhino. The African beauty would be a real pleasure, but he doubted she would last long enough for him to seize that opportunity. The Nazi, Rasta boy, and diarrhea-mouthed Italian would all be foreplay, with the little Japanese geezer a bit more fun due to the fighting skills he had hinted at in the hangar.

The redneck American would probably be the most enticing. He sensed some training in the good ol' boy, which would make the odds more interesting, but he still wasn't a major concern.

After genially allowing himself to be pushed from the chopper, he dog-paddled into a pristine secluded cove and removed the rest of his shackles, never feeling more alive. Under other circumstances, he would have paid for the privilege of competing in an event like this. He was brimming with vitality, already having the time of his life. This island was his Disneyland, and there were nine rides to be had. His chains draped over his shoulder, he set off inland to have some fun.

McStarley was a hundred yards into the jungle when he heard the Nazi die. The explosion brought an instant smile and a fun new mind game as he tried to deduce who had been blown to bits. The sound had come from a good two miles off, which meant someone in the other chopper. Examining the five, the sushi man seemed too fast and shrewd. Rasta wasn't a genius, but he had street smarts. The Nazi was old but still seemed like he had some testosterone pumping through his veins. That left the loudmouth Italian and spicy South African bird. Having no idea that Giangrasso had already been impaled, he hoped it was him.

McStarley continued his stalk, moving like he knew where he was going. He was reeking with confidence, not a modicum of doubt in his mind that he would win.

He heard the unmistakable thudding of chopper blades and looked up. A helicopter flashed between the palms, smaller than the one that had delivered them. It dropped a large black duffel bag attached to a miniparachute. There was no way to miss where it would land thanks to the bright yellow-green smoke trailing from a signal flare. From McStarley's current position, its landing spot looked to be about a hundred yards off. He grinned widely and ran through a swamp toward it.

Saiga was also running, but from a different direction.

He had been hiking in and out of foliage as he made his way around the island. He saw the chopper drop the bag, along with the brightly colored trail of smoke.

Saiga was still wearing his shades when he darted into the jungle after it.

K. C. Mack was practically at ground zero for the drop. He hid behind one of the B-52's engines as the duffel landed a short distance away. He didn't know what the hell was inside it, or why it had been dropped. Then he remembered what the head honcho had said about supplies being delivered. Talk about the right place at the right time!

As all three convicts scrambled for the bag, Breckel watched them on separate monitors. Each was in a dead sprint, and it made for a nice little action sequence. He knew that dropping that bag in the clearing would be like tossing a steak into a pit of junkyard dogs. The spot he had picked, like everything else, had been carefully selected. The crashed B-52 was an incredible set piece.

K.C. reached the bag first and unzipped it. The first items to grace his eyes were bottles of water and wrapped sandwiches. He twisted off a cap and guzzled the water, devouring half a sandwich in one bite, his grin ear to ear. A hand went back into the bag and rummaged around.

It came back with a big hunting knife.

His eyes practically popped out of his skull.

"Now that's what I'm talkin' 'bout!" he exclaimed as he pulled it from its leather sheath.

Saiga arrived at the edge of the clearing and heard K.C. He stopped in his tracks and quietly crept forward. The black dude with the funny hair would be easy to take, though his knife could not be overlooked.

The clearing didn't help either, preventing a surprise attack. He decided he couldn't waste any time waiting for the situation to change—others might've seen the smoke and were probably on their way.

With his kung fu training, Saiga was confident enough to go head-to-head with K.C., right down to keeping his sunglasses on. He stepped into the clearing and made his presence known.

K.C. instantly stiffened. He moved in front of the supply bag as if he were a dog protecting his bone, just as Breckel had predicted.

"Calm down, homey."

Saiga continued forward.

"You try to take my food, I'm gonna have to cut you." He waved his sharp new possession to emphasize the point.

Saiga closed the gap.

K.C. heard a noise overhead and glanced up to see a motorized cluster cam gliding down a cable hung between palms. It stopped and hovered, vulturelike, over both of them. It pissed him off.

Saiga paid the cameras no attention. He was utterly focused, now within striking distance.

12

Conrad saw the chopper. Saw the trail of smoke. Knew exactly what it was. And ignored it.

He was a good two miles away from the drop, which meant about twelve minutes at a decent clip through the hilly jungle, longer if there were cliffs to circumvent. Even if he had been half that distance away, he would have avoided it. Breckel was playing games. He was getting his lab rats to scramble for the cheese and fight over it. Besides, there was plenty of food and water if you knew where to look.

Conrad eyed the topography and made his way toward a ravine surrounded by thick ferns, which required lots of water to remain lush. Sure enough, a creek bed ran through the valley, delivering fresh water from the rain forest farther inland.

He had already broken several thick shafts of bamboo into sections and now filled them with water, sealing them with plugs made of rubber plant leaves. Each homemade canteen held about a pint, which would get him to the weather tower without having to search out more hydration.

This was not the first time he had made bamboo canteens. While on the run in the jungles of El Salvador after his bombing assignment, he had relied on the same technique. Ultimately it had made little difference. Half the El Salvadoran army was after him and created an impenetrable web, making his capture unavoidable. He was supposed to have been pulled out way before that. Conrad had successfully fulfilled his mission, just like always, but this time nobody showed up.

He forced himself to forget about El Salvador and focus on the task at hand. It was time to recheck his directions. He dug a small hole and filled it with creek water, creating a puddle. The magnetized key and seaweed bulb made an encore appearance, pointing the way.

Saiga attacked K. C. Mack, his hands and feet moving in a blur. It was an artful ballet as much as combat, his rate of connection high. Each blow was cumulative rather than delivering a knockout punch. Saiga was putting on a show as much as trying to kill his adversary and plunder the supplies.

Even with the knife, K.C. was on the defensive. He sliced it through the air, but the wiry kung fu dude seemed to be invisible. Twice K.C. thought he had cut him in half, only to have him reappear in a different place. Worse, the Asian could fly—half the time he was off the ground. His feet did more talking than his hands, which K.C. also wasn't used to. After a round of kicks, his knife went sailing into the tall grass.

"What's the coverage here?" barked Breckel as he watched the fight on the main monitor.

"Besides the cluster cams, we've got three lenses on them from the B-52 and a couple others in the palms," answered Goldman, pointing at his other monitors. He was deftly cutting among his cameras, which ranged from overhead tracking shots to ground-level mediums to tight close-ups.

"How many cameras in total?"

"Plenty."

"Let's spice it up. Quick cuts, Goldy, and more close-ups of the blows. Come on, slice and dice."

"Um, I'm slicing and dicing," he grumbled. Breck was beginning to annoy him. "Do I tell you how to do your job?"

Bella and Eddie C were also hovering right behind Goldman, caught up in the action.

"Love this Japanese dude!" Eddie grinned.

"Hell, yeah," echoed Bella. "Who's your money on?"

"Hey, guys, will you do me a favor, will you please go back to your space? Because, this is kinda like *my* space," Goldman bitched.

He had been irritable from minute one, but the quotient had risen since the attack on the South African girl. Goldman felt like he was directing porn or a snuff film. The farther he got into this, the more he realized it wasn't *like* porn or snuff at all—it simply *was*. He had been tarting it up with flashy angles and rapid cuts, but the gorilla was still a gorilla, eight hundred pounds and growing. Now, during this fight, he was subtly cutting wider during some of the worst blows, which Breck was beginning to notice. Goldman decided that once he got through this and collected his hefty fee and profit participation, he was going to take a break from directing reality television.

There in the clearing, Saiga pulled off his sunglasses and tossed them beside the bag. It was time to dial up his attack. He laid into K.C. with a rapid series of kicks, the final blow whacking his head hard. K.C. was as angry as he was worried. He was getting his ass kicked by an Asian dude who was way smaller than him. It was time for some street fighting.

He glanced down and saw the miniparachute draped across the tall grass. The glimpse cost him another foot slam to his head, but that was okay. He fell close to the parachute, and when Saiga came in for the kill, K.C. lunged and covered him with the white silky cloth. Saiga buzzed like a bee trapped in a net, incapacitated long enough for K.C. to slug him in the face twice and knock him to the ground.

He knew his fists were no match against Saiga's feet, which would be flying soon enough. Again he wished for a nine or a .357—any gun, for that matter—but finding that knife had already been too good to be true. He quickly looked around for it, but the grass was too thick. Saiga was already wriggling out of the parachute. It was time to cut his losses.

Saiga yanked off the silk, mad that he'd fallen for such a stupid trick. He sprinted around the B-52 wreckage, darting inside and out, but K.C. was gone. He had underestimated the black man; that would not happen again. Still, his immediate goal had been achieved. He now had the supplies. He just needed to find the knife. As he stepped out of the fuselage and began to search for it—

"Lovely day, don't you think?"

A shaft of sunlight highlighted McStarley like a spotlight. He was standing by the supply bag wearing Saiga's sunglasses, munching on a juicy apple. The knife was in his other hand.

Saiga instinctively took a dramatic fighting stance. The Englishman would be more competition than the black man, quite a bit more. Even so, he had to be taken down in order to win. They all did.

He moved forward and executed a series of warning jabs and kicks, a trained prelude to battle.

"Settle yourself down, son," McStarley said calmly, taking another bite from the fruit.

Saiga attacked one second later with a roundhouse kick toward his face. McStarley dropped the apple and shifted his head as Saiga's foot blurred by. The hand holding the apple punched Saiga in the side, neutralizing him from delivering a follow-up kick. McStarley waved the knife as if it were the head of a rattlesnake ready to strike.

"Bit lively this morning, aren't we, tiger?"

Saiga mumbled in Japanese. He didn't feel the same way about the British as he did the Americans, but losing two fights in one morning would be unacceptable. That's what he told himself as he planted his foot into McStarley's rib cage and knocked the knife away with a right-handed chop. The playing field had just been leveled.

"You wanna play games?" He smiled, taunting the Asian. He was looking forward to the hand-to-hand combat.

Saiga launched into another series of attacks. McStarley countered all of them punch for punch, kick for kick. While the Englishman was only rudimentarily trained in kung fu, he certainly knew his way around karate. Special Forces had supplied him with a black belt.

They went at it again, each blocking the other's blows this time. McStarley decided to do a changeup and lunged at him, pulling him into a headlock. Saiga saw it coming and cinched his arm around McStarley's throat at the same time. They were virtually deadlocked, choking each other to death.

McStarley strained to talk, his grin turning into a grimace. "We could go on for hours like this, little fella. You speak English? You understand?"

Saiga uttered something in Japanese.

"I don't speak monkey talk."

If he had, he would've heard a compliment: *You have learned the martial arts well.*

They both held steadfast . . . and then simultaneously released, backing off a few paces. Each respected the other's abilities.

"I saw you fight the spade," panted McStarley, still catching his breath. "You're pretty ballsy for a little geezer, aren't ya?"

Saiga said nothing, but McStarley's gestures told him he was talking about his fight with the black man.

"The way I see it, you and me will clear some of this

scum up on the island, together." He pointed between himself and Saiga, and then toward the island as he threw some air punches.

"An alliance. You and me." He clasped his hands together, demonstrating a union.

Saiga stared back, noncommittal. McStarley wasn't sure the Asian had understood the proposition, but he had. There was no question that teaming up would be the most efficient way to eliminate the competition. The real question was when the Englishman would turn on him. In the end, the two of them would have to engage in a final battle royale, that was implicit. But the plan did have merit.

McStarley took off the sunglasses, which had managed to stay on his face during their fight. He offered them back to Saiga, essentially declaring a truce. "They look better on you."

Saiga studied him for several seconds and then took the sunglasses and put them on. It was the equivalent of a handshake.

13

Conrad's compass directed him up a steep hill. Once at the top, he hoped he would be able to spot the weather tower somewhere in the distance.

The ground beneath his boots steadily became harder, as well as darker. This was a volcanic island, which explained the extreme topography. Islands like this had been born violently, erupting from beneath the sea in a seismic explosion that created sheer cliff faces and unstable earth in addition to breathtaking beauty. There were ways to die here that had nothing to do with humans. The particular mountain he was scaling would not be forgiving if he fell—jagged black pumice awaited him everywhere. There was also the possibility of lava tubes beneath the ground that could cave in without warning, so he planted his feet solidly as he climbed.

He reached a plateau and saw the west coast straight ahead. The sun was now lower and arcing toward the horizon, which made its directional identification easy. The south shore, where they had all been dropped, was off to his left. He rotated to take in the entire island from his bird's-eye view. The interior was spectacular, with a mini–Grand Canyon and multiple waterfalls cutting a swath through lush jungles.

The northwest corner of the island, where he was going, was partially obscured by another mountain. The weather tower wasn't visible yet, but he knew he was headed in the right direction.

Another slope awaited him at the edge of the plateau. He would have to descend it to stay on course. Conrad couldn't see how steep it was or where it led, other than down. He took a slug from his last bamboo canteen and started forward.

A big, bearded, bald man appeared between two banana trees off to his left, down the slope a ways.

It was Raudsep, the Russian. He pushed his way through the thick leaves with a dead trajectory on Conrad. The Russian was there to kill; he needed to kill as much as he needed oxygen to breathe.

"Hold on right there, big man," Conrad said quietly. "Just slow it down."

The Russian did just the opposite and hoofed like a bull toward a red cape.

Conrad stood his ground and ducked low just before impact, plowing into Raudsep's tree trunk legs. The giant toppled over him and slammed on his back.

"You stay down and we won't have a problem," he advised.

The Russian rose to his feet, all seven feet of him. The slope had shaved off six inches of his height when he had first appeared. Here, on level ground, the giant towered over him.

"We have a big fuckin' problem," Conrad muttered to himself.

At this same moment, Eddie C was watching Conrad's and Raudsep's + signs on his monitor, which were right on top of each other.

"Hey, Breck!" he shouted. "Something's going down!"

Breckel marched over as Eddie pointed at his screen.

"I got two cons right on top of each other"—he entered some keystrokes and read the names—"Conrad and the big guy, the Russian."

Breckel jerked his head toward the monitors, spotting Conrad and Raudsep on one of the tiny screens. They had just engaged.

"Hey, Goldy! What are you, blind? Put that screen up on the live feed. Now!"

Goldman, already frazzled and fending off a few demons, brought it up with no comment. Breckel paced over as Goldman cut among several angles. His technical director had placed three cams up on the plateau, figuring that at least one con would use it as a spot to scope out the competition.

"Very nice," said Breckel. "Very nice."

There on the plateau, Conrad and the Russian were exchanging brutal blows. It was cage fighting without the cage, though Conrad wouldn't have minded an old-fashioned chain-link fence to keep him from flying off the cliff. The mountain he'd scaled was rife with sharp lava rocks that would cut him to shreds if he fell. The slope in front of them remained a mystery, though it had to be extremely steep—the plateau ended abruptly like an infinity pool. Someone was bound to go off the edge before this fight was through.

The Russian's fist felt like a block of concrete as it rammed into the side of his head. Somehow Conrad recovered and ducked the next swing, countering with a string of his best punches. They barely slowed down Raudsep, who gripped Conrad in a bear hug and wrestled him toward the plateau edge.

Conrad struggled to free himself, jabbing his elbow into the Russian's sides and face. He managed to break his nose, but none of it slowed the goliath.

As they approached the plateau's ledge, Conrad got his first look over the side. The initial fifty yards were steep with low ground cover. There were scattered rocks and boulders, but not to the extent of the volcanic side he had scaled to get here. Where it ended was the real problem. It was a sheer drop-off into oblivion. If he survived this battle, he would have to find another route to the weather tower.

The Russian shoved him closer to the edge, pummeling him with more blows. Conrad refused to go off and retaliated with slugs of his own. This infuriated Raudsep, who roared and tackled him. The two went over the side together locked in a death grip. They rolled end over end, plowing into a fern that sat halfway down the slope. The Russian wrapped his massive hands around Conrad's throat and began to choke him. Rather than pry his paws away, Conrad smacked his ears with open palms and shattered his eardrums. Blood from Raudsep's broken nose sprayed

Conrad in the face upon impact. The Russian still held on, but his patience had run out. He released one hand and reached for the red tab on Conrad's ankle bracelet.

Conrad kicked out and cracked the behemoth's chin just as his sausagelike fingers grazed the tab. He pried the Russian's other hand from his throat and slugged him in the face, the momentum of which sent them tumbling again. They slammed through several bushes and came to a halt at the sheer edge of a bottomless cliff. Raudsep, again on top, wound up for a punch that would turn Conrad's lights out for good.

A beeping sound stopped him.

Both of them saw it at the same time. One of their red pull tabs was dangling from a bush they had just rolled through.

Conrad's pupils darted to his ankle. His tab was still in place.

Raudsep looked up from his own bomb and dumbly registered the shock. His tab was gone and his timer was counting down. He wasted two seconds realizing that he had fewer than ten to live.

He wasn't about to die alone. His hands went around Conrad's neck once again.

Conrad punched the Russian directly in his larynx and shattered it. It had no effect.

The bomb continued to beep.

He stared into the Russian's face. His enormous head was ugly and deformed, his beard soaked with blood and saliva, his eyes bulbous eggs. God had been hard on the Texan, but he refused to accept that this was the last thing he was meant to see before leaving this earth.

Conrad reached out with a hand and found what he needed.

It took three hard blows from the chunk of lava rock before the Russian released his grip. Conrad pulled his knees against his chest and recoiled, planting them into Raudsep's torso. The Russian fell backward off the ledge, cascading into space like a paratrooper without a chute.

The explosion echoed through the canyon, which tripled its volume and duration. The Russian virtually disappeared into thin air like a magic trick, leaving behind only a surreal red fireball and plume of smoke. What was left of him fell in pieces for another two hundred feet and scattered in a black crevasse that approximated a portal to hell.

Conrad caught his breath, peering over the edge as the ugly smoke billowed past him.

"Y' shoulda stayed down like I told you," he said to Petr Raudsep, who was no more.

He looked down at his own bomb. The timer now read *23:14:12* and showed no signs of stopping. He clawed his way back up the slope.

Julie watched the fight on her laptop, much like subscribers were doing all over the world. She was alone on the private deck outside of the tent she shared with Ian.

The festive, high-excitement vibe in the control room had disturbed her. She tried to convince herself it was like watching a fight at Madison Square Garden and that people would naturally get excited. Except that here death was not only a reality, it was a certainty. There were ten people in the ring and only one would walk out alive. Two were already gone, she had seen their deaths in graphic detail, and now it looked like Jack Conrad, or the Russian, or both, were about to be next.

She wasn't even sure why she was watching at this moment. Being honest with herself, suspense factored in greatly. She had seen something in Conrad's eyes . . . was it humanity? Julie already felt guilty for writing up the bullshit biography about him, though his true background remained mysterious. He had blown up a building. *Why? Was he a crazy fanatic?* She didn't think so. *Was he working for someone?* Possibly, although that didn't make it right, either. *Who had died in the blast?*

Whatever the answers, she couldn't help rooting for Conrad. The Russian Raudsep was a sick, vicious serial killer. Furthermore, he had initiated the attack on Conrad with fervent glee.

Julie was also watching because *not* watching would be like sticking her head in the sand. Like it or not, she was a part of this now, one of the team. Somehow she had deluded herself into believing it would be morally acceptable since these people had already been sentenced to die. Ian had even told her that a portion of the show's profits would go to improving prison conditions. She'd seen enough of him in action to question his true motives now. The well-being of prisoners was the last thing on his mind. She had allowed herself to be seduced.

Her laptop screen was only fifteen inches diagonal, but the effect was nonetheless huge when Raudsep's body exploded over the canyon. It was a shocking, disturbing sight in any format. The fact that the Russian deserved it suddenly made no difference to her—it was a sick spectacle no matter who the victim. Broadcasting to a wanton audience made it even more despicable. What kind of people paid to watch something like this?

As if to underscore the chasm forming between her and Ian, she could hear hoots and applause coming from the control room tent as the bloody cloud billowed up on her screen.

"Twelve million!" yelled Eddie inside the control room. "We just hit twelve million subscribers. Online, right now."

He pointed at one of his displays with a grin as the last of the Russian literally went up in smoke on the main monitor.

Breckel moved to Goldman and patted his shoulders with a confident smile. He glanced at the monitor as a big red X went over Petr Raudsep's mug shot.

"Hear that, Goldy? Twelve million."

"Twelve million still isn't forty million," he replied, ever the optimist.

"Not yet. But it will be," stated the producer.

Goldy was going soft on him. And Julie was AWOL. Shows like this separated the men from the boys, the loyal from the mutineers. He turned to Bella and Eddie C, who were shaping up to be his biggest allies.

"Bella, Eddie. Replay that fall in super slo-mo until we get something better. Digital push when he blows, freeze-frames, the whole deal. Right away."

"We're on it," said Bella, still psyched from the Russian's death. To her it was an elaborate special effects sequence, the reality of Raudsep's death not even registering. He might as well have been a stuntman shot against a green screen with the explosion and smoke added digitally. The fact that it had made her involuntarily cheer was a testament to Breck's showmanship. The casting, ankle bombs, all of it, was his idea. She stole a glance at her boss and decided he was a genius.

Goldman was also eyeing his longtime friend. Breck had pushed the envelope his entire career, but this was a new watermark in bad taste. Entertainment had crossed into sadism and Breck was reveling in it. His egomania, which was unfortunately a requirement in the entertainment business, was morphing into megalomania. For the first time in their long relationship, he realized that Ian Breckel was a very disturbed man. However this show ended, it wouldn't be pretty—for any of them.

14

The Federal Bureau of Investigation's brand-new Connecticut Computer Crime Task Force facility was located in New Haven. The ribbon cutting had taken place at ten A.M. on June 29, 2004, at the FBI's Connecticut headquarters. It was hailed as a state-of-the-art laboratory and accommodated up to twenty-seven officers from local, state, and federal law enforcement.

The CCCTF was first formed in 2003 to investigate crimes that occurred over the Internet. Among the felonies were computer intrusion, Internet fraud, online crimes against children, copyright violations, and internet threats or harassment. The web was a new frontier, with identity theft, the distribution of hardcore pornography, solicitation of murder for hire, and terrorism investigations soon added to the mix.

The FBI building itself was host to a grand tag team of Internet law enforcement. The bronze seals of the U.S. Secret Service, U.S. Postal Inspection Service, Department of Defense Inspector General, and Internal Revenue Service adorned the walls along with the Bureau itself. Resources were constantly being pooled into a unified attack on virtual crime. There were ninety-two other computer crimes task forces across the country, but the CCCTF was the granddaddy of them all.

The interior was a nerd's heaven. The bustling department was lined with a maze of cubicles, each containing an array of cutting-edge electronics. One field agent was taking a call from a woman who had been victimized by a Nigerian real estate scam. In another, an agent was posing as a teenage girl in a chat room frequented by sexual predators. Two cubicles down, a forensic examiner was breaking passwords and decrypting files in an attempt to gather evidence against a suspected hacker.

Special Agent Brad Wilkins was in one of the labs watching a high-definition flat-screen monitor. Ad banners ran at the bottom third of the screen—alcohol, cigarettes, porn, adult lingerie, and firearms scrolled by along with other fringe products that couldn't secure mainstream advertising. Wilkins paid them little attention, just like everyone else who had plunked down the $49.95 access fee and were logged on to this site.

Above the ads, the Russian was falling for the tenth time in slow motion and then exploding.

Wilkins had been tracking the show since the first blog rumors had appeared. His boss, Assistant Director Alan Moyer, had assigned him to keep tabs. If the show was real, then all kinds of laws were being broken, but Moyer doubted it was legitimate. The webcast was most likely an elaborate Internet hoax designed to scam subscribers. Actors could be hired, special effects used to make them die. In a way it was like

The Blair Witch Project, which had purported itself to be real thanks to a clever Internet campaign and made lots of money at the box office. Either way, the IRS was folded into the investigation to make sure Uncle Sam got its share of the proceeds.

At thirty-five, Brad Wilkins had long outgrown the nerd qualities he had possessed in high school. A late bloomer, he was handsome and smart with fashionably messy hair and a wardrobe out of Abercrombie & Fitch. His khakis were pleated, his button-down shirt crisp and clean with nary a pocket protector in sight.

Long before the Russian's demise, Wilkins was convinced this was no hoax. Intel had confirmed the identities of the participants. The show runner, Ian Breckel, had also been profiled as a man capable of creating this type of "entertainment." People were really dying on that island, wherever it was.

"You're a wanted man. Moyer wants to see you." It was Wilkins's assistant, Stan; while she didn't wear a pocket protector, she was an anomaly—a female geek.

Wilkins nodded and marched out the door. He didn't hate his boss, though he didn't completely respect him. While Moyer was decent enough, he was always worried about offending his superiors. Moyer never rocked the boat. In fact, he wouldn't even take it out of the harbor. Status quo was his middle name.

Assistant Director Moyer was rubbing his temples as Wilkins entered his office. He had recently changed the prescription on his black-framed glasses, which looked less cool than he realized, and they were contributing to his headache. He was in his forties with dyed curly brown hair that paid homage to the late eighties.

"Ian Breckel. What do you have on him?"

"He could be streaming the data to a server from almost anywhere," Wilkins said without hesitation. "I've contacted Interpol. They're collecting data from several other governments. Now, the island—it's somewhere in the South Pacific. I have World War II historians and regional experts examining the images from the web site, but it's not easy. Between Indonesia and New Guinea alone there are more than two hundred tiny islands. It's a needle in a haystack."

Moyer nodded, absorbing only about half of it. The main thing was that Wilkins was on top of it, as usual. Brad Wilkins was his best agent, but he would never tell him that. The belief that Wilkins was after his job always lurked in the back of his mind.

"Ten prisoners in this thing," started Moyer.

"Down to seven," revised Wilkins, who wasn't after Moyer's job. The position required too much kowtowing and not enough nuts-and-bolts crime solving.

"Two of them are American. Still alive?"

Wilkins nodded. "One is Kreston Mackie, aka K. C. Mack. African American from Inglewood, California, age thirty-six. Larceny. Assault. Homicide. Escaped incarceration, 2002." This was all off the top of his head. "Ironically, two years later, he ends up on death row in Malaysia."

"For?"

"Dealing drugs. Hash, lots of it. Officials in Malaysia won't talk to us."

Malaysia wasn't the only roadblock Wilkins had encountered in his research. Every prisoner who was participating had come from a foreign prison. He suspected they had been bought from corrupt prison officials, which constituted another crime, though not under the CCCTF's jurisdiction.

"What about the other guy?" asked Moyer.

"Jack Conrad. Can't find a thing. It's like he doesn't exist."

"Look harder," ordered Moyer, who couldn't think of anything else to say. His headache was getting worse.

An hour later, Stan flagged down Wilkins as he popped between cubicles to check on the progress the field agents were making.

"Just got a tip on the hotline about the American, Jack Conrad," gushed Stan, who had been told by her boss to make the American a top priority.

"Shoot," said Wilkins, hoping for a big break.

"A guy recognized him on the Internet and says they went to high school together. Only he says his real name's Jack Riley."

Stan handed him a folder containing a perfectly organized research file on Conrad.

"U.S. Army, retired," she continued. "Born and raised in Granville, Texas. Dad was a decorated war hero, also Army. Now deceased."

Wilkins skimmed the research and smiled. "Great work, Stan."

Unlike Moyer, he had no problem praising a subordinate.

15

The old Ford pickup with Texas plates rolled along Farm Road 2497 not far from where Conrad had grown up. Downtown Granville was six miles up the road.

Sarah had just come from there. The pickup bed had feed for her chickens and other supplies, while six bags of groceries shared space in the cab. Her boys would eat through all six before the week was over.

She turned down a grassy, unpaved road that was her driveway. Both sides were bordered by a wood and wire fence that kept a couple of horses from wandering off. She bumped along the driveway for a hundred yards until she reached her house, a pale-yellow, single-level rambler with a big porch and no garage. Her closest neighbor was a mile away and out of sight.

Sarah Cavanaugh was a reflection of her surroundings. In jeans, a plaid blouse, and boots, she was down-to-earth and unpretentious. She didn't have as much mileage on her as her pickup, but Sarah wasn't as new as the tractor out back, either. In her midthirties, she was a classic Texan beauty, blue-eyed and blonde, the woman you wanted to come home to.

She climbed out with two grocery bags under her arms and spotted Michael and Scott wrestling in the yard.

"Mikey, off your brother!"

They ignored her. Michael was now nine, Scotty seven. Putting them together was like combining sulfur and potassium, the two main ingredients that make up dynamite. She set down her bags and separated the two hellions.

"Dinner in thirty—now go get yourself cleaned up."

She handed each of them a bag. They ran in the door as Sarah went back for the other groceries.

Sarah's mom, Karen, was watching from the kitchen window. She had let her hair turn gray, but it still looked pretty mixed with her natural blonde. It was easy to see that Karen was once a very beautiful woman. There were good genes in this family.

She came onto the porch as her daughter walked up with two more sacks.

"I swear those boys are gonna eat you out of house 'n' home."

"Sorry I'm late. How were they today—okay?" Sarah asked hopefully.

Karen's whole body said it all. She was dead tired. Her grandkids were a handful with no man in the house. She ran a hand through her daughter's blonde locks and inspected her face. First and foremost, she was a mother.

"Honey, you look tired. You okay?"

Sarah worked up her best smile. The truth was she was getting by, but that was it. The boys' father had been a drunk and she had thrown him out a year after Scotty came along. There were dates here and there, but nothing stuck. She was beginning to think a single life was her destiny . . . and then Jack Riley showed up one day. He had grown up here, he'd told her, had been gone way too long and needed to regrow his roots. The following year had been perfect, almost too good to be true. He told her he wanted to marry her. And then one day he just disappeared.

Even now, over a year later, she couldn't believe that he'd left her and the boys. Sarah was sure that Jack had been madly in love with all of them.

"I'm good, Mom, real good," she said with the best smile she could muster. "Mike offered me a second shift. Can you watch 'm for me tonight?"

Karen's eyes crinkled with a weary smile. "Sure."

They went inside with the groceries and then Karen left to get some rest before her own second shift with the dynamic duo. An old-fashioned radio that Jack had bought her at a swap meet sat on the fireplace mantel playing a country tune, but that was the only visible sign that he had ever been in their lives. Framed snapshots of Sarah, her boys, and Karen sat on a worn end table, but no photos of any men. The kitchen was the biggest room in the house, with a big cast-iron stove that had resided there since 1948, the year the home was built. Sarah had worked hard and bought the property with her own money. She didn't need a man to survive.

The boys, however, were a different story.

Why'd he leave us? she asked herself almost daily.

Maybe something bad happened to him, but that seemed like a long shot. Jack could take care of himself better than any man she'd ever met. One time they'd stopped at a minimart to pick up some milk when two armed hoods barged in to rob the place. Jack tried to defuse the situation, but it looked like they were going to shoot the young clerk and probably them, too. He knocked out both of the thieves in a matter of seconds without a shot being fired. She had never seen anything like it.

No, the odds were that he had left them of his own accord. A lot of people said he took off and left her because that's what most men do—she wasn't one of the spring chickens in her shed, after all, with two high-maintenance kids as baggage. Sarah still couldn't believe it. It just didn't add up.

Ultimately it didn't matter. Jack was gone. That was the reality. She never expected to see him again.

Sarah pushed it all aside, as she did most nights, and went back to slicing the carrots and potatoes for the beef stew she was making.

The phone rang as she dumped the vegetables in the pot. She wiped her hands on the dish towel and answered it.

"Hello?"

"Sarah Cavanaugh?"

She didn't recognize the voice. It was a man, definitely not a Texan.

"Yeah, that's me."

"This is Special Agent Wilkins of the FBI. I'd like to ask you a few questions about Jack Riley."

Her heart stopped cold. It took her several seconds to respond.

"What about him?"

All her feelings came flooding back. She had loved him so much and then forced herself to hate him after he disappeared, which had been impossible. Now the FBI was calling. Was Jack on the run from the law? That, too, was something she found hard to believe.

"His last listed mailing address was yours," continued Wilkins. "I take it you know him."

"He was my boyfriend," she said cautiously. "We lived together."

"When was the last time you spoke with him?"

"About a year ago." *Had it been that long?* "He left. Disappeared."

"Do you have any idea what happened? Where he might have gone?"

"I don't know. Do you know something?" she asked hopefully.

There was a pause on the other end.

From Wilkins's perspective, he was stepping into a gray area now. While he knew very little about Jack Riley aka Jack Conrad, it appeared that she might know even less. Her voice also sounded emotional. At some point he would have to decide how much information to divulge in exchange for facts that might not help at all. If he were Moyer, he would tell her absolutely nothing and play it perfectly safe, regardless of her anguish. But he wasn't Moyer.

"I investigate illegal activity on the Internet," he answered as levelly as possible. "He appears to be involved with a live broadcast currently airing on the web."

Sarah exhaled with relief. He was alive. But it made no sense whatsoever.

"What? What are you telling me?" She was flustered. "What's your name again?"

She turned off the burner under her stew, fearing she would burn the pan. She couldn't concentrate.

"My name is Brad Wilkins, I'm with the FBI," he slowly repeated, giving her his ID number. "Now, this is urgent. I need you to answer a few questions for me right now."

She paced around the kitchen. Jack was in trouble, that much was clear. Would she be hurting him by answering these questions?

"Sarah, please. I need you to answer my questions," he asked a little more forcefully. "He may be a victim in this rather than a willing participant. How long were you two together?"

She decided to go along with it, one question at a time.

"We dated for about a year and a half. He'd recently retired from the service."

"The army, right?"

"Yeah. He came back to town just when I was getting out of a bad marriage. We dated. He moved in. One morning he gets up around five. Packs a bag. Says he's got to leave town for a job."

Saying it out loud made her eyes well. She missed him even more than she allowed herself to admit.

"But he was retired," interjected Wilkins.

From Wilkins's viewpoint, something wasn't adding up. Why would a retired serviceman end up in a prison in El Salvador?

Michael and Scotty came running into the kitchen. They were playing tag and Scotty was it. He tagged his older brother with a squeal and used his mother as a block. Sarah gave them a disconcerted glare and gestured for them to take it outside. Michael reached around her jeans, tagged Scotty, and sprinted out again with his brother in pursuit.

"He did excavating, so he traveled a lot across Texas, Louisiana," she finally answered. "So it was normal. Only this time, he never came back."

"What do you think happened?" he probed. "Did he say anything at all before he left?"

"Just good-bye. And 'I love you.'" She shook her head.

Wilkins could sense her pain and softened his voice. "Where'd he go, if you had to guess?"

She *had* guessed. For more than a year. There was no explanation that made any sense.

"I don't know. Common logic for most people 'round here is he ran off."

"Ran off?"

"You could say I'm no prize," she said quietly. "I'm a divorcée with two kids. A waitress."

She sounded more pitiable than she would have liked. When Jack had left, her self-esteem had taken a nosedive.

"We were getting pretty serious," she went on. "I guess the boys, the responsibility, it spooked him. He ran off."

Again she didn't believe it, even as it rolled off her tongue. It was the town talking, not her. But it was the only logical explanation. She lowered the receiver, composed herself, and then spoke as evenly as she could. "Now, I answered *your* questions. I want to know what's goin' on."

Wilkins looked across the room as Assistant Director Moyer strolled by, poking his head into each cubicle to make sure his underlings weren't bending any rules.

He decided to tell her everything.

16

Rosa Pacheco was in a rock gorge, running for her life.

Eight hours earlier, she had been shoved from the Alpha chopper. She had almost choked on the key as she fell. Salt water ran down her throat and into her lungs when she hit the water. Rosa had yanked the key from her mouth and managed to unlock one wrist, giving her enough freedom to claw her way to the surface and vomit seawater. She struggled to remove her second manacle and leg irons as a wave broke on top of her.

The next thing she remembered was lying on the shore. She coughed up a mixture of sand and ocean and looked around, completely disoriented. Her husband had been pushed out less than thirty seconds before her so he was in the vicinity, but she had no idea where.

Her heart began to thud with profound fear. The ache of separation, and dread that she would never see him again, was not a new feeling.

When Rosa was ten, her father abandoned the family. Her mother moved Rosa and her little sister Trina to Acapulco so they could find work at one of the resorts. The hours were brutal and their jobs as maids barely paid for room and board. They lived in squalor for the next five years until her mother fell sick and couldn't work at all. Trina was too young to work, and Rosa's income alone wasn't enough to pay the rent, let alone feed them and pay for her mother's medicine.

At fifteen, she was already getting plenty of whistles from men. She did what she had to do to survive, and hated the world for it.

Paco had been her savior. He'd found her in a bordello in the heart of Acapulco. By then she was eighteen and he was twenty-two. Rosa had been renting out her body for three years and was numb by now, coldly indifferent to all men . . . but Paco was different. It had been love at first sight. He understood her, didn't judge her, sympathized with what fate had dealt her. She was his "desert rose." Paco's life had been no fiesta either, having grown up on the mean streets of Tijuana. They were two of a kind.

They married right away with no money between them. Paco wouldn't let his bride prostitute herself, so they both took menial jobs back at the resort where Rosa and her mother had worked—she cleaned hotel toilets and he was a busboy. Once again they were living below poverty level. They briefly considered illegally entering the United States, but Paco had already tried that and been deported after spending fifteen hundred dollars on a coyote to get him there. In the brief time he was stateside, he made below minimum wage as a day laborer and shared a tiny apartment with seven strangers, all illegals. They were fucked on either side of the border, he told her. Might as well stay down here.

What Paco didn't tell her was that he was on the run for robberies in the United States, as well as in Baja.

It had been Paco's idea to go on the stealing spree in Guatemala, but Rosa had readily gone along with it. They had come home from celebrating their one-month anniversary to find that their crumbling, cockroach-filled apartment had been ransacked. The *federales* had caught up with him for his transgressions in Baja. Paco punched his fist through the flimsy wall. He had tried to go straight, but the world had shit on him yet again.

Likewise, all the pent-up fear and anger from Rosa's childhood resurfaced. She didn't want to lose Paco like she'd lost her *padre*. On her own, she couldn't make ends meet unless she let other men fuck her. She hated the world as much as her husband did. Rosa told him she would follow him anywhere.

Paco had been in gangs and knew how to shoot a gun, though he had never killed anyone. He didn't plan to now, he told Rosa, but they had to be prepared. He bought a pair of .38 Smith & Wessons from a gang amigo and taught his wife how to use it. The plan was to head south into Guatemala, where nobody would know them.

Their chemistry and mutual pasts mixed into a deadly cocktail during their first robbery. It was a small grocery store in Mazatenango. The clerk made a move for a gun under the counter. Paco and Rosa shot him at the same time, without hesitation.

Having crossed the line into murder, they decided no witnesses could be left behind as they continued their spree through Guatemala. Thirteen robberies occurred over the next month, resulting in seventeen shootings. They always picked small businesses during off-hours, but occasionally an unfortunate patron showed up. It had been their bad luck, according to Paco. Since life hadn't been fair to him, why should it be fair to anyone else?

One of those patrons survived and identified them. A year later they were on death row. Two more years went by before Ian Breckel intervened, saving Rosa and Paco from their planned executions. Which, ironically, happened to be scheduled for today.

There on the sand, Rosa suppressed her darkest thoughts and got to her feet, hoping she would find him soon.

The distant explosion stopped her cold. Somebody's bomb had gone off. Like Paco, she prayed it hadn't been him. If anything happened to her husband, she might as well be dead herself. She tried to concentrate and then remembered what Paco had whispered in the helicopter. He'd told her to get off the beach *rápido* so she wouldn't be exposed and to hide in the jungle. The island wasn't that big—he would find her as quickly as he could. The explosion came from the beach, which meant it probably hadn't been him. At least that was the hope she clung to as she quickly moved inland.

There had been no place to hide at first, but eventually she found a river that led to a huge rock gorge with a natural pool. Rosa gulped down fresh water and washed off the dried sea salt. The gorge was well hidden, too. A perfect place to wait for Paco.

Some time passed before she heard the second explosion, which obliterated the Russian. This one came from the island's interior and reverberated down into the gorge. Her heart skipped again. There was no way of knowing who had died, but she prayed once again that it hadn't been her husband and that he would find her soon.

Another hour passed, the gorge beginning to dim as the sun dipped. Her fear began to ratchet up. Would Paco locate her down here in the dark? The island was bigger than it had looked from the air—would he find her at all, even in daylight?

She decided to take a look around before blackness completely swallowed her surroundings. Rosa cautiously followed the river downstream. A quarter of a mile later her vista substantially widened, with afternoon light still streaking through the trees.

Rosa heard movement in the foliage and ducked behind a tree. She almost called out Paco's name, her faith in his arrival clouding her common sense. She stopped herself and peeked out from behind the trunk.

McStarley was staring back at her from across the riverbed with a broad smile. The sunlight glinted off the knife in his grip.

Rosa ran. For her life.

She tripped and fell in the riverbed, her right hand landing on a rock. She felt a sharp pain but didn't have time to contemplate it. Her head darted backward and forward, and she caught a flash of his clothing passing between two trees. McStarley was closing the gap.

Hope you can run your feet as fast as your mouth, Breckel had told her after she'd spit in his face. Rosa picked herself up and sprinted on. She was definitely fast, but whether it was fast enough remained to be seen. Right now she was staying alive moment by moment.

Rosa wound her way back into the gorge, her lungs gulping in air as she ran. She hazarded another glance backward and saw nothing. Maybe she had lost him. She ducked into the shadows and allowed her breathing to catch up to her heart rate. Her hand was throbbing. She lifted it and saw blood oozing from her palm.

Rosa silently kneeled and rinsed it off.

She heard his footsteps behind her one second later.

Rosa spun around and gasped as he rushed toward her.

"Paco!"

"Mi amor," he said, practically in tears.

Paco dropped his chain and scooped her up. They hugged and kissed, Rosa sobbing with joy and relief.

He saw the gash in her hand and grimaced.

"¿Qué sucedió?" he asked, wanting to know what had happened.

She explained in a flustered mixture of Spanish and English that "the big white one" from their chopper had been chasing her but that she'd gotten away.

"He's close by," she said, trembling.

"I'll kill him," he said defiantly.

"Baby, *él tiene un cuchillo*," she warned, telling him that McStarley had a knife.

"I'll break him with my hands, I'll make him beg," Paco uttered through gritted teeth. The thought of anyone touching his wife incensed him.

He lifted her hand again. "Let me take care of this."

He helped Rosa sit down on a rock and then tore a piece off his T-shirt, wrapping it around her wound.

She glanced at her ankle bracelet as he tended to her. The timer was ticking down from *17:32:41*.

"Paco . . . are we going to die?"

He ran his hand through her dark hair and looked into her huge brown eyes, which were welling again. He had no answer for her, at least not an honest one. Only one person was going to survive this, and their competition was overwhelming. Those were the hard and cold facts. He was going to do everything to ensure that Rosa was that person, but their odds were bleak.

He answered her question with a tender kiss.

Their respite was cut short by an admiring whistle.

"Very romantic."

McStarley was standing only twenty feet away, blade in hand.

"I can't remember—did I tell you how sexy I thought your missus was?" He grinned.

Paco snatched his chain and jumped up, readying it as a weapon.

"Go! *Vaya!*" he ordered Rosa.

Rosa didn't want to leave him, but Paco knew what was best. She scrambled to her feet and ran farther into the gorge.

Paco leaped forward and swung his chain. McStarley ducked and punched him with his left hand, then sliced with his right, cutting Paco across the forearm. He gasped at the pain.

"Speed, baby, that's what that is!" McStarley blustered. "C'mon! What else we got?"

Paco swung again and caught McStarley in the kidneys, following up with a series of punches to his face. The Brit was big, but Paco was fast and a good street fighter. His ass had been kicked by other gang members in his youth and that knowledge came to his aide now. He dove into McStarley and tackled him, his knife splashing into the shallow river.

There was a loud scream.

Paco leapt to his feet and spun around.

It was Rosa.

Saiga had just tackled her. He was clamping McStarley's shackles around one of her ankles.

"Paco!" she shrieked.

McStarley instantly grabbed a branch from the riverbed and cracked Paco in the left knee, shattering it. Paco collapsed, howling in agony. The big Brit casually retrieved his knife from the water and held the blade at Paco's throat.

"Don't you just love it when that happens?"

The Englishman glanced at Saiga, who was just about finished chaining up Rosa. Their alliance was off to a very good start.

17

Five minutes later, Paco was hanging from a tree by his own chain. It had been looped around his wrists with his back against the trunk, his feet dangling a few inches off the ground. He had an unobstructed view of Rosa, only ten yards away.

Paco moaned, realizing what was about to come. His physical pain was enormous, but it paled compared to the thought of what these animals were planning to do to his wife.

McStarley could read every one of the Mexican's thoughts, and it was a real page turner. Torture came in many forms. In this case, forcing a man to witness his worst nightmare was much more horrific than any physical pain he could endure, though that would come soon enough as well. The Mexican would die, no question, but the fun would be in everything that led up to it. McStarley relished the fact that Paco knew what was about to happen and his agony was in not being able to prevent it. This was as much of a turn-on as what he'd be putting his missus through.

He gently stroked Paco's brow like a little baby, enjoying his power over him.

"Calm yourself down," he said soothingly. "This won't take too long."

Paco spat in his face. Part of him wanted to be put to death right then and there rather than watch what was about to happen. Another part wanted to kill McStarley so badly that any form of retaliation was better than none. Spitting was all he had, the ultimate insult.

"I'll fuckin' slap you if you keep on," snapped McStarley, wiping his face. He shrugged and calmed again, as if it hadn't happened. "I wanted us to be friends," he said patronizingly. "I didn't want this. How is that knee?"

He slammed his fist into Paco's already shattered knee. Paco screamed.

Rosa cried out, feeling his pain. She struggled against her restraints but was chained to the tree by her ankle. She wasn't going anywhere.

Saiga was standing beside her, hungrily looking her over. He hadn't been with a woman in three years, ever since his incarceration.

McStarley stroked Paco's head again. He sniffed the air.

"Y' smell that?"

He sniffed harder.

"That's *love*. Love in the air, that is. See, you, you're a lucky man. That is one fit bird you got there."

He focused his ravenous gaze on Rosa.

Paco involuntarily followed his glance. Saiga was starting to mess with her, tearing at her blouse.

"Rosa!" Paco cried out, his shattered knee all but forgotten.

McStarley moved along the gorge toward them. "Easy, son, easy, easy," he said to Saiga, motioning for him to get up.

Saiga glared back and then climbed off Rosa.

"That's no way to treat a lady," he scolded. He smiled at Rosa. "Is it, sweetheart?"

He leaned down to stroke her long black hair and she kicked him in the shins.

It hurt, but McStarley liked it when they fought back. Up to a point.

"Ooooo, fiery little thing, isn't ya? Wildcat!"

He laughed, winking at Saiga.

"Let's see those titties . . ." He reached for her breasts.

Rosa cracked him across the face, catching him by surprise. She was not the fighter her husband was, but surviving on the street as a teenager had taught her a thing or two about defending herself. If she was going to die, she was going down fighting.

McStarley snapped. For him, rape was all about violence, not sexual gratification, and the foreplay had officially ended. He dragged Rosa to her feet and decked her with a full punch to the jaw. She fell to the ground and he kicked her hard.

Paco screamed, struggling with all his strength to get free and murder this madman.

Rosa's nose was bleeding now. Her vision was cloudy but clear enough to see McStarley hovering over her with his knife. He slapped her once for good measure and then sliced open her blouse.

*　　*　　*

Julie walked into the control room hearing Paco's and Rosa's screams on the speakers. The room was eerily silent otherwise, Breckel's crew staring at the big plasma with a mixture of awe and repulsion.

Julie had shut off her laptop shortly after seeing the Russian's death repeated in slow motion ad nauseam. She had wandered around the compound, trying to come to terms with what Ian was producing, along with her involvement in it. She'd made up her mind to confront him about it, but the screams combined with silence in the room put her plans on hold.

The image on the screen favored Paco, with only an obscure view of the others in the background. Glimpses of McStarley hitting, kicking, and slashing his knife could be seen, though Rosa was blocked behind the tree that held her in place. She was crying for mercy as her husband screamed at the top of his lungs.

Like the others, Julie watched in utter disbelief. She saw Ian move to Goldman, who didn't look like he was enjoying this at all either.

"How many angles do we have on this?" he quietly asked.

Goldman turned away from the screen, having reached his saturation point. "This is all we got."

"Well, this coverage is no good," he said matter-of-factly.

Goldman just stared at him.

Breckel turned to Eddie C, who was fully caught up in the action. "Eddie, where's the live unit?"

The young hacker reluctantly pulled his vision away from the big monitor and checked his display, bringing up the map with the + signs. A blue camera icon was blinking a short distance away from the cluster that represented McStarley, Saiga, and the Pachecos.

"Not far."

Breckel moved to his security chief Baxter, who was watching the screen stoically.

"Get the live unit over there. Now."

There, in the gorge, McStarley took his sweet time. He knew he was being photographed and didn't mind it at all. He wanted to put on a good show for the folks at home.

Not far away, the jungle moved.

At first it appeared to be someone rustling a bush, but then the bush itself moved. It was a human in full camouflage. Mask, gloves, every inch of his body was covered in leafage—along with a camera. He was invisible unless he moved.

Beneath the elaborate camouflage was Donaldson, the cameraman who had videotaped the Russian's audition in Belarus. He had been in the field for more than eight hours now and hadn't shot a thing, but he wasn't complaining. Donaldson had heard enough in his headset to know that three people had already died violently, and now two more were in the batter's box. He realized that he was about to document a cold-blooded murder.

"Move," ordered Baxter in his headset, who was watching the grid in the control room. "Or it'll be over before you get there."

Donaldson pressed on, another bush moving behind him. This one was holding an MP5 submachine gun. Donaldson had a backup guard in case the talent discovered him and got any funny ideas.

Rosa was still alive when they arrived. They blended in with some foliage about thirty yards away. Donaldson stared for a few seconds. He knew it would be better once he hid behind his viewfinder and the reality changed to grainy pixels. But he was wrong. Especially when he zoomed in.

"The live unit's in position," Breckel sternly told his technical director. "Bring it up."

When Goldman reluctantly cut to the live cam view, people in the room audibly gasped. Thanks to Donaldson's skilled photography, Rosa's sadistic demise now filled the big plasma in glorious close-up.

Breckel didn't smile. His look was more awestruck than anything.

"Eddie . . . numbers . . ."

Eddie punched them up as quickly as he could. He didn't want to miss anything either. What was happening was almost surreal, an NC-17 horror film that was not only real, but happening live. He'd seen beheadings on web sites frequented by Islamic militants, but the grainy videos had been rendered in low resolution and uploaded after the fact. This was high definition and going down right now, the real deal. It made him sick—how could it not? But it was too incredible not to watch.

"We're climbin', around fifteen mil."

"Stop this . . ." Julie finally found her voice.

Breckel casually turned to her. She was back, which was good, and her protest had been fully anticipated.

"What? She's a convicted murderer," he said straightforwardly. "And a whore."

"She's a human being."

"Who went on a killing spree with her husband," he added. "They were going to electrocute her in Guatemala—today, as a matter of fact. Remember?"

Her face began to flush. "No. This is wrong. This is sick." She said it loudly enough for the entire tent to hear.

Now Breckel started to turn red. Julie was supposed to be on his side. He didn't need this shit, especially not in front of his crew. It undermined his authority, his power, his *control*. If he couldn't handle his own woman, how did he expect anyone there to respect him?

"Please, Julie," he said in a frighteningly calm voice as he pierced her with a stare. "I want the drama up there—" He pointed at the monitor. "Not *here*. Okay? Please?"

His look said it was not a request. It was an order.

She stared back. She'd been doing perfectly fine, thank you very much, before he came into her life. Julie had never been anyone's subservient concubine and she wasn't about to start now.

"Ian, how can you let this go on? It's reprehensible."

He glanced around the room. People were pretending they didn't notice, but he knew they were all listening. He needed to defuse her.

"It's just happening. And we're shooting it," he said with no hint of anger or frustration, though both were pegging the needle. "You're right. It is reprehensible. But it's not my doing."

"It *is* your doing. You set it up."

"I put ten people out there," he quickly countered, abandoning the Mr. Nice Guy approach. "What happens, happens. Pure reality. Right? RIGHT?"

Everybody was looking at them now, silent and nervous, like kids who didn't know what to do when Mom and Dad were fighting. He needed to assert his authority right away, lest his crew get any ideas of mutiny.

"Here's REALITY," he stampeded on. "This woman was going to die. I didn't pass the sentence—a jury in Guatemala City did. Here, she had a fighting chance. But, me, I do not intervene because that would *not* be reality, would it? I couldn't have stopped her electrocution, so why should I stop it now? She's GUILTY. The story will unfold as it unfolds. For all of them."

His speech was intended for the entire room, not just Julie. Several heads nodded in agreement, especially Eddie's and Bella's.

Goldman couldn't look at him, or at the screen. Like Julie, he was deeply disturbed.

"How rich do you need to be?" Julie asked him point-blank.

It took all of his strength not to slap her across the face, though it barely showed in his expression. He moved very close to her, his voice turning into a whisper. "It's not the money, Julie. Millions and millions of people are watching a show that I created. I'm good at this. The best."

He was dead serious, as honest as she'd ever seen him. That scared her more than the lies.

She left the control room without another word.

Breckel turned to Goldman, his longtime friend, his number one lieutenant, but Goldy wouldn't look him in the eye. Not only that, he got up from behind his console and walked toward the door.

"Hey, hey, Goldy. Where the hell do you think you're going?"

"Fresh air," he said without looking back.

Breckel couldn't let him go without a browbeating. He needed to make his point of view clear-cut to everyone.

"What? Are you getting soft on me? Am I going to hear a crybaby story from you, too? Suddenly you're having a crisis of conscience over a bunch of murderers and rapists?"

Goldman looked back, anxious and flustered, his voice stammering. He *was* having a crisis of conscience. He'd been having one ever since the first death. The fact that he hadn't walked out then is what was eating him up. Goldman had never walked out on a show, or a friend. His limits were being fully tested now.

"No, Breck, no, I, just, I, this—" He pointed to the plasma. Rosa was no longer screaming, but that didn't stop McStarley from continuing his business.

"This is not exactly easy to watch. But I'm with ya, I'm with ya . . ." He was trying to convince himself as much as Breckel.

"Good," Breckel answered skeptically. Goldy was a

longtime friend, but at this point in the production, only one person on the team was not replaceable, and that was himself. Eddie or Bella could take over if Goldy folded on him.

"Eddie? You with me?"

"Hell, yeah," he answered. "I love this job."

"Bella?"

"I love what I do. We're a team."

Breckel smiled broadly. "You know, Eddie and Bella, you two give me hope for the future."

He glanced at Goldman after he said it, letting him read between the lines. Goldman felt the sting and looked away just as a red X went over Rosa Pacheco's photo.

As the drama began to subside in the control room, it showed no signs of diminishing on the other side of the razor wire.

McStarley rose from Rosa's corpse, completely covered in her blood. Saiga watched dispassionately from the sidelines, miffed at having never gotten his chance with her. The Brit strutted over to his Japanese ally and guided him away.

"You didn't miss much. That's one angry bitch."

One second later, Rosa's ankle bracelet exploded and what was left of her vaporized.

Now it was Paco's turn.

When the smoke cleared, they saw that he had vanished, along with his chain.

McStarley took it in stride. The man had a shattered kneecap, after all. "Don't worry about him. He won't get far."

18

Sarah Cavanaugh hung up with Special Agent Wilkins and stood in a daze. Jack Riley, whom she just found out was also named Jack Conrad, was alive. There was fleeting relief in the news that he wasn't dead, but it was soon overshadowed when Wilkins told her about Jack's imprisonment in El Salvador and the brutal reality show he was participating in. There was no doubt that Jack had been living a secret life, but she still couldn't shake the belief that he truly loved her.

Sarah had an old computer in the house she used for word processing and letting the boys play games as a reward for good behavior. It had a dial-up Internet connection that was snail slow. Wilkins had told her it wouldn't be able to handle the webcast's streaming video, although he recommended that she not watch it in any case. The content was graphic, repulsive, and would serve no purpose other than to disturb her. Not only that, she would have to pay almost fifty dollars for the privilege of being sickened.

Sarah phoned her mother and asked her to come right back—there had been a change of plans and she had to go to work early.

Karen had just stretched out on her couch for a nap to recharge her batteries.

"No problem," she told her daughter, driving the five miles back from her two-room clapboard on the edge of town.

No sooner had her mother pulled into the driveway than Sarah hopped in her truck and raced back to town. She hurriedly parked in front of the Blue Boot Bar & Grill, where she worked as a waitress. Once upon a time, horses had been tied up in front of the Blue Boot with a water trough lining the wooden sidewalk. Concrete had replaced the wood, but the building's walls were still rustic pine. Inside was a classic Texas barbecue joint with American beer on tap and slow-smoked beef served on paper plates. Country music was floating from an old jukebox, with a football game on the big screen at one end of the long bar.

Mike Sanders, the owner of the Blue Boot, was serving up beers to a couple of locals as Sarah came in. Mike was in his forties, clean shaven, happily married, liked by all. He was a big brother to her.

"You're early." He smiled at Sarah as he handed a young cowboy a mug of draft.

"Mike, can I get on your computer?"

"Sure."

"You got high-speed, right?"

She was all business, looking very worried.

"Why? What is it?"

"It's Jack."

His expression changed instantly. Mike knew all about Jack Riley and had liked him a lot. Jack didn't talk much, which wasn't a bad thing—Mike had suffered his share of loudmouthed carousers in here. When Jack spoke, it was always worth listening to. He was a straight shooter, didn't drink too much, treated Sarah like she walked on water, and took to her boys like they were his own. Like Sarah, Mike couldn't understand why he had left them without any explanation.

He opened up the hinged door and let her behind the counter, knowing better than to ask any more questions. Jack Riley was a sensitive subject.

She breezed past him to his laptop, which was resting at the opposite end of the bar. Sarah opened his browser and typed in the site name that Agent Wilkins had reluctantly given to her.

The home page came up with dramatic graphics, almost like a movie poster. Rusty prison bars were in the foreground with a stunning tropical island behind them. Gallows and an electric chair were incorporated into the image, along with illustrations of the cast. Yasantwa's gorgeous face was in close-up, as was McStarley's psychotic visage. Others were smaller, running through the jungle or jumping off cliffs. Jack was missing since Breckel had commissioned the artwork before his last-minute casting.

A digital clock was ticking down in the corner of the screen, currently at *17:33:08*. It was impossible for Sarah to know this, but McStarley would be murdering Rosa in less than five minutes.

Jack missing from the artwork gave credence to her hope that this was all a big mistake. Forty-nine ninety-five was also a chunk of change for a single mom to waste, so she hesitated before subscribing. Possibly Wilkins had mixed him up with somebody else, but the agent had been adamant. He'd already seen Jack fight and kill a Russian on the program and described him to a T. It had to be her Jack.

Sarah clicked on the "subscribe" box, which brought up a window asking for credit card information. She pulled out her Visa and entered the information. Sarah Cavanaugh had officially become another one of Ian Breckel's patrons.

Mike walked up behind her, his concern and curiosity getting the better of him. "What's going on?"

"It's loading," she said, not knowing where to begin.

A page came up with a stylish menu that included:

RULES

CONTESTANTS

GO TO LIVE!

IAN BRECKEL—BIOGRAPHY

Sarah clicked on *Contestants*. A page opened featuring the ten boxed mug shots. A red X was over three of them, an Italian, Giangrasso, a German called Bruggerman, and a Russian named Raudsep.

She saw Jack's mug shot and instantly felt lightheaded.

He had bruises on his face and an icy, detached look that she had never seen before. Sarah gazed at the image in disbelief, bordering on denial. It was like a mother watching her daughter in a porn film. She couldn't believe what she was seeing . . . and she hadn't seen anything yet.

"Jack," she uttered.

A couple of regular patrons, Buck Farland and Brad Burdick, were leaning over the bar, good ol' Granville boys. They'd also been friendly with Jack and knew the whole Sarah situation. In a town the size of Granville, there were no secrets.

"Holy shit, that's Jack," said Farland, voicing what Mike was thinking as well.

"Yeah, I know, I know," said Sarah, almost defensively.

She clicked on his image and brought up his bio.

It was exactly as Breckel had dictated to Julie. Born in Arkansas. KKK member. Set fire to a Baptist church in Little Rock, Arkansas, in 2004, fled the country to El Salvador and bombed a clinic for the handicapped and mentally disabled in 2005, had killed women and children . . .

She stopped reading, her eyes glazing over. This was impossible. The Jack Riley she knew was not this Jack Conrad. He may have been keeping secrets from her, maybe had a few skeletons to reckon with, but none of them were of the caliber listed in this supposed biography.

"KKK member?" Farland read incredulously.

"What's it say?" asked Mike, looking around for his reading glasses.

"It says he burned down a church and bombed a clinic for the handicapped and mentally retarded in El Salvador," relayed Farland.

"What?" Mike said in disbelief.

"It's lies," said Sarah. "It's all lies."

"Yeah, it's bullshit," agreed Farland. "Jack was livin' here in 2004—how could he gone an' blown up a church in Arkansas?"

Sarah shook her head. Even if he hadn't been living with her at the time, she refused to believe a word on this web page.

She went back to the main page and clicked on the *Rules* link. It was just as Agent Wilkins had told her—this was a reality show where people were fighting to the death. It was almost impossible to believe. Who would put on a show like this? She read Breckel's superlative-laden biography and realized she had watched a couple of his early shows, which she'd found tasteless. This was also the man who had lobbied to put prison executions on pay-per-view.

She quickly skimmed some of the other bios to see what Jack was up against. There was no way of knowing if they were true, based on the lies in Jack's, but his competition read as a who's who of the worst criminals in the history of mankind. She prayed that this wasn't real, but there was only one way to find out. She needed to actually watch it.

With much apprehension, Sarah clicked on *Go to Live!*

The screen filled with McStarley slashing a half-naked Rosa, captured in vivid close-up by the live unit. The screaming and crying made it unbearable.

Sarah gasped. This was not a hoax. This was for real.

"Holy Christ," said Farland, unable to believe his eyes.

By now, Mike had his glasses on and just stared. He was a tough man who'd worked in a slaughterhouse before buying the Blue Boot, but what he saw turned his stomach.

Twilight had befallen the island. The horizon was rimmed in magenta with pink-orange clouds drifting over an indigo sky. A billion stars had begun to make their appearance. Palms were rustling in the warm evening breeze. It was the perfect romantic setting.

That had been Breckel's intention, anyway. Business and pleasure always went hand in hand on his shoots. He didn't want to spend a month of prep and thirty hours of production away from the comforts of a woman. Even after her defiance in the control room, maybe even because of it, he remained extremely attracted to Julie. Bedding her presented more of a challenge now, adding another layer of titillation.

He found her sitting on the deck outside his private tent, taking in the afterglow. God, did she look good in this light. He had expected her to be there, his ego too huge to think that any woman would walk out on him. It had been a spat, that's all. It was time to kiss and make up. Sex after a fight was always better anyway.

"You hate me?"

He was holding a pair of iced lattes that Bella had made for him. Julie liked to sip a latte at sunset; it was one of their rituals.

She nodded back a yes. She *did* hate him right now. Not him, exactly. She hated what he was doing. Her feelings were complicated. He hadn't cheated on her, hadn't really lied to her either, though he'd certainly spun the details to make the excitement and innovation whitewash the gruesome details. He was a passionate man, so his enthusiasm was forgivable up to a point. Nobody had put a gun at her head and forced her to come. Julie was just as angry at herself as she was with him.

"I told you what it would be," he said softly. "You knew what this was. Right?"

She looked at him and found herself nodding again.

"If you don't like what I'm doing, why did you come?"

Julie said nothing, but they both knew the answer. She was in love with him, at least before the timers had started ticking down. It was hard to completely shut off those feelings, even now.

He set down her coffee and gently kissed her. Julie returned it tentatively, then got swept up like she always did. As they embraced, she forced herself to ignore what lurked beyond the romance. She wouldn't watch the screens anymore—that would solve it. Eighteen hours from now, it would all be over, an unpleasant memory that time would blur.

The indelible image of Rosa being slashed to death suddenly flashed in her mind's eye.

She broke off the kiss and stared at him, unable to separate Ian from the images of death she had seen.

"I can't do this."

Julie went inside the tent without a word, curling up in a chair. There would be no lovemaking tonight, probably not for a long time.

Breckel stood on the deck. He had never tolerated rejection well, certainly not from a woman. Having watched McStarley go to town with Rosa, he had a primal urge to march in that tent, rip off Julie's clothes, and take her whether she wanted it or not. They were in the middle of a war out here. Wartime rules applied.

He suppressed the urge for the benefit of his show. Julie was becoming a distraction. There were six convicts to go, and five had to die spectacularly on camera. He needed to stay sharp.

19

Conrad hadn't stopped moving since he'd sent the Russian off the cliff. Afternoon had turned to dusk and dusk to darkness, but there was no time to sleep. The timer on his leg showed no signs of slowing down, so neither could he.

The massive canyon that had almost claimed his life stood in the way of his route to the weather tower. This had forced him to take the polar route back down the same lava rock mountain he had previously scaled, followed by a trip through the rain forest. He arrived at the base of the canyon by nightfall and waded across the river, stopping only to gulp down water. His bamboo canteens were long gone after tumbling with Raudsep.

Sound waves carried strangely on this island. At times he could hear distant waves breaking, and then they would go away, replaced by the amplified chattering of birds. The sound of a powerful waterfall cut through at one point, but as soon as he'd traversed a ridge, it vanished. He never heard Rosa's cries or her husband's agonizing screams in protest, though the explosion after McStarley detonated her bomb cut through. Conrad didn't waste time speculating who it was. All that really mattered was that there was one fewer of them.

The moon eventually rose, not quite full, but enough to speed up his trek with dim illumination. He had been moving stealthily anyway, just as the army had trained him when cutting through sniper territory. He hadn't seen any signs of company since his interlude with the Russian. No tracks, no broken branches, no scent of urine or defecation. He was alone out here.

Midnight arrived with no fanfare. He was now hiking two miles upstream from the gorge where McStarley had committed his grisly act. By Conrad's guesstimation, he was more than halfway across the width of the island. If he kept on at this pace, he would make it to the weather tower before sunrise, which was critical— he knew he stood little chance of sneaking into Breckel's compound during the light of day.

He spotted tracks in the damp ground. They were irregular, one track much heavier than the other. The boot size eliminated the women.

Conrad stopped and listened, moving his head slowly to focus his hearing.

Breathing.

Someone was heavily breathing nearby.

He quickly scanned his surroundings. There was a big tree up ahead, its trunk covered in vines. The tip of a boot was exposed on the other side of it.

The breathing turned into shuddering sobs.

Conrad crept forward, carefully rounding the tree.

It was Paco. One of his wrists was still shackled thanks to McStarley, the chain dangling from it.

He didn't even look up at Conrad. Paco was in another world. It was as if he had already died.

"What happened?" Conrad asked quietly, glancing around the entire time to make sure this wasn't an ambush.

Paco continued to cry, delirious in his grief.

"Amigo, talk to me. What's going on?"

He finally looked up. Conrad could see he had been beaten badly.

"I'm gonna kill them, I'm gonna kill them . . ." he choked out.

"Gonna kill who?"

The Mexican's face became crazed. He desperately grabbed onto Conrad's leg. "You help me kill 'm—together we can kill 'm both."

"You're not making any sense," Conrad said, still looking around. Whoever Paco wanted to kill was probably still in the vicinity.

"My Rosa . . . they took her like a dog. The big one cut her and they made me watch. When he was done, he set off that bomb on her leg and she . . ."

He trembled and then found his hate again.

"You help me KILL 'M."

Conrad digested what he'd heard. If it had been Sarah, he would want to kill them, too.

There was also important information here. Paco had said *they*. Two of the cons had teamed up. Since the Russian was dead, the "big one" had to be McStarley.

"HELP ME KILL 'M," he repeated louder.

Conrad heard a branch break in the distance.

"Keep it down. We got company."

He listened and looked. Fifty yards away there was movement through thick trees. Two figures stalking together, one big, one small. McStarley had teamed up with Saiga, the Japanese con, who knew his way around martial arts. He and Paco needed to get out of there.

"I'll help ya stay alive. Now get yourself together. Get up."

"I can't, *esai*. My knee's broke."

Conrad sighed. This explained the irregular footprints, which McStarley and Saiga were probably tracking. A wounded bird was just what he needed right now. He was on the wrong side of midnight, with dawn only a few hours off. He didn't need to be slowed up, didn't need his toughest competition hunting him down. But Conrad wasn't the kind of soldier who left a wounded man behind.

He lifted Paco and slung his arm around his shoulder, carrying him off.

K. C. Mack waited until nightfall before returning to the B-52 wreckage. After decking Saiga, he'd decided to cut his losses and run into the jungle. He told himself he would find another bag, another convict to kill.

Neither had happened.

He guardedly made his way back to the clearing. The contents of the supply bag had been pilfered, but maybe there was something he could use inside that fuselage.

After locating his old spear, which he had tossed after finding the knife, K.C. held it ready as he peeked inside. Without the sun's help, it was pitch-dark.

Hell no, he said to himself, backing away.

He listened for five minutes, hearing only silence.

The choice was simple. He could stand out there all night, or be a man and go for it.

K.C. lunged through the opening and thrashed his stick around. Lots of stuff fell, but no people. He was alone.

It took a few seconds for his eyes to adjust. He saw a few old sardine cans and picked one up. The metal was rough and corroded, circa 1940s. K.C. hated sardines, but right now they sounded fantastic. He pried off the key and peeled back the lid. The foul smell practically knocked him down. K.C. tossed it outside and kept looking. There was another can on the ground in a different shape but with the same corrosion, its label having disintegrated. He figured it had probably spoiled as well.

What the hell, it was worth a try.

K.C. peeled it open, bracing himself for the stench. He hazarded a small sniff from a distance. So far, so good. He sniffed closer. Not bad. Dipped his finger inside and tasted it.

A flood of memories hit him.

Mama . . .

His mother had fried up Spam when he was a kid, serving it on toast, noodles, cabbage, everything. They had been poor and the mystery meat was cheap, but it had done the job.

More than two decades later, here on this death island, it would do the job again.

It tasted as good as he remembered it. That was the good part. But the bad part was thinking about his mother. Right now he couldn't bear the thought of facing her. She had faithfully visited him at Soledad State Correctional Facility after he'd shot a fellow dealer and ended up on death row. He told her he had found the church, that he'd confessed his sins to God. He was a changed man. He was ready to pay for his transgressions against society.

A week later he escaped while being transferred to the maximum security prison at Folsom. K.C. had been planning the escape for months—Soledad was notoriously racist and he knew he was about to be moved. His cell mate had turned him on to a hash dealer in Kuala Lumpur, so Malaysia became his destination of choice. Apparently they didn't like drug dealers in Malaysia, especially ones who moved in on other dealers' turf, and he ended up on death row. K.C. never called his mother to tell her where he was, knowing it would break her heart. She knew he had escaped from Soledad, had to know, which meant that everything he'd told her about reforming was a lie. She probably didn't know about his activities in Malaysia, and he wanted to spare her another pile of grief.

And what would she think of his current situation? Her son being hunted down like a wild animal, killing others just to stay alive? He hoped she didn't know a thing about this.

K.C. slurped down the ancient Spam, his hunger overcoming all thought.

Movement caught his eye through a hole in the plane's side.

He pressed up against the fuselage and peered out. His pupils had adjusted to the inky darkness inside, so the moonlit clearing looked bright, almost like he had night vision.

Yasantwa, the South African babe, was moving past the wreckage like a scared deer. She stared straight at the plane, right at him. Nothing registered on her face.

She can't see me or she'd be flyin' outta here.

He hoped she would come closer to explore it. Ambushing her would be easy.

She started to do exactly that and then changed her mind. It was hard to read her expression due to the distance and dim light, but to him it looked like her body language spelled fear. While she didn't run, she didn't linger, and moved on at a brisk pace.

K.C. crept out and began to stalk her, not exactly sure what he would do when he caught up. Unlike the others, rape wasn't on his mind, but he still needed to win this contest.

From Yasantwa's perspective, the plane had looked like possible shelter and a place to sleep, though K.C. had been wrong. She *had* seen movement inside. Yasantwa knew if she ran, whoever was in there would give chase. Deceiving people, especially men, was her forte. Better to let them think she was oblivious.

She wouldn't have been able to sleep anyway. After the day's events, fear would not allow any shut-eye until this was over. She'd nearly drowned and the German had come very close to raping and murdering her. After killing him, she hadn't stopped moving. The thought of winning this insane contest hadn't even crossed her mind. Right now it was all about survival.

Yasantwa pressed on, letting her ears be eyes in the back of her head. She knew she was being followed, but like a cat encountering a dog, running would only incite her attacker.

She heard leaves mashing right behind her. The thudding of her heart against her rib cage nearly drowned out the footfalls. It took all of her conviction not to run.

There was a dead fallen tree a few feet ahead. It was now or never.

Yasantwa stepped around it, hoping her attacker wouldn't be able to see her for the few moments she needed to surprise him. She spotted a dead branch the size of a walking stick and snapped it off. With luck, he would think she had just stepped on deadwood.

She could hear the footsteps again. Her pursuer had just rounded the fallen tree.

She kept her back to him and continued to walk on, careful to keep her weapon obscured. Her senses were fine-tuned. She could hear his breathing between the crunching of his boots. He was now close enough for her to smell his body odor.

Yasantwa turned and swung, cracking K.C. across his shoulder blades. He fell on his back. She was on him like a leopard, shoving the tip of her branch against his throat.

One of his hands shot out and knocked it aside, the stick stabbing the ground beside his ear. He kicked out, tripped her, and flipped her on her back. K.C. snatched up the stick and dived on top of her, pressing it against her chest.

He was pumping with residual adrenaline from his ass kicking by Saiga and was ready to break her neck. At this moment, she wasn't the same woman he had semibonded with in the hangar and chopper. She was the enemy.

"Come on, man. Take her out! TAKE HER OUT!"

Eddie C was watching them on the monitor with Bella, both of them totally fired up. It was the wee hours and everyone else was fighting off fatigue.

Breckel strode in and joined them. He had no intention of sleeping until the thirty hours were up and a winner had been declared. Julie was a write-off for the time being, though he was confident that once he was wrapped here, he could patch things up.

Goldman was more of a concern. He'd told Goldy to take a break, though the truth was he wanted to get him out of his sight for a while. He was pissed at Goldy for wimping out during McStarley's performance, but as he watched K.C. and Yasantwa on the screen, his respect for the man was renewed. Goldy had installed superbright lenses and night-vision software that made everything visible, no easy task with two black-skinned cast members fighting in near darkness.

Still, the clever technology meant nothing if his cast didn't perform.

The evening had gone slower than he had expected. No deaths, no interaction at all since McStarley had slaughtered one of the Mexicans. Thank God for the limey—at least he was putting on a show. He hoped these two would as well.

"It's about time." He snorted, watching as the drug dealer from Inglewood prepared to kill Breckel's sensuous female lead. With any luck, he would take more than just her life.

Yasantwa continued to struggle, but she was physically outclassed. She'd gotten lucky with the Nazi and knew it. It would take another miracle to survive this time around.

"Calm down, just calm down," she heard her attacker say. "Y' were gonna kill me."

She felt the pressure ease up on her chest, though he still had her pinned.

"I was just scared," she told him, shaking.

"I don't want t' kill ya. I jus' wanna get this bomb off my leg."

"Is killing me gonna do that?" she said, still fearful.

There was a long pause.

"No . . ."

He'd spent a fair amount of time on the fence deciding whether or not to kill her. His survival stood on one side. Pragmatically, she needed to die. It was the only way he could win. He had murdered plenty of men and a couple of young gangbangers in his lifetime, but never a woman, although there had been a couple who deserved it. He was no fool—women were less violent but could be just as evil. Why take the chance? Kill this bitch.

On the other side was her luminous face. That alone was almost enough to sway him, but what finally pushed him over was his mother. How would she judge him if she was watching right now? He could justify killing the others in self-defense, but not a female who was smaller and weaker than him. He'd already done too many bad things in his life. If somebody else killed her, that was fine, but it wasn't going to be him.

As he gazed down at her, the connection he'd felt earlier resurfaced. She had a sweet, innocent face, doelike eyes, and perfect lips. Jesus, was she attractive, but it was more than that. They had something, the two of them.

She stopped shaking and relaxed her muscles, giving in to him.

"You can trust me," she said softly.

"Last time I trusted a woman I ended up on death row," he said skeptically.

He was not exaggerating. K.C. had killed a competing drug dealer in Malaysia and told his girlfriend about it, a stunning Asian he'd hooked up with in a strip club. It turned out she was a plant in the dealer's organization, hired to get close to K.C. and scope out his growing operation. He'd bought everything the bitch had told him, every single lie.

That was not going to happen again. His eyes were staying wide open this time. And right now they were on Yasantwa's gorgeous face and slender body.

K.C. climbed off Yasantwa and pulled her up.

"He's letting her go?" Eddie complained as he watched them on the plasma.

Bella shook her head. "That really sucks."

Breckel was livid. "For fuck's sake, what is this? *Friendship Island*? What do I have to do to get some goddamn killer instinct out there?"

Eddie saw his boss heading for a meltdown, which would not be a pretty sight. In the few shows they had worked together, he had seen Breckel unceremoniously fire entire crews simply because he was in a bad mood. Right now he was on his boss's good side, but that could change faster than the naked celebrity photos slide-showing on Eddie's screen saver. He brought up the subscription page, hoping for some good news. It was already daylight in many parts of the world, which meant more people online.

"Easy, boss, epic news. As of this moment, over twenty million viewers have logged on, and PAID, for entry onto our site."

The information assuaged Breckel, but not completely. "Halfway there."

He glared at the screen. Sucking in a Super Bowl–sized audience would be impossible if the action remained flat. If somebody didn't die in the next hour, he would have to make it happen.

20

With Paco as an appendage, Conrad crisscrossed the river in two places to cover their tracks. The Mexican limped along as best he could with a walking stick, reminiscent of a wounded soldier hobbling through a battlefield. McStarley and Saiga were surely hunting them and could move much more quickly. Conrad's plan was to find Paco safe cover and then resume his course to the weather tower. He would make his tracks obvious so the pair of killers would track him and leave Paco alone. His amigo was going to die—there was no doubt about that—but better to perish instantly at the thirty-hour mark than be tortured by an English madman and his cruel sidekick.

Satisfied that they had lost McStarley and Saiga for the time being, Conrad let Paco rest and hiked up a small hill, hoping to get a better view of their surroundings. He could see the top of the weather tower less than a mile away across a ravine, its metal roof glinting in the moonlight. That was the good news.

A very important detail suddenly clouded his mind, one that threatened his entire plan. He glanced down at his ankle bracelet with a deep frown. He should have thought of this before.

GPS.

They knew his exact position on the island at all times. They were tracking his every move. Night or day, they would know he was coming.

He had to find a way to disable it, but first things first. He needed to get Paco settled.

Conrad surveyed the area. It was hard to see much in the darkness except that the topography was fairly open in this part of the jungle. It would be easy for McStarley and Saiga to find them there.

He studied the ravine and spotted a wooden bridge through the foliage. It looked wide enough to hold a jeep. Crossing the narrow canyon looked to be a cinch, with better hiding spots on the other side.

He rejoined Paco and they made their way for the bridge, hiding their tracks as best they could. As the bridge came into full view, Conrad saw that the structure had been bombed out by a mortar. Its middle section was gone, cutting off access to the opposite side. Rusty support cables still spanned the gap, but he could never get Paco across.

Conrad considered it carefully. Something of importance had to be near that bridge, or why would it have been bombed? Whatever it was, the allies had tried to cut off access to it.

Another fifty yards of hiking confirmed his theory. An open-walled structure with a plank loading dock, stacked wooden crates, and a stone bunker was on their side of the ravine, hidden in the jungle. It would be a good place for Paco to lay low. They might even find something inside that he could use to defend himself.

Conrad got them to the command post and sat Paco down on the loading dock. His knee had swollen to twice its size. Conrad knew he had to be in pain.

"How's your knee holdin' up?"

"Can't walk, can't fight, can't do nothin' but limp 'long with a fuckin' stick." The Mexican grimaced. His eyes rolled up to Conrad. "You kill 'm for me. Kill both of them for me?"

Conrad knew the main reason Paco was hanging tough was due to his thirst for revenge. He thought about telling the grieving man what he wanted to hear, just to ease his mind, but Conrad wasn't a liar. While he might end up having to kill them out of necessity, his mission right now was to contact Sarah, not be somebody's hit man. He'd been there, done that, working for the army.

"Sorry, amigo. I got somethin' I gotta do."

"What you gotta do?"

"I saw a weather tower on the northwest end of the island. There's gotta be a radio in there."

Paco's expression changed. "You call for help?" The American had just given him another reason to stay alive.

Conrad thought about the question. Calling in the cavalry had originally been part of his agenda, but the more he thought about it, it seemed like a stretch. Who would he call? His own military had abandoned him. The odds were that he was going to die out here. All of them were.

"We're light-years from help, man."

Paco nodded back. Living without Rosa seemed pointless anyway. All he could do now was avenge her death.

"So who y' call?"

Conrad said nothing. It was nobody's business but his.

"Y' got a woman? Y' got a wife?"

He gave the Mexican another glance. Right now, Paco was the closest thing he had to a friend. The man had just lost everything, and Conrad could empathize. He, too, had lost all that was important, but way before this island. He never should've left Sarah and accepted the assignment in El Salvador.

"Yeah. Somethin' like that."

They both looked off, Paco fighting back tears.

"Here we are, *esai*, on this island . . ." He shook his head. "Maybe this is the price y' pay for the sins. The Bible's hell. Me, I killed some *jefes*. You?"

Conrad didn't answer, at least not verbally. The look he gave Paco said yes. Definitely yes.

Paco nodded back and looked off again.

"I was on the run. Came 'cross Rosa in a bordello in Acapulco. Das what she was, man, that's what she had t' do—for her mama, her lil sis. I took her from there, with me. She learn real quick y' can make a lot mo' money with a gun in yer hand than yer back on a bed."

Paco paused as he looked back on their life together, the edge of his lips going crooked with a bittersweet smile.

"We hit everythin', me and Rosa, we raised some

fuckin' hell." His mouth began to tremble. "Without her, I don't know what I got."

Neither of them noticed the camera mounted at one end of the loading dock.

Breckel was frowning at Conrad and Paco on the big monitor as they commiserated. The image abruptly cut to McStarley and Saiga, trudging through the dark jungle like a pair of good buddies. It then cut to a tree-cam angle looking down on K. C. Mack and Yasantwa as he led her by the hand back to the B-25 wreckage.

The show was going nowhere fast.

Goldman had returned to his console and was doing the cutting himself, giving his assistant JJ a break. He was feeling better for the time being. Nobody was dying. They were getting along, in fact.

Naturally, Breckel's disposition was exactly the opposite.

"What the fuck is going on?" he railed.

"Nothing," piped up Eddie, stating the obvious. "It's dead out there. No one's engaging."

"Yeah, no shit," spat Breckel, as if Eddie were a moron. "What are their relative positions?"

Eddie dutifully brought up his grid map with the six remaining + signs, now grouped in three pairs.

"It looks like the hottie and the homeboy are on their way back to the B-25 wreck." He pointed, still smarting from Breckel's condescension. "Conrad and the Mexican are at the Japanese ruins."

"I can see that. Where's McStarley? What's his proximity to the others?"

Right now the Englishman was the only one Breckel could count on for brutal excitement. McStarley was camera savvy. He didn't just kill, he performed.

Eddie pointed at a pair of + signs not far from the pair that signified Conrad and Paco. "Right here. A few clicks east of Conrad and Señor Paco."

Breckel moved to Baxter, who was on his fifth cup of coffee. It was time to shake things up.

"Drop a Christmas bag to McStarley," he said discreetly, though Goldman heard every word. "Give him the works. Send him to the Japanese ruins."

21

The chopper set a course inland per the coordinates that Baxter had given the pilot. It came in at a low altitude, barely skirting the treetops as it dipped into a valley. Their destination was a small glade halfway between the Japanese command post ruins where Conrad and Paco were positioned and the valley that McStarley and Saiga were traversing.

The latter two had been following Paco's tracks, which had soon joined up with another set about a mile upstream from where they'd had their fun with the Mexican whore. McStarley had a pretty good idea who made those tracks because the owner had managed to send them all over hell and back. The American bloke knew what he was doing.

McStarley had suspected for a while that Conrad was military—army, Special Forces, a SEAL, something like that, judging by the way he'd sent Breckel's head of security on his ass in the chopper. In their present situation, only somebody with training could've hidden his tracks so well, especially with a lame duck in tow. Why Conrad was helping the Mexican made no sense to him, but it was a card he might be able to play down the road.

He and Saiga heard the chopper, looked up, and saw a bright red glow floating down from the sky about a kilometer up ahead.

"Santa just dropped us another bag o' toys." The Brit grinned, sprinting for it.

They arrived with the flare still burning. McStarley quickly snuffed the fire in case anyone else was around and then tore into the big black duffel. It was chock-full of all the essentials, and then some.

"Merry fucking Christmas." He beamed. "We got sandwiches, knives . . . oh, look at this, someone up there likes us, boy—cigars!" He slapped Saiga on the back. "We've hit the fucking jackpot, mate."

The booty didn't stop with food and tobacco. There was a compass, a professional bow with a quiver of arrows, a three-foot machete, jars of gasoline, and several packs of matches among the goodies. The two convicts were in heaven.

McStarley reached in and pulled out another sweet treat: a map of the island. "You are here" was written in a circle. Not far away, two blood-red Xs were marked at the abandoned Japanese command post. It didn't take a genius to figure out their next victims were waiting there for the taking.

A few raindrops splashed on the map, followed by a rumble of thunder. McStarley folded it and grabbed the bow and arrows. The bow was styled on classic Turkish weaponry but had been made in the good old U.S. of A. Weighing in at twenty pounds, it was state-of-the-art, constructed from a wood, fiberglass, and aluminum composite, employing a micropulley system to increase its efficiency. Its sleek graphite arrows were designed for hunting wild game, not for archery.

Meanwhile, Saiga was playing with a pair of bolo knives. Eighteen inches long with a curved tip and a handle made of caribou horn, they had been imported from the Philippines. The lethal knives were normally used for killing pigs, chickens, and cows. Humans were about to be added to that list.

"You better limber up, son. We've a show to put on," McStarley said with a wink.

Saiga did a series of cartwheels and flashy kung fu moves. The Englishman deadpanned him. His Japanese mate was just a little bit *too* gung ho.

"Settle yourself down a bit."

The truth was that McStarley was just as excited. He now had all the toys to do what he loved to do most.

The rain began to fall in earnest as they marched on, now less than twenty minutes away from their intended targets.

Conrad and Paco had no idea they were coming.

They had heard the chopper but hadn't seen the flare. The command post was secluded in the jungle and the drop had been made behind a hill. Conrad considered the possibility that another food supply bag had been delivered close by, but it didn't change his plans. He needed to disable his GPS and get to that weather tower.

He had first searched the bunker built into the hillside. A one-foot viewing slit had been carved in its rock face, with a rusted Type 91 ten-centimeter Howitzer sticking out. The huge gun was completely corroded and of no use to them.

Conrad entered the bunker, which was nearly pitch-dark. Using his hands, he searched its innards and found several unused artillery shells. At some point they might come in handy, but not at the moment.

He returned to the command post's loading dock, where he had left Paco.

"What choo doin'?" asked Paco.

The Mexican had crawled inside for shelter as the downpour fell in earnest. Conrad stepped past him without taking time for an explanation. He began to rummage through the World War II remains as rain leaked through holes in the roof. There hadn't been much left behind—a few wooden bowls and rusty silverware, but no weapons, ammo, or food. What did remain had mostly decomposed in the tropical heat.

He finally spotted something that could potentially help. A circa 1943 lead-acid battery was resting beside a Japanese radio. The radio was corroded and useless, but he wasn't interested in that.

Conrad glanced around to make sure there wasn't a camera spying on them. He had already spotted the lens mounted high on the loading dock. After careful inspection, he noticed a lens wedged in the corner of the interior. Conrad casually tossed some crates around until the lens was blocked. He wanted them to think he was too stupid to have noticed it.

Satisfied they weren't being watched, he smashed the battery against the corner of the concrete wall and broke it open.

"See that? GPS," he finally answered, pointing at a component on his ankle bracelet. "I don't like being tracked."

Inside the battery were thin, malleable plates of lead. He pried two of them out and sandwiched the plates between the electronics surrounding his GPS unit. In theory, the lead would act as a shield and keep it from transmitting his location. He wasn't sure it would work, but he would have to take the chance.

Conrad placed the old wooden bowls under the roof's leaky holes. They quickly began to fill up.

"Y' got some water here. Take this—"

He picked up a rusty steak knife he'd found on a shelf and handed it to Paco. It was a gesture of moral support more than anything else. Conrad hoped the rain would erase any traces of their tracks leading to the compound and his friend wouldn't need to use the knife.

Conrad began to exit and took a last look at Paco. He started to wish him good luck, but no amount of luck was going to save him. It was just a matter of time—hours, minutes, and seconds that were relentlessly ticking down on both their ankles. He gave him a final look of commiseration and started to leave.

"Hey, *esai*—"

Conrad turned back just before he disappeared out the door.

"*—Gracias.*"

Conrad barely nodded back. He hadn't done anything special. He did the right thing amid a bizarre gathering of people who did everything wrong, nothing more.

The rain started to come down hard as he left the command post and made his way to the bridge.

There was no way for him to know that McStarley and Saiga had a map and would be there in about fifteen minutes, with Paco a sitting duck.

At the same time Conrad was smashing the battery, Eddie C was checking the subscription numbers and blogs. Bella, who also hadn't slept, was cutting together a highlights reel to keep viewers from nodding and/or logging off. McStarley and Saiga should be about to end the lack of violence, but Bella wanted to be proactive just in case. Breck had been in a shitty mood the last few hours, and she didn't relish getting raked over the coals like Goldman had; even Eddie had taken some verbal abuse.

Finishing his blog check, Eddie returned to his grid map to check on McStarley's progress. Two green + signs were steadily moving toward another pair.

Right before Eddie's eyes, one of the + signs at the Japanese compound disappeared off his grid.

"Whoa, whoa. Hey, Breck. Conrad just kinda vanished."

Breckel was busy watching the main monitor, featuring a close-up of McStarley. The de facto star of his show was trampling through foliage with the supply duffel on his back and a bow in his grip. Saiga was right behind him with the bolo knives.

"What do you mean, vanished?"

"He's gone. He's not on my grid." Eddie pointed it out. "I just lost his signal."

"How the fuck did this happen?"

Technical malfunctions were the last thing needed right now.

"Gotta be a problem with his unit," he answered, bracing himself for another reaming. "Software's fine."

Breckel decided it was a waste of his energy to yell at Eddie since he had nothing to do with the GPS units. He instead went to Goldman, who hadn't said two words since the bag of goodies had been delivered to McStarley.

"Goldy. Find him."

Goldman nodded, anxiously searching his myriad of camera angles. At this point he just wanted to get through this so he could go back to shooting college football. One of the convicts—*murderers*—was off the grid and could be anywhere. This was definitely not supposed to happen.

It didn't help that the lens mounted inside the Japanese command post was blocked by a crate. Conrad could still be in there, but Goldman decided not to count on it.

Several minutes went by with the Texan AWOL.

"Found him," Goldman finally said with some relief in his voice.

He brought up Conrad on the big monitor. He was dangling upside down, his arms and legs wrapped around the bridge cable as he worked his way across the ravine.

Breckel squinted at the dim image, trying to read Conrad's mind. "Where's he going?"

"I don't know."

"Keep an eye on him."

Duh, Goldman said to himself. He had been keeping an eye on *all* of them with hundreds of cameras—that was his job. Another comment like that and he would explode, though not at the magnitude of the Nazi, Russian, and Mexican woman, which he had so gloriously captured on video. The whole thing was making him sick, just as it had Breck's latest conquest, Julie. Goldman hadn't liked her at the outset—she had zero experience working on a reality series and had suddenly been handed the costume designer gig. Now that they were in the thick of it, his opinion of her changed. It seemed like he and Julie were the only two people on this island with a modicum of morality.

Special Agent Brad Wilkins was also watching Conrad crawl across the ravine on his laptop.

He was still waiting for more information about his background and what he had been doing in El Salvador. His conversation with Sarah Cavanaugh had yielded little, save a confirmation of facts he already knew. Conrad's birth name was Jack Riley and he was from Granville, Texas. He had been in the army and had supposedly retired, but then he turned up in El Salvador in 2005. The bio on *The Condemned* web site was mostly erroneous, except that he had indeed bombed a building and was on death row.

Army officials had confirmed that Jack Riley was a decorated soldier who had saved lives during the Gulf War. His service record from the mid-1990s onward was hazy. He officially retired in 2003. Wilkins knew that he lived with Sarah from then until early 2005, at which point he mysteriously ended up in San Salvador, the capital city where the bombing took place. There were a whole lot of holes that still needed filling in.

His assistant Stan knocked on his door with a worried look. "Moyer wants you in his office right away."

"What's going on?"

"I don't know, but he sounded nervous."

Wilkins reluctantly got up and walked down the hallway to Alan Moyer's corner office. The assistant director was behind his desk with a nice view of downtown New Haven and the Connecticut countryside framed in the windows behind him.

"You wanted to see me?" Wilkins said from the doorway.

"We have to drop the investigation into Jack Riley."

Wilkins stepped into the office with a baffled expression. "Drop it?"

He noticed a man sitting in the corner wearing a stylish dark suit and patent leather shoes. He looked to be about forty-five, his hair dyed a youthful brown and coiffed with some sort of shiny product. Moyer didn't introduce him.

"It's over," his boss said bluntly.

Wilkins eyed the mystery man again as he spoke. "Two Americans are trapped in this thing—"

"Brad, Brad, this is not a conversation, okay?"

He could tell that Moyer was running scared. He didn't want to lose that nice view, didn't want to make any waves.

"Just hours ago, you told me to get to the bottom of it," Wilkins protested, ignoring the admonition. "Jack Riley, U.S. Army, decorated soldier. Now you're telling me to drop it?"

The man in the corner reached over and slowly nudged the door shut, never leaving his chair.

"When you started digging into Jack Riley, you caused a lot of people a lot of stress where I work," the man said. His voice had the smug lilt of a Washington bureaucrat.

"And where's that?" Wilkins asked pointedly, not the least bit intimidated.

Moyer cleared his throat and answered for him. "The Pentagon. This is Wade Meranto, DIA."

Wilkins's stomach began to sour. He knew all about the Defense Intelligence Agency. Their slogan was, "Committed to excellence in defense of the nation." If you believed the watercooler gossip and conspiracy theory experts, this translated as more worldwide covert operations in play than the CIA and FBI combined in any given year. Officially, the DIA was all about the integration of highly skilled intelligence professionals with leading-edge technology at their disposal. This sounded a lot like what Wilkins did, but in fact it involved shades of Rambo. The DIA frequently used highly trained military operatives to achieve the mandates of defense planners and national security policy makers.

"Your investigation is over," Meranto said with zero emotion. "We know all there is to know about Captain Jack Riley."

Maybe this DIA agent did, but Wilkins wasn't about to roll over and play dead like his boss Moyer.

"Is he a killer or not?"

Meranto offered up a knowing smile. "He's probably killed more men than anyone on that island."

"What was he doing in El Salvador?"

"Enough, Brad." Moyer was sweating under his collar.

"It's okay," Meranto told him. He always enjoyed flaunting his position of superiority when he visited sister agencies. In the intelligence business, knowledge was definitely power.

"He did fourteen years, Special Forces detachment, Delta," he began. "He retired, but his old boss, *my* boss, calls him up from time to time. Black ops. Year ago, he was sent down to El Salvador to demolish a Vallejo drug plant. The profits were being used to fund our enemies. Got the job done, killed several men, all Vallejo cartel. He traveled with bogus papers under the name of Jack Conrad. His real name and who he worked for were never uncovered, although they tried. The prison warden was cozy with the cartel."

Wilkins digested this. Special Forces Delta, black ops . . . Jack Riley aka Jack Conrad was a serious component of America's military defense operations. He had been following orders when he blew up that drug plant, and our country had left him to hang out and dry.

"So you let him fry in a Central American prison for an entire year? You let him get executed?"

"Guys like Jack Riley get paid well," Meranto casually replied. "And they get hired for the same reason they get fired—to keep DC brass clean." He crossed his legs and smoothed out his expensive tropical wool. "We can't have you rattling doors that need to stay shut."

"It's politics," chimed in Moyer, concerned only with not making waves.

Wilkins gazed at both of them. "This is bullshit." He started to open the door.

"I know—you want to go out and make some noise, don't you?" the DIA agent said. He could tell that Wilkins was headstrong, which could end up being a problem.

Wilkins didn't answer.

Meranto locked eyes with Moyer, reinstilling the fear he had planted upon arrival. "That can't happen."

Moyer stiffened. "It won't. That's a guarantee."

Wilkins got the trickle-down effect a second later: Moyer's hard stare left no room for interpretation. Jack Riley-Conrad was officially off the books, along with *The Condemned* webcast.

22

Julie couldn't sleep.

Falling asleep had been no problem. Her body and brain were begging for some shut-eye, so she'd passed out within two minutes of lying down. It was her dream that refused to let her rest.

In it, she had been one of the convicts, and the Nazi was trying to rape her. She continually tried to reach for the red activation strip on his bracelet, but it was always dangling just out of reach. She punched, kicked, and clawed. Her hands and feet went through him as if he were a ghost. Other apparitions began to crowd around and watch the assault—American and Japanese World War II soldiers in uniform, some missing limbs. A few familiar faces were among the dead, including the Italian Giangrasso, Raudsep the Russian, and Rosa Pacheco. All of them were gazing cruelly at her.

She looked back at the Nazi. He was beginning to slowly change into another man, who eventually materialized as Ian Breckel.

Julie bolted up in a cold sweat. No amount of sleep would make the reality of her situation go away.

She came out of her dazed fear and realized she needed to do something about this. Certainly she couldn't be the only one disgusted by this show. Goldman was definitely disturbed by it; maybe if the two of them cornered Ian, they could talk some sense into him. Everyone seemed to be afraid of him. If her dream was to be taken seriously, that group included her.

Julie walked down to the control room, the rain drenching her. She was fully aware that part of her power over Ian was her attractiveness. Looking like a drowned rat would not help her cause, so the insecurity she had felt in the dream resurfaced. She would talk to Goldman and maybe a few others first. Get some support behind her.

When she arrived, Ian and Goldman were in the middle of a serious conversation. She stayed back and listened.

"Okay, Breck. As you can see, the American, Yul Brynner, he's gone. He's off my monitors completely, along with the grid. I had him and then I lost him. And the reason I lost him is that he is headed toward us, and I did not rig cameras where we are at. And quite frankly, um, it's disturbing."

"Relax," said Breckel, not the least bit concerned. The only thing that disturbed him was the possibility of missing Conrad's death once McStarley and Saiga caught up to him.

"I'm going to relax when killers and rapists are on the *other* side of the island, Breck. Is that cool?"

Goldman popped another antacid and chased it

with his anxiety medication. He lifted his walkie and ordered three new security cams installed right outside the compound.

Breckel almost smiled. At least Goldy was showing some emotion again.

Not for a minute was the producer worried about one prisoner infiltrating their compound. Conrad was weaponless. Armed guards were everywhere. And what was his motivation for coming here? Goldman was being paranoid, that's all.

Baxter was nearby and wasn't taking the news quite as cavalierly. His left eye was starting to turn a deep shade of purple thanks to Conrad's elbow. Nobody had ever surprised him like that. Having the redneck coming this way presented an opportunity. The boss might not like it, but he saw a chance to kill Conrad himself.

"I'll find him," he announced, marching out.

Goldman watched him go, Baxter's exit bringing Julie into view. The two locked eyes. Both were on the same page—the show and its creator were both reeling out of control. But now was not the time to broach the subject, not until Conrad was located.

Conrad, in fact, was just outside the village compound. He surveyed the ten-foot fence topped with razor wire. Beyond it was another circular fence that encompassed the compound proper, not unlike a wartime demilitarized zone. The setup reminded him of the El Salvadoran drug factory he had infiltrated. Conrad peered through the fence just as the tropical rain stopped. Along with the weather tower, there were elaborate tents constructed inside the DMZ, one larger than the others. He also spotted the huge satellite dish he had seen from the chopper. He counted roughly a dozen armed guards milling about, though there were probably more. This was definitely Breckel's headquarters. What the man was distributing wasn't all that much different from heroin or crack, but stopping the broadcast wasn't part of Conrad's agenda right now.

Thoughts of El Salvador were hard to suppress. He had never met DIA Agent Meranto, but the bureaucrat had stretched the truth about Conrad's "keep the DC brass clean" mission. He had never agreed to be expendable, nor had it even been suggested. They had also guaranteed him backup. Lastly, if he were to be caught, they would use every diplomatic measure at their disposal to extract him from the country. None of these promises were ever kept. His own country sold him out.

There had been men with automatic weapons at the drug plant, just like here. He felt like he was behind enemy lines all over again, though he didn't have his usual arsenal of black ops weapons and supplies this time around. He would have to find a simpler way in.

In El Salvador, Conrad had clipped the fence wires, crawled in, and silently taken out two guards before he arrived at his target. He had knocked out the first guard and stabbed the second in self-defense using his combat knife. Neither of these incidents were ever reported, nor was he charged with them. The three cartel kingpins who died in the explosion got all the attention. Some people's lives were worth more than others'. Right now his own was worthless.

Conrad didn't have the fence cutters or combat knife, but he would be following pretty much the same game plan. Entering through the main gate was out since it was too heavily guarded. Gunfire would end the mission cold, just like the drug plant, so he needed to remain stealthy.

Peering through the fence, he spotted a locked access gate on the opposite side of the compound. A big Samoan grunt worker was installing a security camera just outside the gate per Goldman's orders. The weather tower was a short distance away, with one man inside. There were two human obstacles. Once again, it mirrored El Salvador. Conrad wasn't a superstitious man, but he didn't like the parallels.

The main gate opened, allowing a jeep with armed guards to exit. At the same time Baxter and three other men walked out on foot, all armed with MP5 automatic machine guns. Baxter had a leashed, snarling German shepherd with him. They exchanged words that Conrad couldn't hear and then split up. Two guards passed within six feet of him, having no idea he was ducked behind a bush. He waited until they were out of sight and then circled the fence toward the smaller gate.

The Samoan worker had just finished mounting the camera when Conrad arrived, its red LED power light still off.

He needed to do this before the camera was activated. The big Samoan climbed down his ladder and pulled out his keys, unlocking the gate. Conrad sprang just as he swung it open, slamming the heel of his hand into the worker's surprised face. The man crumpled to the ground with little fanfare. Conrad yanked the wires from the camera. He eased the gate shut but kept it unlocked; he would need a quick exit as soon as his business was finished.

The DMZ began about twenty feet away, its fence free of barbed wire. Conrad easily scaled it and made his way to the rickety stairs leading to the top of the weather tower. The dark, predawn hours made his infiltration possible, just as he had surmised.

While he was relatively invisible, Breckel's village wasn't. Pools of light illuminated the grounds at essential spots, including the main gate and tent entrances. There was a work light at the foot of the stairs, which he would have to pass through. He waited until the guards weren't looking in his direction and then darted through the light. As he climbed the stairs, he saw Eddie C leaving a portable latrine and walking back to the control room tent, along with more guards milling about. He knew from the hangar briefing that Baxter's security staff was not made up of professional soldiers. Even so, he was unarmed. A bullet was a bullet.

Conrad eyed the big tent again. It had to be the show's nucleus. For a few moments, he considered taking it out and ending Breckel's broadcast. He could kill a guard and get his gun easily enough, drive a jeep into the tent, wreak all kinds of destruction. Hell, with that ankle bracelet still strapped to him he could even be a suicide bomber and hold people hostage.

He shelved the notion for the same reason he didn't kill the Samoan. What would it accomplish? Breckel and his security head deserved the worst, but innocent people would end up dying. There was a good chance he would get killed, too. Conrad needed to stay alive at least long enough to talk to Sarah and make things right for her and the boys. He'd think about taking down Breckel after that was accomplished.

Conrad continued up the stairs to the tower's upper deck, which wrapped 360 degrees around the structure. He peered through the dirty glass. It was a square space, about fifteen by fifteen feet, with a single China hat lamp dangling from the exposed beam ceiling. As he suspected, two walls were lined with newly installed weather-tracking and satellite communications equipment. A thirty-something technician of slight build was manning the equipment, his back to Conrad. The man looked unarmed.

Conrad opened the door and walked right in.

"Howdy."

The technician turned around to greet whoever it was. Conrad's bald head was directly under the China lamp and shining like a beacon. The technician knew who he was in a split second. He opened his mouth to scream bloody murder, but Conrad cracked him with his right fist, silencing him.

As he dragged the man aside, he spotted a half roll of duct tape in a box of wiring and other components. He thought about taping the technician's mouth shut and securing him but scrapped the idea—he would be long gone by the time the tech woke up. The tape might come in handy later, so he shoved it in his pocket before taking a seat behind the console.

His black ops stint included communications training that incorporated satellite and GPS. There were more than 150 communications satellites in orbit, with at least a hundred of them in geosynchronous orbit. The geosynchronous satellites were the ones Conrad needed to utilize. They orbited over the earth's equator and made communications to any part of the world possible twenty-four hours a day by bouncing signals from one satellite to another. Digital phone carriers relied on this technology, but none of the wireless networks had towers out here. He needed a satellite phone to make his call.

While the geosynchronous satellites were also used for broadcasting television and Internet content, they had nothing to do with global positioning. GPS used a small network of low-altitude satellites—only twenty-four of them in total—to cover the entire globe. Besides tracking the prisoners, the island's exact location could be pinpointed using GPS technology. He had told Paco they were "light-years from help," but that was based on nobody giving a shit about them as much as their remote location. El Salvador had taught him not to expect a rescue mission, and he didn't expect one now. Still, he decided to give Sarah his coordinates if he was lucky enough to get her on the phone.

For the time being, he ignored the tower's GPS system and went straight to the satellite phone. The chopper flight, which he was now sure had originated in Papua New Guinea, hadn't been long enough to take them out of the South Pacific, but they were definitely out of the United States. With that knowledge, he preceded Sarah's number with the international prefix code.

His eyes closed with relief when he heard the phone ringing.

It was morning in Granville when Sarah's kitchen phone rang. She had been up all night at the Blue Boot watching the webcast and was dead tired. Mike wouldn't let her work and sent her home at sunup to get some sleep. Her mother was asleep on the couch when she got in. Michael and Scotty were already up, their motors revving and stomachs growling, so she fixed them breakfast.

Sarah put two heaping plates of bacon, eggs, and pancakes in front of them, answering on the fourth ring.

"Hello," she said wearily.

"It's me, Sarah."

The voice on the other end momentarily paralyzed her.

It had been more than a year since she'd heard Jack's voice. There had been nothing in the interim—no calls, no letters, nothing. And then comes a mysterious call from an FBI agent less than twelve hours ago, followed by a Pandora's box of disturbing information, an Internet broadcast where the man she loved was competing to the death, and now his voice on the phone.

She staggered out to the porch where nobody could hear her, the cordless phone trembling in her grasp.

212

Sarah wanted to stay calm, but her words fell on top of each other as they left her mouth.

"Jack, what happened? Are you okay? What the hell is going on?"

"Just listen," he said quietly. "I don't have much time."

There in the weather tower, Conrad glanced down at the compound as he talked. Sooner or later the Samoan would be found and the place would be on red alert.

"Why haven't you contacted me?" she asked in a voice that broke his heart.

"For your own safety. Did ya think I walked out on you?"

He was greeted by silence.

Conrad shook his head, feeling her pain. How could she *not* think he'd up and left her? He had gone off with no big good-byes and then never came back. It killed him to keep his covert career a secret, but it had been for her own good. If she'd known anything about what he did or his current mission, she could have been a target for the Vallejo cartel or any number of organizations he had brought down. And there was also the DIA, his employer, to think about. Sarah would have come after them tooth and claw if she knew they had abandoned him in El Salvador. The DIA liked tidy little packages with no messes—he wouldn't put it past them to keep her quiet by whatever means necessary.

"I didn't know what to think . . . I've been through this before," she eventually answered, trying not to cry. "And then, you leave me—"

He interrupted her—his time was ticking away fast.

"Sarah, listen to me. I did not walk out on you. I love you and I love those boys of yours like my own. You understand that?"

The tears came fast. He loved her. Deep down she had known that, but hearing him say it, hearing him *alive*, was overwhelming.

"Jack, I—"

"Hold on, hold on, I'm not through. Grab yourself a pen, write this down. Cross National Bank, 25434-56 . . ."

He had carried the account number around in his head since El Salvador. There was over two hundred thousand dollars in that account. He'd tried to call Sarah from prison to give her the information, but they wouldn't let him near a phone. The money had been put there for her, Michael, and Scotty in case something bad happened. Well, it *had* happened. And was still happening.

"Jack, what is this, what are you doing?"

"I got some money saved up. I'll feel better knowing you have it. It'll help things around the house. It's for you and the kids."

"Money? You know I don't want money, Jack. I want you."

"I want ya t' take this, just in case—"

The lack of sleep and overload of emotion made her snap. "Just in case! A year ago you say you're leaving for work and I don't hear from you till now. Where've you been, Jack? The FBI called! Why is the FBI looking for you, Jack? What did you do?"

As Sarah poured out her heart, Conrad spotted Baxter rounding the outside fence perimeter with his German shepherd. The dog was jerking hard on his leash toward the access gate, where the Samoan lay unconscious.

"You're on the Internet, on this, this sick horror show," she went on. "They're saying you killed some people. Jack, tell me what's going on—you gotta tell me right now!"

"Just listen to me, Sarah. I gotta go. Write down this number—"

The money meant absolutely nothing to her, which he should have known. There was no way for her to know that he was about to be caught and possibly killed.

"No! No! I DON'T WANT IT," she shouted, loud enough to wake up her mother. "I want YOU. I want you back here with ME. That's all I want. I want you to tell me you're coming home."

She began to cry hard. He started to offer words of comfort, but then the German shepherd began to bark.

Down at the access gate, Baxter was staring at the unconscious Samoan as the dog went crazy. Armed guards were already on their way over.

"Breck, we got a breach of the east gate," Baxter spoke into his headset.

Breckel was perched in his leather lounger when he heard the words. His face flashed with uncharacteristic concern. He said nothing and stepped away from the others.

Goldman saw his expression and immediately cornered him. "What's going on?"

"It's Conrad," he said levelly. "He's here."

"Oh, great, how nice," he blurted, hit by a wave of panic. "Right here with us."

Simultaneously, Baxter's vision began to move like a rifle scope. The weather tower was the closest structure, so his eyes naturally went there. The booth looked empty. It wasn't supposed to be. He moved until he could get a better look inside.

He saw Conrad's shiny head behind the console.

"He's in the tower," he told everyone in his headset.

Breckel immediately turned to Goldman. "Shut the tower down. Kill the generator."

Goldman didn't question it, hurrying off.

"You do whatever it takes, you play this sick game, but I need you," Sarah begged Jack. "I need you here with me."

"All right, all right. Just calm down," he told her, giving up on the money.

He glanced out the window and saw Baxter and several guards scaling the tower stairs. His escape route had just been cut off.

"I gotta go. Everything's gonna be all right," he lied, unable to think of anything else to say. The odds were he wasn't going to make it out of this, but at least he had heard Sarah's voice one last time and, he hoped, given her some comfort that he genuinely loved her.

Sarah spoke as he started to hang up. "No, wait!

Jack! I spoke with an FBI agent. Where are you? You gotta tell me something, 'cause they got nothin'!"

He processed her words in an instant. Maybe he was wrong. Maybe somebody out there *did* give a shit.

He quickly turned on the GPS system, knowing Baxter and his men were seconds away. Like any car or handheld device, the unit had a transmitter pinpointing its exact position. The visual display was of no value since he couldn't transmit images to Sarah, so he went right to the numeric coordinates.

"Write this down: latitude 7.549282, longitude—"

The power went out: lights, console, the works.

"Sarah? Sarah?"

The line had gone dead.

23

"Jack? Jack?"

She was greeted with a dial tone.

Sarah hit star 69 and got a fast busy signal. Jack had been cut off.

She hurried back into the kitchen and wrote down the coordinates he had just given her.

Her mother was off the couch with a concerned look. "Honey?"

Sarah held up a hand to silence her, straining to remember the numbers as she jotted them down. She dug into her purse and fished out the slip of paper with Agent Wilkins's phone number and quickly dialed it.

"May I speak with Special Agent Brad Wilkins, please? It's urgent."

Conrad dropped the phone and paced the tower interior like a caged lion, looking for an escape that didn't involve the main stairs. He could feel the tower vibrating with the weight of Baxter and his guards as they climbed toward him.

He moved to a side window and scanned the compound below . . . coming face-to-face with Ian Breckel.

The producer was standing outside the control room staring up at him, not the least bit intimidated. They held each other's gaze for several seconds. Conrad broke it off first. Every second was crucial if he was to make it out of this. He rushed to the door and swung it open.

Bullets riddled the deck and shattered the windows beside him. Baxter and his men were right below and coming up fast.

He ducked the gunfire and dove for the corner of the deck, crawling around to the opposite side. The tower was a good three stories tall, perched right beside the inner DMZ fence. It was another fifteen feet to the outer perimeter fence and its razor wire, which abutted thick, lush foliage outside the compound.

More shots rang out, blasting more glass behind him.

There was only one way out of this.

Conrad climbed onto the railing and dived off the edge, free-falling over the razor wire into a cluster of dense bushes, which helped break his fall. The stunt would have crippled most men, but his thick bones were hard to break. He crashed through the bushes and thudded hard on the ground, receiving rude shocks to his ribs, arms, and legs. More bullets rained down on him and he instantly scrambled for cover. Baxter and his cohorts were lining the tower deck, firing at him like they were in a shooting gallery. If they had been military trained he would've been dead. Luckily he was able to scramble into the darkness of the jungle without taking any lead.

He was back in the game, whether he wanted to be or not.

Yasantwa and K. C. Mack were huddled inside the B-52 wreckage. A small fire was burning with a colorful bird roasting over it. K.C. had managed to spear it with the same stick Yasantwa had tried to kill him with.

He pulled the bird from the spit and tore off a chunk of meat, handing it to her.

"What a woman like you do t' end up here?"

"Plenty."

She devoured the meat, saying nothing else.

He also said nothing but barely ate his. He had done plenty himself and didn't feel good about it, especially now that his date with death was almost upon him. The timer on both of their ankles was showing *08:02:23*. They had a little over eight hours to live.

K.C. began silently swearing to himself. He wanted to say it out loud, but it would just be whining. He still had his pride.

He looked up at her. Yasantwa's face was glowing in the firelight. She was absolutely beautiful, in the prime of her life. What a waste.

"You know we're gonna die," he said quietly.

"Maybe not," she replied in a hopeful tone.

He admired her naïve optimism. Unfortunately, he didn't share it.

"I've been off 'n' on death row like a toilet seat. Death row ain't real. It's a waiting room, politics." He glanced at his bracelet again. "This bomb on my ankle . . . this is real."

"I fight till the end," she declared.

His smile was bittersweet. What were her chances? He'd been able to take her down with very little effort. The other cons out there were even bigger and stronger. They also had absolutely no compassion and would make her suffer. She didn't stand a chance.

"This is the end," he conceded. "Wake up and have a cup."

He rubbed his sore neck, which hadn't improved over the last twenty-four hours, and basked in his misery.

"You okay?" she asked with a lilt.

"When they threw me from the chopper, I landed wrong. We shouldn't be offin' each other, we should be offin' *them*, the ones who brung us here."

She scooted closer and began massaging his neck. "How does that feel?"

His eyes involuntarily closed. At this moment, it was the best thing he'd felt in his whole life.

"Awful, just awful." He sighed. "Stop, please stop."

She leaned closer, whispering seductively in his ear. "You want me to stop?"

"Oh, yeah, stop." He smiled. *"Please* stop."

Yasantwa worked her way down his back. She knew what he was thinking. She knew what *all* men were thinking. In his case, it wasn't just about sex.

"You say the last time you trusted a woman, you ended up on death row. What happened?"

K.C. opened his lids. He wasn't an idiot. He'd made sure there were no weapons close by in case she got any ideas. On the other side of the coin, there had been several opportunities for her to attempt another attack or just run off. But she hadn't. For all her big talk, he figured that she knew the boat she was in and how fast it was sinking.

"I grew up in LA, Inglewood. You know it?"

She nodded. "Heard of it."

By now her hands had slipped under his shirt and were working his sides and chest. It felt too good for words.

"They call it the Bottoms," he told her, his whole body starting to relax. "Three of us sold all the dope. Me, Sugarbooga, and Big Y. I meet this girl. Right off, we was tight. Now, I'm a player, but I fell hard. She comes over one night, she's all cryin', she's all beat up, sayin' it was Sugarbooga. I snap—I get both my guns and I go and shoot the motherfucker so many times . . ."

He tensed at the memory. Yasantwa's hands pressed harder, melting it away.

"It was a setup. Murder one on my ass. This girl I fell for was Big Y's bitch. In one night, I take out Sugarbooga and they send me straight t' death row. Big Y owns my blocks now. Anyway, I escaped t' Malaysia, but that's another story, 'bout another bitch."

He looked off and spotted a camera lodged inside the fuselage, the firelight reflected in its lens. K.C. angrily grabbed a rusted sardine can and heaved it, smashing the lens.

In the control room, Bella and Eddie watched the image of K.C. and Yasantwa turn to snow. Goldman and Breckel were gone, still dealing with the fallout of

222

Conrad's infiltration. Goldy had left JJ in charge of the console.

"JJ, switch to the other camera," barked Eddie. "What are you? Retarded?"

The woman glared back and changed camera angles, bringing up an overhead shot in the same location. All of them were operating on short fuses due to the lack of sleep, the demands of their superiors, and an intruder in their midst. They watched Yasantwa scoot around and face K.C. straight on, continuing to rub his chest.

"I think they're gonna get it on." Eddie grinned.

"Hundred bucks says no way," countered Bella. "She's setting him up."

They shook hands and turned back to the show. The only thing missing was popcorn.

"Why don't you lie down?" purred Yasantwa, pulling off his shirt, unaware that she was being watched by the camera above them.

Right now K.C. was living in the moment, and it was a fine one indeed. He hadn't had sex in years, not if you discounted the near rapes in prison. Spending the last few hours of his life with this goddess wouldn't be the worst send-off for a man.

He voluntarily slumped onto the plane's floor. Yasantwa leaned over him, running her hands through his dreadlocked hair.

"I don't blame you for not trusting women." She smiled sympathetically.

He nodded back. The memories were bittersweet, with the emphasis on bitter.

"Well, get this. I'm being transferred to Folsom. In transit, I bust out 'n' make my way to Mexico, then I'm off to Malaysia. Got nothing when I get there, set up my own hash op."

He didn't bother to mention that he'd double-crossed a drug dealer there to set up his operation.

"Start seeing this native girl—beautiful, sweet, sexy. Now I'm in heaven. I'm rich, free, and in love . . ."

His mind drifted to the past as Yasantwa's hands drifted south, rubbing his thighs. She was just the therapy he needed, mental as much as physical. He closed his eyes and let it all out.

"So she gets nailed on some bullshit possession charge 'n' she gives me up. Cops come, I got fourteen pounds of hash under my bed. Know what that means in Malaysia? Death row. *Again*. I guess it's just gonna take me some time b'fore I let my guard down, know what I'm sayin'? You feel me?"

Yasantwa remained silent.

He heard a beeping sound.

K.C.'s eyes flashed open just in time to see her bolting from the plane. He looked down at his bracelet. Red lights were flashing on it, the timer ticking down. He had fewer than ten seconds to live.

"MOTHERFUCKER!" he shrieked, trying to rip the device off his leg. "BITCH GOT ME AGAIN!"

Yasantwa was running away from the plane as he continued to holler.

"GODDAMN, MOTHER SON OF A—"

The fuselage exploded, flames ripping it apart.

Several miles away in the mess tent, Goldman heard

the explosion along with everyone else. After Conrad had been chased out, he had finally gone to eat something. Even before the first death, his appetite had been nil. Taking his medicine on an empty stomach hadn't been the smartest thing either—his intestines were burning and diarrhea wasn't far away. There was a nice spread of shrimp, prime rib, pasta, and an assortment of salads and desserts. Breckel always fed his crew well, knowing he would get a better performance out of them.

Right now, hearing that explosion, none of it looked appealing. He tossed the plastic plate and silverware. He wouldn't be eating until he got off this wretched death island.

Goldman dragged himself back to the control room, entering just in time to hear cheering.

"That's my girl!" shouted Bella, clapping her hands. "She sucks 'm in and spits 'm out. That's my style! Old school!"

"Settle down, toots," said Eddie as he fished five twenties from his wallet and handed them over.

"Scoreboard, baby! Scoreboard!" Bella taunted, pocketing her winnings as a red X went over K. C. Mack's mug shot.

"What the hell just happened?" interrupted Goldman in a far less festive tone.

He was looking up at the main plasma, which featured a wide shot of the burning B-52 wreckage with black smoke billowing.

"Another one bites the dust," muttered Eddie, much more disturbed about his loss of cash than the loss of human life. "The black American dude. *Boom.*"

He gestured a mushroom cloud effect with his hands for emphasis.

JJ had no reaction either way. The show had stopped being real for her a long time ago. She just wanted it to be technically perfect and not get yelled at. Right now, she was doing a slow push on the flames.

Goldman couldn't take much more of this.

"Get this off and bring up something else," he ordered, giving all of them a disgusted look. "Now! Okay? Change it!"

JJ quickly brought up another camera, the one mounted at the abandoned Japanese command post.

McStarley and Saiga were dragging Paco onto the loading dock. They began to beat the defenseless Mexican, the big Englishman grinning at the camera between blows.

24

Paco had heard them coming.

His first and only instinct was to get on his feet and attack them with the knife Conrad had given him, though he had no illusions about his chances. Before the end came he wanted to kill at least one of them.

He stood just inside the command post entrance as their feet creaked across the dock's wooden planks. He readied his blade as they got closer. Paco had been in a few knife fights as a gang member and knew what had to be done—the first stab would go into the kidney to incapacitate the fucker, with the second, third, and fourth going for his heart. He prayed the English gringo would step through the door first. Before leaving this life, he at least wanted to avenge Rosa's death.

Paco had no way of knowing that McStarley and Saiga already knew he was hiding in there thanks to the heads-up from Breckel's map. The pair had snuck up from the opposite side and peeked through a decomposing hole in the wall expecting to find both the American and the Mexican in there. They saw only Paco, who was slouched on the floor. This was both disappointing and somewhat of a relief. While killing two birds with one stone had been their plan, taking them both on at the same time would definitely be more challenging than one at a time.

They moved back to the dock and purposely made enough noise to let Paco know they were coming. McStarley wanted to make him think that he held the element of surprise. There was no reason for this except to humiliate him further when they turned the tables.

McStarley figured he would be hiding just inside the door. He silently motioned for Saiga to fly through the threshold rather than creep in. In the Mexican's distraction, he would disarm him and then the merriment would begin.

Saiga understood the hand gestures well enough and flipped through the entrance in a blur.

Paco tried to stab him but missed by a foot. McStarley sprang a split second later and grabbed the arm gripping the knife. He twisted it, snapping Paco's elbow joint.

The pain was excruciating, just like it had been when the English convict shattered his knee.

"Surprise, surprise," quipped McStarley as he decked him with a punch.

Paco and his plan for revenge hit the ground hard. His survival instincts kicked in and he crawled behind some crates. McStarley knocked them aside and grabbed him by his ankle, hauling him out.

"Little help 'ere," he said to his partner.

Together they dragged Paco onto the loading dock, where the sadistic Brit had seen a camera. He wanted everyone to see what he had in store for the crippled Mexican.

Paco shouted for help. Part of him wanted to die anyway, but there was enough revenge left in his veins to maintain his will to live.

The beating began, both men taking turns on their defenseless victim. McStarley knew how to inflict as much of it as possible without letting him pass out. Saiga wanted to kill him quickly, but the limey wouldn't let him. There was too much fun to be had first.

It was all on display on the big control room monitor.

"Our boy Paco is FUUUUUCKED," exclaimed Eddie, the loss of his bet with Bella fading to the background. "McStarley's back—this is gonna be gnarly."

"The sun ain't even up and the Mexican havin' another bad day," she mocked, just as pumped as her coworker.

Goldman stared at both of them. The convicts had ceased to be real human beings to these two—it was as if the prisoners were digital 3-D creations from *Halo* or *Grand Theft Auto*. In those games, the players also died very graphically, except that they had multiple lives and could earn health credits. And they *weren't real*. This wasn't a video game, cartoon, or action movie, but Breck's young crew no longer seemed to realize that. Maybe it was because the people out there were already sentenced to die, but he didn't think so. Eddie and Bella had become completely desensitized.

"Twenty-eight million IDs are logged on," proclaimed Eddie, glancing at his display. "Twenty-eight million!"

Goldman left without saying a word. He moved off into the shadows behind the tent and vomited. No solid food came up, mainly the burn of pills that hadn't decomposed in his stomach. He was sick as a dog, but not from any illness. He spit out the rancid taste and turned to leave.

Julie was standing there.

Ten silent seconds went by before either spoke. He knew exactly how she felt; her very public argument with Breck earlier left little room for interpretation. His own feelings were no mystery either. She had just seen him throw up yet didn't ask if he was okay. He *wasn't* okay, and she knew it.

"He's my boss and yet he's my best friend," Goldman started, looking off with an ugly smile. "He's good. A genius. The man could sell dirt to a ditchdigger."

"We've both been sold," she said coldly.

He wiped his mouth on his shirt sleeve, his expression completely pallid. "I know."

"Although he gives you shit, you're the only one he respects," she told him. "He'll listen to you."

"I doubt it."

"Goldy, we have to stop this."

He realized she was right.

As they made their plans to confront him, Breckel was resting in his private tent, which by no means meant that he was sleeping. His bed was still made and would remain that way for the duration.

His quarters were like what a general would have on the outskirts of his battlefield, only more posh, with rattan furniture and a wet bar. Right now he was occupying the same chair Julie had curled up in earlier, watching his live broadcast on a small plasma display. He had the sound turned down so he could concentrate on his thoughts. Only half of his cast members were dead, yet more than twenty-four hours had passed. The pace needed to pick up or there wouldn't be a winner. All but one had to die within the next six hours. Otherwise his audience would feel cheated.

He watched the screen dispassionately as Paco slowly succumbed. At least things were moving in the right direction. McStarley was now beating him with a chain as Saigo repeatedly kicked him. With the audio off, Paco's screams were silent, but his cries would have fallen on deaf ears regardless.

Julie entered first, Goldman behind her. Breckel glanced at both of them. He knew what this was about, had expected it, in fact. He had decided not to let these two upset him and dismissed their presence with a turn of his head. His relationship was with the screen now, nothing else.

"This is *not* reality," Julie said emphatically. "You manipulated this. You sent them there so they could do this to an injured man who's already watched his wife get—"

She stopped herself. When Goldman had told her about Ian giving McStarley an unfair advantage, she had wanted to scream. Julie felt herself rapidly approaching that point again. She was not going to lose it. If she did, he'd win. She'd be just another emotional woman who couldn't handle the pressure, the weaker sex.

"Don't tell me you won't intervene, because you already have," she tried not to shout.

Breckel's eyes remained on the screen, his voice conversational. "Twenty-eight million people are watching something I created, and not one network gets a piece of it."

They both just stared. This wasn't the same man they knew, or thought they knew. The producer sitting there was a certifiable megalomaniac.

Goldman stepped between Breckel and his screen, forcing him to meet his eyes. He looked pale and severely depressed.

"Breck, it's too much for me. I knew what this was originally, but it is not okay now, it's too much. We've crossed the line that's beyond the line I thought we were gonna cross."

Breckel studied him. Goldy hadn't slept. He was a soldier with battle fatigue, maybe a little weak of character, too. But he still believed his loyalty was salvageable.

"All right, all right," he said with unexpected empathy. "Some of it is a little difficult to watch, I know. But it's essential. To create drama you need good guys, bad guys, and victims. That's storytelling."

Goldman couldn't believe his ears. "This isn't some teleplay we're writing, this is real. It's too fuckin' real and I can't hold down food."

Breckel's face was starting to flush, his patience with these two rapidly waning.

"Real? NOTHING IS REAL," he erupted. "Movies. TV. Reality TV. The news. Magazines. Newspapers. IT'S ALL JUST ENTERTAINMENT."

"Entertainment? Do you really believe that?"

Goldman had sadness in his voice, which almost made Breckel laugh. No wonder he wasn't a show runner.

"CNN. ABC. MTV. It's all manufactured and manipulated just like this—to entertain," he said condescendingly. "Most of what you see isn't the truth—you of all people should recognize that."

He saw that Goldman and Julie were looking at him like he was . . . what was that in their eyes?

They think I'm insane.

He had to keep himself from laughing in their faces. If anyone were crazy it was *them.* How could they not understand the magnitude of what he was doing?

"Remember, one will live," he explained as if they were schoolchildren. "And that's one more than fate had planned. We are saving a life."

"By torturing others," Julie angrily countered.

"You gotta stop this," echoed Goldman.

Breckel angrily pointed his finger at the screen. "You think this Mexican had more dignity awaiting the electric chair in Guatemala City? Do you?"

Goldman forced himself to look at the image. Paco was curled up in a fetal position begging for mercy, but the blows kept coming.

"Yes. I do."

That was it. The straw. Breckel bolted to his feet, his fists clenching as tight as his teeth. He wanted to do the same thing to Goldman that McStarley was doing to Paco.

"You ungrateful son of a bitch. I've made YOU a

dollar or two—you ain't hurtin' THANKS TO ME. All I ask is a little fuckin' loyalty. DO NOT COME IN HERE AND TEAM UP AGAINST ME WITH HER."

He pierced Julie with an icy stare. It unnerved her, but she didn't look away.

Breckel suppressed his rage, shoving the beast back into its cage. He was past the point of physically assaulting them but seething nonetheless.

"You both knew what you were getting into. I'm done debating this."

He stepped within inches of Goldman's face. "Make a choice right now. You're either with me or against me, but you do not waver until this gig is over. Stay with me and there's a very sweet bank account waiting for you in the Cayman Islands. I'm giving you participation in the show's profits, remember? It's up to you, Goldy."

Goldman had never planned on walking. He was a saber rattler. His intention, his hope, had been to persuade Breck to make some big changes so they could salvage some of their morality. He had been kidding himself, of course. Ian Breckel would not give in—he had never backed down on any show, why should he now? Breck was also dead right about Goldman having known what he was getting into. He'd never walked out on a job because of content issues and hated people who did. Crew who did that kind of stuff were blackballed in the industry real fast. He was not a quitter. Especially not when a friend was involved.

These were all the things Goldman told himself so

he could justify selling his soul. He didn't want to face the notion that the big payday he'd be receiving was a factor in his decision.

"I want an answer right now," Breckel demanded after five seconds of silence.

"I'll finish the show."

Julie gazed at Goldman with total disillusionment. "Goldy, you just can't—"

"I don't want to hear it, Julie," he interjected, shutting her down before she could launch into him. God knows he deserved it.

"I'm going back to the monitors." He walked out, a beaten man.

Breckel stepped over to Julie and slapped her hard.

She never saw it coming. The impact made her dizzy with shock. No man had ever hit her before. Her whole face felt like it was on fire.

"For the past twenty-four hours, do you know how ridiculous you've sounded?" He was like a parent disciplining a misbehaving child. "Preaching, begging, crying—for what? To save some killer? To save some Mexican whore?"

Her eyes began to well. "I was trying to save you," she whispered.

Julie drifted out of the tent.

Breckel felt better now that he had vented his emotions. He sat back down and watched his show, which was finally picking up some speed.

25

Conrad had disappeared into the jungle before Baxter and his guards could shoot him. It made no sense for them to come after him now since he was back in play with the others, though he continued to look over his shoulder. He sensed a personal vendetta from the security head—why would they shoot at him once he was out of the complex? Surely Baxter's boss wouldn't approve. The big cheese wanted all the deaths on camera.

Before things went belly-up in the weather tower, Conrad had weighed the idea of taking Breckel as a hostage and using him as a bargaining tool. This rumination fell by the wayside now that the element of surprise had evaporated. Even though he remained invisible on their grid, daybreak was only minutes away, more surveillance cameras had been installed, plus Baxter and his men would be on extra-high alert.

Speaking with Sarah had given him some peace of mind, but not enough. She now knew he hadn't run out on her. That was good. But she'd been stubborn about the money, which ate away at him. Short of surviving, providing for them was the only good thing he could do to make up for the anguish he'd caused. Sarah had gotten only partial coordinates, so a rescue mission remained unlikely. And if it did happen, it wouldn't arrive in time to do any good anyway. His odds of seeing tomorrow were a long shot at best.

He swallowed the unpleasant facts and tried to think proactively. Having heard Sarah's voice, Conrad wanted to survive now more than ever.

Dancing to Breckel's music was something he refused to do. There had to be another way out besides killing the others, only right now he couldn't think of what that was. He retreated the way he came, hoping for some inspiration.

His hike became a sprint when he heard Paco's screams filtering through the rain forest. By the time he reached the bombed-out bridge, the sounds were more than somebody merely dying. Paco was being tortured. He rushed to the edge of the bridge and got a full view of the loading dock.

Sunrise was starting to break, allowing enough light to see that Paco's face was nearly gone, beaten to a bloody pulp. McStarley and Saiga were taking turns as the Brit puffed on a fat cigar.

"Stop it!" shouted Conrad.

Both bullies looked up. Paco couldn't see or hear anything at this point. They had beaten him senseless.

"Hey, Yank! Where you been all night?" a grinning McStarley asked.

"He's had enough!" Conrad yelled back.

"Enough? You think this little Mexican geezer has

237

had enough? Shit. We haven't even started!" He turned to Saiga, making a kicking motion. "Hit him again."

Saiga released a brutal kick into his chest. Paco moaned rather than screamed. He was rapidly slouching toward death.

McStarley pulled an arrow from his quiver and paced back a few steps.

"What do you think? I might hit him from here, Yank?"

Paco made one last feeble effort to stand and retaliate against his attackers, though he was nearly blind.

"Hold still, fucker."

McStarley drew back his arrow. He was at a point-blank distance. There was no way he could miss.

Conrad watched impotently as he fired. The arrow pierced Paco squarely in the heart. The Mexican staggered for a beat and then collapsed. He was dead by the time he hit the deck.

"You're out!" howled the Englishman. "You like that, Yank?"

Conrad transfixed him with a gaze. If winning the contest meant killing these two, so be it, but that's not what would drive him from this point forward. They were evil men who didn't deserve to live.

"Yo, Yank, I got you down as military, like myself—Special Forces, SAS." McStarley pointed proudly at himself. "Me and you, we got a lot in common."

Conrad continued to gaze at him from the bridge. "We got nothin' in common, you 'n' me."

The Texan's stone-cold expression told McStarley

everything he needed to know. Conrad was the enemy. The Brit's smile went crooked.

"That disappoints me. That makes you soft. Not me. I'm the real deal."

He snapped his fingers and pointed at the supply bag. Saiga pulled out one of the jars filled with gasoline and poured it all over Paco.

"This, I'm gonna do to you."

He flicked his cigar onto Paco.

The Mexican's body caught fire, quickly turning into a roar of flames. It cast a bright orange glow across McStarley's beaming smile.

"You're a SICK MOTHERFUCKER," bellowed Conrad, his voice reverberating through the ravine. He wanted to leap across the bombed-out gap in the bridge and kill these two with his bare hands, rip their heads off.

McStarley knew he had pushed the right buttons. He wanted his foe fuming and irrational. Asserting his power, the Englishman loaded another arrow and took dead aim at the American.

Conrad looked him straight in the eye with pure defiance, not retreating one inch.

McStarley released the arrow. It sliced through the air across the bridge.

Conrad didn't move one muscle as it rammed into a rotten beam only inches away from his head.

"Game on," he said to himself.

He stepped off the bridge and disappeared into the jungle.

*　　*　　*

DIA Agent Wade Meranto strutted across the shiny floor of the FBI lobby with Assistant Director Moyer dutifully escorting him.

"I trust you'll stay on top of this," Meranto said as a final warning. He didn't want Moyer's underling Wilkins stirring any more pots.

"Absolutely," replied Moyer as he opened the door for him.

As he started to exit, Special Agent Wilkins hurried into the lobby with a message in his hand. "Jack Riley just contacted Sarah Cavanaugh with a coordinate."

Meranto stopped in the doorway, Moyer looking very uncomfortable.

"It's not complete, but the island is somewhere between the seventh and eighth parallels. I got it right here." Wilkins held up the piece of paper with the partial coordinates on it.

Meranto eyed it without taking it.

He was weighing all the complications if he accepted this information without acting on it. There had obviously been a cover-up and this new information wouldn't help the cause. If the press discovered the truth about Jack Riley and their lack of intervention, it could blow up in the DIA's face. His boss would be very unhappy.

Wilkins saw that he wasn't going to take it.

"Please tell me we're going to do something?"

More silence. He started to lose his cool.

"No? We're just going to stand around and do nothing?"

"Brad, understand, it's a situation that needs to be finessed," said Moyer, nervously eyeing the DIA agent.

Wilkins ignored him and focused on Meranto.

"Have you seen what's happening on this island? It's sick. It needs to be stopped, not finessed. Jack Riley did a year in a Salvadoran prison, interrogation, torture, he never gave up a word—all to protect you, your boss, our country. He deserves more than *finesse*. More than goddamn bureaucratic politics."

"Brad . . ."

"What the fuck is wrong with you two?"

His boss was shocked to silence; Meranto said nothing either.

Wilkins gestured at the entire building. "What is wrong with *us?*"

Moyer wouldn't look at him, but Meranto did. This young agent had balls, which is more than he could say about his boss, and maybe even himself. The thought of standing up to his own superior like that was a fantasy he didn't see happening, though Wilkins was right about everything. Ignoring this new information was the coward's way out.

Meranto stepped forward and took the slip of paper from Wilkins's grasp, looking it over. "I'll have the navy run a jet over this coordinate," he said, hoping he wouldn't regret it.

Wilkins nodded with relief as Meranto left the building. He walked back to his office, leaving his own boss in the dust.

Moyer wanted to fire him on the spot but stopped himself. He couldn't terminate Wilkins without creating lots of paperwork to justify it. It would also expose himself to scrutiny because Wilkins would almost certainly fight back. The tension headache he had been fighting all day came back in full force as he lurched back to his office.

Mike Sanders was hooking up his laptop to the big screen above his bar.

It was a little past noon on a weekday and a small crowd had already gathered, mostly men but a few women. Word had spread fast in Granville that a local boy was on the Internet fighting for his life.

Mike found the S-Video input on the rear of the big TV and plugged it in, along with a pair of audio cables.

"Got it?" asked Brad Burdick, who was holding the remote control.

He and buddy Buck Farland had been at the Blue Boot into the wee hours the night before watching the webcast. They'd both gone home for a quick nap, cashed in one of their sick days at the machine shop in Lufkin where they worked, and raced back down to Mike's. Like Sarah, neither had high-speed Internet and didn't feel like shelling out $49.95 if they did have it. They also wanted to watch it with friends.

"Got it," answered Mike, finishing the connections and hopping off the bar stool.

Burdick pushed a button on the remote and ESPN vanished, bringing up *The Condemned*. It was seventeen hours later in this part of Oceania and the sun was just coming up.

People in the bar didn't quite gasp, but their reaction was instant. A bloody Mexican man was being beaten by a big white guy and a smaller Asian who knew karate or something like it. Was this for real? The murmurs around the bar quickly confirmed that it was no put-on.

"That's Jack!" somebody said as the view cut to Conrad, standing on the bridge. He was shouting at the big one, telling him to stop.

Sarah walked in just as McStarley planted the arrow into Paco's chest, the patrons responding in shock. After the initial recoil, she took in the crowd with dismay. This was a private matter as far as she was concerned. Mike, Farland, and Burdick had turned it into a Super Bowl party.

"The boys okay?" Mike asked as she came closer.

"Yeah, they're with my mom." She gestured around the room. "What's this?"

At least thirty people had gathered now, every eye glued to the screen.

"That's goddamn sick," said a cowboy wearing a worn brown Stetson, echoing the others' sentiments. McStarley had just set Paco's body on fire

"Everybody wanted to see Jack," Mike explained. "He has a lot of friends here. I thought I'd rig it up so they could all watch."

She knew Mike well enough to know that he wasn't exploiting the situation for business, but it still bothered her.

"Here? On the big screen? I kind of wanted to watch this alone, in back."

Lyle, the cowboy with the brown hat, overheard her. He had gone to high school with Jack Riley.

"I don't got high-speed either, Sarah. Jack's an old friend—I just wanted to watch this. We all do."

Sarah looked around and understood. Jack was universally liked and respected. She couldn't claim sole ownership of him. But it would be too difficult for her to watch this spectacle with others around, especially if it went badly.

Everyone bristled as McStarley shot the arrow at Jack and barely missed him.

"I can't stay. I can't be here for this," she told Mike, then headed for the door.

He caught up and stopped her.

"Sarah, you've got nothing but friends here, you and Jack both. We all care about Jack. Stay here with us."

Sarah glanced at all the faces again. If it did go badly for Jack, these were the right people to be with, to share in her grief.

"Okay," she whispered.

26

The sun was fully up over the Japanese command post. Saiga was pacing the dock sporting his expensive Ray-Bans, impatiently swinging his bolo knives. He stepped over Paco's charred remains, barely smoldering now, and kept a watchful eye out for Conrad. The American would be coming back for them—he had to if he wanted to win this contest. Saiga was looking forward to it.

McStarley was up on the roof with his bow and quiver, taking in his kingdom from his elevated perch. The command post was his. He owned it. He ruled the entire island. The shiny-headed American was out there somewhere making a weapon or devising some cock-eyed plan to kill him, which excited him. McStarley liked competition, loved a challenge. So far he'd been swatting flies. It was time for some big-game hunting.

He glanced down at Saiga. The little Asian was a good soldier and had come in handy. However, he was just another arrow in his quiver. Sooner or later, the arrow would become disposable.

"No sign of the geezer yet," he called down, "but he's on his fucking way. You want first crack at 'm?"

Saiga understood enough of it with the help of McStarley's gestures. He responded by slicing the air a few times.

"That's what I thought." The Brit grinned.

Meanwhile, Conrad had backtracked and hiked into the ravine below the bridge. He forged himself a six-foot bo staff from a dead branch and sharpened its tip between river rocks, grinding it down like a giant pencil sharpener. Like McStarley, Conrad had received martial arts training from the military, but not to the extent of Saiga's. A bo staff was an essential martial arts tool. Conrad knew he would need all the help he could get.

He waded up the river, leaving no footprints. He didn't think he was being tracked since he had followed a careful listen-look-move strategy, but he didn't want to take any chances. Adding up the explosions he'd heard plus Paco's death, there were only four convicts left besides himself, maybe only three. There were plenty of ways to die besides a bomb going off on your ankle, though yanking that red tab was definitely the popular mode of expiring the competition. The Russian had almost pulled his, which he didn't want happening again. Just like blocking the GPS signal, this vulnerability would have to be dealt with before he faced the enemy.

The concrete foundation of the bombed-out bridge came into view as he trudged upstream. There was a huge footing at its midsection, its support beam having been blown out. The concrete itself had also been hit and was cracked and crumbling, exposing a skeleton of rusty iron rebar.

Conrad decided that McStarley's bow and arrow, along with the knives and gasoline, came from that helicopter he'd heard in the night. The competition had been given an edge, which was nothing new for the Texan. Like always, he would deal with it.

He grabbed one of the iron rebars, bending it backward and forward until it snapped. Fifteen bars later, he had what he needed. Each piece was about a foot long, roughly the length of his forearms and shins. Conrad pulled out the duct tape he'd stolen from the weather tower and taped four bars to each arm and leg. He hoped this would give him the armor he would need when the battle began.

Next up was the bomb. He unspooled the tape and wrapped it around his ankle bracelet and red tab, making it impossible for someone to yank it out. He made sure to leave the timer exposed so he could keep track of how long he had to live. Conrad stared at the numbers: *4:43:23*.

He doubted that McStarley and Saiga were still hanging around that command post, but it was the best place to start tracking them.

Footsteps on the bridge directly above him changed his theory.

He ducked out of view behind the concrete. Conrad caught a glimpse of Saiga through the rotting beams, swinging his knives. The Asian was still there, which probably meant both of them were.

They've been waitin' for me to come back, he thought. This meant less tracking on his part. Saiga wasn't acting the least bit inconspicuous either. The man was

247

arrogant and overconfident, just like his partner—also a good thing.

Conrad formed his plan.

Above him, Saiga was growing restless. He wanted the American to hurry up and show himself so he could kill him. After that, he would take on his cocksure English partner. Saiga had let McStarley assume he was in charge to give him a false sense of control, but the kung fu expert had carefully thought it out. Counting up the explosions, there was only one more convict for them to kill after the American. It was quite possible that someone had been dispatched quietly, but the death had to be confirmed regardless—the rules were nine dead in order to win. McStarley would keep him around for the time-consuming search before he tried to kill him. Saiga had other plans: he would strike unexpectedly, right after the American was murdered. Whoever was still out there would be far less competition than the Englishman, if they were alive at all.

As the Asian contemplated a future attack on his partner, Conrad crept up the side of the ravine. Peering through thick leaves, he spotted McStarley on the compound roof. He was mostly facing the bridge, making an entrance from the back Conrad's only option. He snuck through the thick plants and circled behind the compound, which was bordered by a rock wall. The taped-on iron bars restricted his movement and threatened to clank against the wall as he scaled it. Somehow he managed to succeed without drawing McStarley's attention. It would be impossible to surprise him on the rooftop, which made Saiga first up by default.

Conrad flattened himself against the wall and watched the Asian continue to pace on the bridge. If he could make it to the clump of foliage adjacent to the bridge without being seen or heard by either man, he had a chance for a surprise attack.

He gauged the distance, reminding himself that McStarley was armed with a bow and arrow. The span from the rooftop to the bridge was closer than McStarley's last shot at him across the ravine. He would need to keep moving during his fight with Saiga; otherwise his odds of being hit were high. Arrows reloaded slower than bullets, so the quicker he took out Saiga, the better. He would then sprint in a zigzag pattern for the compound and deal with the Englishman.

His strategy began as planned, though it was a waiting game—he had to move when both men were facing in opposite directions. Saiga paced to the edge of the bridge and looked down just as McStarley checked the rear of the compound. Conrad made the dash into the foliage undetected.

He could see the Asian through the leaves only twenty feet away. He was turning around and pacing back in his direction.

Wait, Conrad told himself.

Saiga stopped. Conrad got a firm grip on his bo staff.

A little closer.

Saiga took another step forward.

NOW.

He sprang onto the bridge and lunged at Saiga's heart with his sharpened staff. Conrad was going for a quick kill.

Saiga easily dodged it. Not only that, he hacked two chunks out of the stick with his knives.

McStarley heard the noise and turned. His comrade was shouting in Japanese as he came at Conrad, slicing his knives like a crazy sushi chef. It made the Brit grin. McStarley wanted to kill the American himself, but he was content to watch his associate put on a show. There was also the possibility that Conrad would triumph. Either scenario was fine with him. The winner would illustriously be awarded a sharp graphite arrow through his rib cage.

Conrad's plan had taken a wrong turn and he knew it. He now had to trade glances between Saiga and the arrows that would be flying soon. He managed to slam his wooden staff against the side of Saiga's head, but the wiry Asian was tough and answered with a kick jab into Conrad's left kidney. He recovered and lunged at Saiga again. The Japanese fighter quickly whittled down Conrad's stick and finally chopped it up completely. Saiga came at him with both knives and hacked at his face. Conrad blocked the blades with his arms, sparks shooting out as metal struck metal. The iron rebar was doing its job.

Saiga didn't expect this and Conrad took full advantage, ramming his fist into the Asian's gut. Conrad then backhanded him in the head, his rebar slamming against Saiga's skull. The bolo knives clattered onto the wooden bridge as he dropped them.

The playing field had just been leveled weaponwise, but Saiga's martial arts talent was no match for Conrad's experience and sheer strength. Every kick was blocked and countered, every jab was answered with a punch. He came at the Japanese warrior with both fists flying. Conrad kicked him with his iron-clad leg and slammed him with an old-fashioned right hook that sent him on his back. He began to pummel him toward unconsciousness.

McStarley saw where this was going and pulled out an arrow. He took careful aim . . . and then hesitated. His odds of hitting Conrad were slightly better than fifty-fifty from this distance, which was not good enough. The American would be finishing off his erstwhile partner in short order and probably wouldn't hang around for archery practice. He would get only one or two attempts before the redneck ran off.

He jogged to the edge of the roof and made an impressive leap to the dock below. The Brit smiled at his prowess, as well as with anticipation as he paced forward. He lined up his shot, slid the arrow's notch into the bow's taut gut, and drew it back.

Conrad was on top of Saiga now, reaching down to break his neck, when instinct told him to look up.

The arrow came at him almost invisibly due to its speed. Conrad rolled as it grazed him, ripping a slice off his shirt as a souvenir. Another arrow would be on its way in three seconds, so he had no choice but to dash. He made it to the side of the compound just as the next arrow pierced the beam where his head had been a split second before.

The bunker came into view. If he could make it inside, McStarley wouldn't have a good shot. He would be forced to enter and engage in hand-to-hand combat.

Conrad made the final dash, tumble diving into the bunker's side entrance. An arrow ricocheted off the rocks beside him as his head banged against the hard bunker wall inside. A slice of daybreak through the viewing slot brought slight illumination, but it was still nearly dark in here.

He saw two white eyes gazing at him from the void.

He was not alone.

Meanwhile, Saiga was back on his feet and running over with his knives, bloody but resilient. McStarley motioned him over to the supply bag on the deck. He had a crooked grin that the Asian immediately interpreted—there were two more bottles of gasoline in there.

The eyes inside the bunker stepped into the sliver of light.

It was Yasantwa. She was gripping a sharp metal shaft she'd retrieved from the B-52 crash site after detonating K. C. Mack.

The young seductress had been hiding in there for hours, having shown up while McStarley and Saiga were torturing Paco. Still planning to win, she'd been waiting for one of them to check out the bunker, but neither had. Conrad had been the first one in. She didn't plan on letting him out alive.

He just stared at her.

"Y' gotta be kiddin' me," he muttered.

Conrad hadn't expected her to be alive. She was tough, no doubt about it, but half his size.

"Try me," she hissed back.

They squared off in the dark. Her pupils had fully adjusted to the darkness and his hadn't, plus he'd just banged his head. It still wasn't a contest. When she lunged, he easily grabbed her wrist and slammed her against the wall, pinning her weapon hand. Their noses were an inch apart, their bodies touching. She relaxed her grip, along with her tough expression. The sweet, vulnerable, victimized look she had used so effectively on K. C. Mack washed across her face.

"Please," she said, her voice trembling. "I thought you were going to kill me . . ."

He said nothing.

Her sultry eyes went to work. "You can trust me . . ."

"Sweetheart, I trust one woman, an' it damn sure ain't you," he replied with no hesitation.

There was a whooshing sound.

Yasantwa's body jolted. Her eyes went wide and fluttered. She opened her mouth to speak and nothing came out.

Conrad pulled her back from the wall and found an arrow in her back. It had come through the slit in the bunker, which he had pressed her up against.

"Bull's-eye!" crowed McStarley from outside. "C'mon, Yank! You're next—show yourself!"

The Englishman cautiously moved closer, motioning Saiga toward the bunker's side entrance. The latter had fashioned a nice pair of Molotov cocktails and was lighting them up. McStarley wasn't about to take any chances with the big Texan, who had proved to be very sprightly.

Conrad set Yasantwa down. She was moaning, still clinging to life. The two were staring at each other as a bottle of gasoline flew inside and shattered against the wall. The cave erupted with flames. The fire was lapping at the artillery shells.

Conrad could come to only one conclusion. They were fucked.

"Give me the bunker! I want to see the bunker!"

Breckel was shouting now. Thanks to Goldy's low-lux night-vision lenses, they had witnessed the South African babe try to attack Conrad in the darkness, but the fire from Saiga's Molotov had just fried the circuitry.

"Both cameras inside are torched. We got nothing," Goldman said, feigning disappointment. He had witnessed McStarley and his Asian sidekick sadistically torture and kill the Mexican and his wife. In stark contrast, Conrad had helped Paco when he could have killed him. Watching him in the bunker, it didn't look like he planned to kill the woman either. McStarley had taken care of that job yet again.

Going into this project, Goldman hadn't given a rat's ass about who would win—and still didn't—but he was sure about who needed to lose. McStarley and Saiga were evil incarnate, especially the psycho from England. Jack Conrad seemed to be the only one capable of taking them down, but it looked like he was about to die. Goldman didn't want to witness that.

Conrad was *not* about to die, at least not in his own mind.

As a member of black ops, he had studied scenarios for virtually every war that America had ever been involved in, including strategies devised by the enemy. The Japanese lost World War II as a result of Hiroshima and Nagasaki, not because of a lack of intelligence. Japanese war strategies in the South Pacific theater were top-notch, including ground warfare. They would never let themselves be cornered, especially in a crucial artillery bunker like the one he was now trapped in.

There had to be more than one exit.

As the flames began to spread, Conrad looked around for another way out. The bunker had been built against a rocky hillside, making a tunnel in the back wall improbable. He was already on his knees to avoid the smoke, so he crawled around the dirt-covered floor and began to slam his fist. It was packed earth for the first five feet, and then a hollow sound thumped back. Conrad quickly cleared the dirt and found a wooden trapdoor. He pried it up and found a small chamber below it.

He reached through the smoke and grabbed Yasantwa's hand.

"Let's go!"

She wouldn't move. He saw that her free hand was reaching for the red tab on her ankle.

"No," he told her, not ready to give up on her.

The arrow was still in her back and she was an inch from death, in complete agony. The flames lapped at her face and her lids fluttered again.

"Please," she begged.

Conrad appraised her. They both knew she was not going to make it. She was suffering. She wanted to go quickly.

He let go of her hand.

She pulled the tab.

Conrad gave her one last look and then disappeared down the hole.

The crowd at the Blue Boot gasped as the bunker exploded. Thanks to the artillery shells, it was a gargantuan blast. McStarley and Saiga were both knocked on their ass from the impact.

Everyone had seen Jack go inside and struggle with the black woman. He hadn't come out. And then it was obliterated.

Jack Riley was dead.

"NO!" Sarah cried out, her hand going to her mouth.

Mike tried to hold her, but she couldn't be held. She gazed at the screen as the blood drained out of her, along with tears.

Silence fell on the bar. People shook their heads, some holding each other. Buck Farland kicked over a bar stool and went outside to cool off.

Sarah drifted away from Mike and sat alone at the bar, her whole body slumping with grief. A small TV was on by the cash register with the volume turned down low, but she was oblivious in her heartbreak.

"What about the children?" said the voice on TV. "Kids all across the planet can log on and witness live murder?"

She slowly looked up. Donna Sereno, the well-known journalist, was conducting an interview with Ian Breckel, the creator of the show that had just killed the man Sarah loved. He was wearing a spotless khaki shirt without a bead of sweat, as if he were on a rich man's safari.

"Sure they can," he answered. "Anybody can watch if they have a credit card. But as entertainers we can't tailor-make everything we do for children. It's the parents' responsibility to monitor what their kids watch, not mine."

Sarah had never hated anyone in her life. Up until now.

At this same moment, Ian Breckel was watching Sereno's broadcast on a small screen in the control room as the big plasma continued to display the fallout at the bunker. He was feeling better now that two more contestants had been eliminated. There were a couple of hours left, with only a pair of competitors remaining. It was down to McStarley and Saiga, and he had no doubt who would win. The Englishman had put on an extremely good show for him so far—the sadistic murderer-rapist had definitely risen to the occasion.

He'd watched raptly as the bunker blast sent McStarley and Saiga on their backs. The smoke was thick, but both men were definitely alive. The suspense toward climax was building exactly as he had envisioned. Although his cast had been allowed a wide degree of improvisation, he'd "written" the show by strategically supplying his star with weapons and a map. It was just like every other reality program he had ever produced—Breckel was a master at manipulating his subjects to heighten the storytelling.

He smiled at himself on TV. Having been interviewed countless times over the years, Breckel was camera savvy and knew how to convey confidence and power in his posture. His nose looked straighter from the left side, so he'd made sure to have the camera on Sereno's right, and not too low so the tiny scar under his chin from a childhood bicycle accident wouldn't show. Accidents were something that didn't happen to him. His life, just like his shows, was orchestrated to perfection.

"That's a cop-out, Ian, and you know it," Sereno continued on TV. "You have to take some responsibility."

Breckel almost laughed as he watched. She was so stupid. Did she not realize that vilifying him was only helping his cause?

"Donna, I'm not forcing anybody to log on and tune in," he replied with firm poise. "I didn't create the demand. It was there long before the Romans. The coliseum. The guillotines in Paris. The witch trials in Salem. People like to watch violence, always have, always will."

God, am I good.

The interview cut to Sereno live in her newsroom with a generic shot of a tropical island matted behind her.

"When I finished this interview, I was angry at one man, Ian Breckel," she spoke to her viewers. "I now realize my reaction was simplistic. Over the past twenty-four hours, millions have logged on to his web site. With his success, I am no longer angry. I am sad. Sad for us, sad for the world we live in."

"Perfect . . . simply perfect," he said out loud as he watched. He couldn't have scripted it better himself. Donna Sereno had just guaranteed him another ten million subscribers.

"The question is not how do we stop men like Ian Breckel, but rather, Who are we? What are we?" Sereno said emotionally. "Those of us who reward him, those of us who watch—are *we* the condemned?"

Julie was standing a short distance behind Ian, watching the broadcast over his shoulder, though he was too caught up in ogling himself to notice her arrival. Like Donna Sereno, she was far more than simply angry. She was sad—for herself, for him, for Goldman, for the world.

Julie looked over at Goldy, who was also watching the interview as JJ manned the console. He wouldn't meet her eyes, though his disturbed expression told her they still shared the same mind-set. Their mission had been reduced to getting through the next two hours and then getting off this island. Ian Breckel would be out of their lives forever after that, though the horror of what they had been a part of would never go away.

"Until tomorrow, this is Donna Se—"

Breckel remoted it off, beyond satisfied. He turned and saw Julie standing there. He hadn't expected to see her for the duration of the show, but here she was. She might not like him right now, especially after that slap, but he knew he was irresistible. Women loved power and expected to be mistreated now and then. In the world of reality entertainment, he was a rock star.

Rather than try to patch it up, he walked away from her. He wanted Julie to come crawling back to him.

Breckel shifted his attention to the main screen. It was almost time for the last contestant to drop. He had little doubt that his star would make it a spectacular finale.

27

The force of the bunker explosion nearly knocked Mc-Starley and Saiga unconscious. Both were pelted with chunks of rock and shrapnel. They hadn't known about the leftover artillery since they'd never been inside the bunker.

Both of them were down for a good thirty seconds. Their heads were pounding and ears ringing when they came to. As the smoke began to clear, so did their disorientation. Both came to the abrupt realization that they were the last of the ten.

They stared at each other through the dissipating haze. The two killers were separated by about thirty feet. Saiga still had his knives; McStarley's bow was in hand but his arrows were a few feet away. The question was whether or not Saiga could attack him before he was able to retrieve an arrow, load it, and fire.

They both stood frozen, waiting for the other to make the first move.

"C'mon, ya little geezer, let's see what ya got," goaded McStarley.

Saiga's mind had been wrapped around a surprise attack. That was his forte. He had already learned the hard way that direct confrontation didn't always produce the desired result. A case in point had been his fight with the black American, which had ended with a parachute over his head and his victim escaping. The Englishman was twice the competition of the black man. He and McStarley had already gone head-to-head and toe-to-toe. He knew what he was up against. The odds of hacking him to death before he got off a shot were a toss-up at best.

McStarley forced himself not to go for the arrows. That would likely scare off the little bugger. There was no doubt in his mind that he would plant an arrow in Saiga's chest before the runt arrived to do his slice 'n' dice. He would probably nail him through the heart at ten paces. He wanted Saiga to make the first move.

Saiga read his mind and indeed made the first move.

McStarley lunged for his arrows, but not quickly enough. Saiga had disappeared into the jungle.

"Fucking hell," he grumbled to himself.

He glanced at his timer: *02:00:03*. Two hours to find the Asian half-pint, kill him, and claim his crown. Plenty of time.

He checked his quiver, which was depleted to only three arrows. He moved to the supply bag and fished out the machete for insurance.

Simultaneously, Saiga ran past the rotting bridge along the edge of the ravine, trying to put some distance between him and the big Englishman so he could form an ambush plan. He considered leaping into the river, but the drop was nearly a hundred feet and the water depth impossible to gauge. He pressed on.

Just below him, an ancient drainage pipe jutted from the side of the ravine. Dirty rainwater from the recent storm poured from its three-foot mouth into the river.

Three seconds after Saiga ran by, a muck-covered hand emerged from the darkness inside the pipe. Conrad pulled himself out, his entire body covered in black slime.

He had gone through the trapdoor in the bunker floor into the hidden, pitch-black chamber beneath it. Crawling around, he found the drainage pipe within three seconds and scrambled inside. Another five seconds passed before the explosion, which was tantamount to being at ground zero during an earthquake. Chunks of earth and concrete fell on his legs as the pipe caved in behind him, but he managed to pull himself free and continue into the blackness on all fours. Dirt and slime had gotten into his eyes, though it made no difference—it was so dark in here that he would have been blind regardless.

He crawled on as if he were blindfolded, the grit stinging his eyes. It smelled of dead animals and rat shit the farther he went, along with rotting roots, mold, and decay. The blindness was a blessing as he crawled over rodent carcasses, their bones crunching and guts squishing under his weight. A couple of tree rats were alive and squealed; he knocked them away but not before one bit his hand.

He heard the roiling of water up ahead. After fifty

more yards of crawling, the pipe intersected with another carrying rain runoff. Common sense told him to follow the flow of water.

Eventually there was light at the end of the tunnel, literally.

He tumbled into the river and washed the grime from his eyes, his vision returning. Glancing upward, Conrad caught a brief glimpse of Saiga darting along the ridge. He was looking over his shoulder as if he were being chased.

McStarley's after him.

That was good. The two were now separated and against each other. They both thought he was dead, too. All of this would work to his advantage.

For the next half hour, it was a game of cat, mouse, and cat, though McStarley and Saiga had no idea that Conrad was back in the mix.

Nor did anyone else.

Occasionally Conrad momentarily appeared in one of Goldman's tiny windows that displayed each lens on the island, but these cameras were ignored in favor of tracking the final two competitors. Everyone else was dead now, rendering all other angles obsolete. Thanks to the battery lead covering his GPS unit, Conrad was also off their grid.

Julie remained in the control room tent, in a state of suspended animation. Like Goldman, she took Conrad's death hard. She still didn't know his true history, but his actions of the last twenty-eight hours belied the charges against him. Conrad was far from the murderer-racist–child killer per the biography Ian had dictated to her. He had shown bravery and humanity. She secretly hoped that whatever he'd been doing in the weather tower would bring an end to Ian's madness.

Thousands of miles away in Texas, everyone was hanging around the Blue Boot attempting to console one another. The webcast was still in progress on the big screen, but Mike had turned down the sound. Now that Jack was gone, everyone's interest had waned, though a few revenge-minded diehards wanted the satisfaction of seeing at least one of Jack's killers pay the ultimate price. Mike offered up drinks on the house and turned the afternoon into a wake.

Up on Mike's big screen, Saiga was darting into the jungle.

They couldn't hear his thoughts in Granville or anywhere else, but he was now more confident about winning than he had been since the contest began. The first time he and McStarley had confronted each other had ended in a draw, which wouldn't be the case this time around. The Englishman had very few arrows left. Once they were used up, the bombastic Brit would be at a distinct disadvantage. Saiga had a wonderful pair of knives and he knew how to use them.

McStarley, meanwhile, was equally positive that he was going to prevail. He would likely bring Saiga down with an arrow, but if not, he had that big machete tucked under his belt. He also had savage strength that he hadn't fully tapped yet. The squirrelly Asian had risen to the occasion when they'd first introduced themselves at the plane wreck, that was true, but he was worn out now. McStarley had energy to spare as he ran into the jungle after him. He spotted Saiga skipping over rocks, occasionally swinging between branches as he made his escape.

Bugger's a little fuckin' squirrel monkey, McStarley said to himself as he watched him swing. He was within firing distance now and loaded an arrow.

Saiga slowed down and held still. He knew McStarley was behind him and wanted to draw his fire, to use up those arrows.

McStarley let one fly, Saiga darting behind a tree at the last split second. He ran hard, but not too hard, and coaxed another arrow from his attacker, diving behind a rock as the arrowhead ricocheted across it. The Asian peeked from behind the boulder and saw McStarley loading his final arrow. His timing had to be flawless in order to seduce the Englishman into thinking he had the perfect shot.

Saiga dashed into open space and tripped on purpose, narrowing the gap between them. He then got up and ran in a straight line, giving McStarley an easy target.

After missing with his first shot, McStarley knew exactly what the competition was doing, but his confidence was such that he was positive he would bring him down with the second. When that arrow missed, he was pissed. The third would not be wasted. The monkey had just done a face plant, probably on purpose, but his back might as well have been a bull's-eye as he stood. McStarley planted his feet and let his final arrow fly.

Saiga leaped up and swung over a branch as the arrow sliced his pants, taking a chunk of flesh with it. His thigh had a bloody gash, but the price was worth it—the Englishman was out of arrows.

He swung back down like a gymnast on the parallel bars and saw McStarley toss the bow, exchanging it for the machete.

Saiga's face sank. He hadn't counted on that.

It was back to plan A, a surprise attack.

He swung off the tree and dashed into the rain forest. McStarley was bigger, but he was quicker. One minute later he disappeared into the green void. Saiga hid behind a tree and waited for his pursuer to come to him.

By now, everyone at the Blue Boot was watching as McStarley stalked past the tree that Saiga was hiding behind. Goldman's placement of the lens showed the sneaky Asian big in the foreground.

Saiga silently crept out and tiptoed toward McStarley, raising his knives as Jack's friends watched in suspense. They wanted both of these felons dead for what they had done to Jack, but McStarley was clearly the more sadistic of the two. They all were pulling for Saiga.

Suddenly Conrad stepped out from behind another tree and clocked Saiga with a punch that sent him splashing into a swampy pool.

The bar went into an instant frenzy.

"Jack's back!" shouted Farland. "He's back! He's alive!"

Sarah spun on her stool, knocking over the shot of

whiskey Mike had given her. She gazed at the big TV, her emotions roller-coasting again. Jack was up there on the screen. Alive!

Saiga had flopped in less than a foot of muddy water, dazed but conscious. His hands rose from the muck first. Both were still grasping his bolo knives.

"Let's go, sweetheart," growled Conrad. He marched into the swamp, all business.

Saiga got to his feet surprisingly fast and swung his weapons, Conrad dodging and deflecting every swipe. The iron bars were still taped to his arms and legs, which saved his life and allowed for brutal retaliatory hits.

McStarley had spun around the moment Conrad had surprised Saiga. He watched as the Asian sailed onto his back with Conrad trampling after him for more. This time he wasn't going to wait for his former partner to cut down Conrad. The likelihood of that seemed remote anyway, based on the redneck's amazing resilience. There was no question in his mind now about the American's background—only Special Forces, black ops, SEAL training, or sheer luck could keep a man alive after what he'd been through. McStarley didn't believe in luck. That meant military.

He decided the only way to take Conrad out of the game was to reunite with his little buddy. Saiga would probably welcome it, seeing as how he was getting his ass kicked.

As McStarley moved toward the Texan with his machete, he flashed on a killing from his past. It was during one of his peacekeeping tours in Africa, specifically

Rwanda. He loved the military and their euphemisms. Where else could you murder and torture people and get a commendation as a "peacekeeper"? There had been insurgents supposedly holed up in a shanty, though the intel was hazy. He and three others in his company stormed inside and found three civilians—two men and a woman, all terrified. McStarley roughly corralled them as his men searched their tiny abode. They were poverty-stricken field-workers and possessed only the bare essentials, including rudimentary eating utensils and torn blanket bedrolls. There were no weapons, save a machete used to clear sugarcane that still had bamboo wedged in its blade. McStarley grabbed it and waved it over their heads, trying to persuade them to confess to crimes they didn't commit. His comrades told him to stop, but he ignored them, telling them to get out and let him do his job.

He did his job, all right. After decapitating both men, he raped the woman and then sliced her up as well.

Thinking back on it now, his only regret was that he hadn't killed his own men, who had later turned him in. The executions, however, had been indescribable and almost worth the punishment. Gripping that machete right now brought his bloodlust back in full force.

He stampeded toward Conrad with his arm arched. He was going to behead him with one powerful slash.

Conrad punched Saiga and swung around as the machete swiped through the air. He ducked and deflected it with his iron-barred forearm, rolling to the side and quickly righting himself.

McStarley and Saiga were now standing on both sides of him. He could take each of them down individually, but his odds went way down if they ganged up on him.

Saiga sensed the same dilemma. McStarley had been stalking him, yet he was now motioning for the pair of them to jointly attack the American, essentially realigning their alliance. The American had taken on mythical proportions to the Japanese fighter so the idea held instant appeal. He was the kind of folk hero his ancestors talked about around campfires. An explanation as to how he survived that blast eluded him, plus Conrad had silently surprised him and was a powerful fighter. The American scared him. The sooner he died, the better. The only way that was going to happen was with the Englishman's help.

They attacked Conrad at the same time, three blades swinging to his none. Conrad blocked their initial attack with every one of his limbs. He was unable to throw any blows himself, too busy defending himself.

People were screaming at Mike's big screen, cheering Jack on.

C'mon, bud! Hang in there!" yelled Burdick as he pounded his fist on a table.

Farland was shouting on top of him: "Fight, Jack, fight!"

Sarah could only hold her breath. Once again, it looked like Jack was about to die.

There in the jungle, Conrad's adversaries paused after round one to catch their breath. Conrad knew he had to think of something fast before round two began. His forearms were crisscrossed with lacerations like a baked ham; one of his legs was also gashed down to the shin bone. If he remained on the defensive, he'd be dead after the next attack. His only hope in turning the tide was to fight back hard.

When they came at him again, he roared like a lion and charged with both arms swinging. His right arm caught McStarley across the face and sent him stumbling backward. The Brit tripped and fell, his head slamming into a fallen log. Conrad received two more slashes from Saiga before connecting with an anvil punch, sending him to the ground.

McStarley, semidazed, was not eager to rise up for another beating. Saiga, however, was too full of pride to stay down and came at Conrad like a true warrior. Conrad blocked the swipes and knocked one knife from his grasp. Saiga lunged with the other, on a direct course for Conrad's heart—but the military hero grabbed his arm, twisted it around, and rammed the blade up into Saiga's rib cage.

The Japanese murderer stared at him face-to-face, blood trickling from his half-open mouth. The knife had gone all the way through him, the blade puncturing his lung on its way through his heart and out his back. He took his last breath and went limp in Conrad's arms.

Conrad dropped his body and turned his attention to McStarley, who was still on the ground. He picked up one of Saiga's bolo knives and gazed at the English sociopath. Showing his true colors, McStarley got to his feet and ran away.

The Blue Boot cheering section went absolutely nuts, just like the rest of the world who had logged on to this unparalleled bloodfest.

Eddie C bolted out of his chair. "Conrad! Conrad's back!"

Everyone stared in awe as Conrad sprang from behind the tree and beat the hell out of Saiga.

Breckel watched the action unfold, shocked at first. He was rarely wrong about anything, but he had underestimated the big bald Texan. Putting his ego aside, he decided this was a wonderful thing. Breckel loved surprises as much as the next guy—just as long as they were in his favor, and this unequivocally was. Conrad's reemergence was a classic twist for his audience: kill off a formidable bad guy and then bring him back in a shocking reveal. The way Conrad had popped out from behind the tree to ambush Saiga couldn't have been staged any better. Better still, the audience hated him more than the little Asian—how could they not, based on that wonderfully detestable biography he'd invented for the Texan? Pitting the two most despicable killers on the planet against each other for the final showdown was the ultimate crowd pleaser.

"Thirty-five million servers logged on, boss."

The producer smiled at Eddie, watching the plasma as Conrad took off after McStarley.

"Let me know when it hits forty."

28

Special Agent Wilkins stared numbly at his computer display and dropped his head. He had just seen Jack Riley-Conrad die in a fiery explosion.

He hadn't been sure if Meranto would go to his DIA superiors to authorize a flyover of the coordinates he had given the agent. If so, Meranto would likely receive a rejection. The only way around it would be to take matters into his own hands and send off a plane without running it by his boss. This, too, seemed improbable, except that he'd seen a look in Meranto's eyes when he'd taken the slip of paper. It was almost as if the DIA agent respected him for being a pain in the ass. The more he thought about it, they were in the same boat. They both had bosses who preferred sweeping it under the rug to cleaning it up properly. In situations like this, you needed to dive into the mess yourself rather than wait for approvals that would never come in time, if at all. He hoped Meranto was doing exactly that.

But that was before the bunker blew into a million pieces with Conrad inside of it. Rescuing him was a moot point now, though locating the island and bringing charges against Ian Breckel still justified the use of government resources.

Wilkins went for a cup of coffee and tried to console himself that he had done everything he could to save the Texas military hero. He wasn't sure that Sarah Cavanaugh knew her boyfriend was dead, which also bothered him. He'd advised her not to log on, but in her shoes, he would've ignored his own advice and gone somewhere with a high-speed Internet connection. Wilkins didn't know Sarah well enough to know if she'd taken that initiative and therefore felt an obligation to give her the news. He fully expected to take the heat from her for not rescuing Jack Riley in time, but it had to be done.

He went back to his office and picked up the phone, dialing Sarah's home number.

A young boy answered, his Texas accent still in a high range. "Howdy, Cavanaugh residence."

"Is your mother home?"

"Naw, but Gramma's here."

Wilkins hesitated. He didn't want Sarah getting the bad news secondhand.

"Where's your mom?"

"Down at the Blue Boot—that's where she works."

Wilkins heard an older woman's voice in the background. "Who's that, Mikey?"

"Thanks very much," Wilkins said, and then hung up. He dialed information and got the number for the Blue Boot Bar & Grill, glancing at his computer monitor as he started to dial.

The Japanese convict was stalking the British Special Forces killer on his screen.

The phone began to ring.

Conrad jumped out from behind a tree and slugged the Asian.

Wilkins did a double take.

A male voice picked up the phone. "Blue Boot—" Wilkins heard voices in the background: "Jack's back! He's back!"

Wilkins hung up, riveted to his screen. Sarah was watching, all right, along with a whole lot of others. He didn't need to tell her that Jack was dead because he wasn't. He, Sarah, and everyone else were seeing it unfold in real time.

Conrad was on the run, only now he was the pursuer. McStarley had tortured, raped, and killed over the last twenty-nine hours mainly for the pleasure of it. He deserved to die even more than the terrorists and drug lords Conrad had taken down at the behest of the Pentagon. Unlike McStarley, the Texan had never enjoyed killing anyone and took great effort in accomplishing his assignments with the minimum loss of life. The stakes of this mission were different, however. He had personally watched Paco's torture and murder at the hands of this sociopath, not that his brief friendship with the Mexican absolved Paco of his crimes. Still, the joy McStarley had taken in the doing deserved a swift punishment. Weighing in even heavier was hearing Sarah's voice. The satellite connection was crisp and clear with no digital delay.

It had sounded like she was in the next room. He wanted to hold her and wrestle with the boys. He wanted to live now more than ever in his life.

Living meant winning this piece-of-shit competition. McStarley had to die—no ifs, ands, or buts. In a perfect world, that asshole producer who put everyone out here would have to pay a price as well, but that comeuppance had to go on the back burner.

McStarley was every bit as fast as Conrad, which kept the distance between them consistent for the next three hundred yards. The Englishman veered toward the ravine again, running down a path that ended at a steep, rocky ledge. The gorge below was a vast void of darkness with only the roar of a waterfall to give any kind of perspective to its depth. There was no way out except back the way he came, or down into a chasm that never saw direct sunlight.

For all his experience with death, McStarley didn't savor the thought of being on the receiving end. He knew the Yank had a soft spot when it came to others dying, but he didn't think that would apply to him. Talking his way out of it wouldn't be an option. Winning the battle, at least under present circumstances, also seemed to be a difficult proposition. For the first time in his life, McStarley began to question his confidence.

Conrad ran up and saw that he had a clear advantage. McStarley was cornered with nowhere to go. The question was how to take him. Shoving him into the gorge would be the gentleman's way of dispatching him—no muss, no fuss. Except that the pit below was an unknown. Death had to be guaranteed. No, the only way to finish this was hand-to-hand combat. Conrad didn't like himself for feeling this way, but the truth was that he wanted to take McStarley's life up close and personal to avenge what the madman had done to Paco and Rosa.

"Let's go, just me 'n' you now," he told McStarley as he shortened the gap between them. "Let's dance, asshole."

He was close enough now to see fear in the lunatic's eyes. When all was said and done, McStarley was a coward, like most sadistic killers. He preyed on the weak to satisfy his impulses. It was time for him to taste his own medicine.

"Not today," answered the Brit.

He turned and leaped into the abyss.

At first Conrad thought he had committed suicide— again, the coward's way out. But the splash, which came after several seconds of delay, told him the killer was probably still alive.

The rules of the game had been very specific. In order to win, everyone else needed to die. If both of them were alive at the thirty-hour mark, then nobody would win and both would go up in smoke.

Conrad looked down into the gorge. He couldn't see the bottom. He glanced at his timer: *00:59:01.* He might die jumping, but would be dead in less than an hour if he didn't.

Like McStarley, he took a leap of faith.

The fall seemed to take minutes. Dark rocks and moss blurred past him as he fell into the void, a branch roughly scraping his back. He wondered if he had made a stupid mistake—McStarley could easily be dead, having landed in shallow water and broken his neck on barely submerged rocks. His fate might be the same.

Time slowed down even more as the smear of passing rocks and ferns turned to murky gray and then darkness. He was on his way down into hell, having just left purgatory. Like many people during what they thought were the last seconds of their life, select events flashed before his mind's eye. There was a brief image of his mother kissing his dad as she served them homemade stew. She was wearing a yellow flowered apron and a sunny smile. He saw his own blue eyes in his mother's face, a resemblance he had never noticed before.

Then he was walking along the beach with his dad, picking up seaweed and popping it between his fingers. His dad chased him across the mirrorlike low-tide sand. He could see his dad's shadow catching up in the afternoon light. A second later he was flying as his dad scooped him up and tickled him until he couldn't breathe.

And then Sarah . . . it was their first Christmas together and her face was glowing with colored light cast by Christmas tree bulbs. She opened his present and glowed. It was an antique radio he'd picked up at the Antique Barn in Granville. She turned it on and a Hank Williams song came out of it. The boys began to dance, Sarah joining in. She grabbed his hand and tried to get him to join them, but he had two left feet and refused. The boys jumped onto each of his huge legs and he tried to shake them off, moving like a robot as Hank sang "Honky Tonk Blues." "Nice moves!" Sarah laughed. Conrad laughed, too . . . harder than he had in his whole life.

Sarah's laughing face was the last thing he saw before impact.

The water felt like a sheet of cement he had somehow shattered. There was a roar in his ears for a fraction of a second, and then all sounds became muffled. He couldn't tell whether his eyes were open or shut since everything was black. His boots hit the bottom hard, but not enough to break his legs. He planted his feet, shoved, and launched himself upward.

Conrad exploded from the surface, and the loud roar flooded his ears again. It was dark, but not pitch black. He had landed in a sizable pool with a strong current. Saiga's knife was still in his grip, which surprised him since the impact had been so great.

He looked around. Behind him was a massive waterfall cascading over prehistoric boulders. The entire basin was filled with massive rocks. If he'd landed a few feet to his left, he would've been instantly killed.

To his right was a huge cave, which the water was flowing into.

Conrad slowly turned a full 360 degrees. McStarley was nowhere in sight.

There was only one place he could have gone. Conrad swam into the cave, the current helping him along.

There on the island, as well as at the Blue Boot, the FBI facility, and several million homes all over the world, people were asking the same question that Ian Breckel was: "Where the hell are they?"

He was practically hysterical. "What do you have, Goldy, what do we have? Find them!"

"I'm looking," Goldman said, his neurosis shifting into high gear. He truly wanted to find them now—he needed to see the good guy win, not necessarily in graphic close-up, but McStarley had made him literally vomit over the last twenty-nine-plus hours. Like many others, Goldman wanted Conrad to permanently take the sadistic Englishman out of the game.

"For God's sake, find 'm!" ranted Breckel. "Don't you have a camera down there?"

"Do I look like Jacques Cousteau?" He switched through all of his cameras, trying to find any kind of angle. "I don't do inaccessible underwater caves. Hence, dead spots."

The best he could find was a view of the waterfall from a high angle. He hadn't anticipated that anybody would be crazy enough to jump, and neither had Breckel. Like everyone else watching, they had no idea if either man was dead or alive.

"Eddie, what do you have?" the producer hollered, giving up on Goldy.

Eddie castered over to his grid monitor. There was one + sign remaining on the grid.

"I got one of 'em."

"Which one?"

He clicked on the symbol and brought up McStarley's stats.

"McStarley. But we lost Conrad's signal a while back, so he could still be alive, too."

"For Christ's sake," cried Breckel. His finale had just gone off a ledge and disappeared into a dark pit.

Ironically, he was now praying for Conrad's survival. Breckel had big plans for the ending, but they would be worthless without someone to take on his golden boy McStarley.

"What's going on? What happened?"

Sarah was asking everyone around her as if questioning her own eyes. Mike, Farland, Burdick, Lyle, and all the others didn't know anything more than she did. They had all watched McStarley jump into oblivion and Jack follow him fifteen seconds later. The next thing on the screen was a shot of a big waterfall. The entire room was tense with anticipation; it was as if somebody had cut out the most crucial part of a movie with no explanation. Had Jack survived the fall? Where did he end up? What happened to the bad guy? Some hoped the limey had killed himself, but most didn't. As Breckel knew all too well, his audience wanted to see a showdown.

In Connecticut, Special Agent Wilkins and his staff were equally baffled as they watched the live broadcast. After learning that Conrad had survived the bunker blast, he'd put Stan in charge of routing the webcast to the conference room so their colleagues could watch the events unfold.

He had assigned research tasks to several groups, so everyone in his department was aware of the Jack Riley aka Jack Conrad situation. Rumors had spread that a navy flyover was in the works to locate the island, though the grapevine had elevated it to a full rescue operation. Wilkins still didn't know the actual status because Meranto wasn't returning his calls.

They had all seen McStarley and Conrad take the plunge and disappear. Currently a waterfall was on the conference room screen, which abruptly changed to shots of the jungle that lingered for only a few seconds. It was either clever editing to create suspense, or the people running the show had lost them and were trying to get them back on camera.

In actuality, with Goldman at the console, it was a little of both. He *was* trying to find them, though his showmanship was hard to suppress. Bella kicked into gear as well, subtly playing suspenseful jungle music to heighten the anticipation. She'd put on a marine field cap and was really getting into it.

Five excruciating minutes went by before one of their stars was back on camera.

29

The river created by the waterfall rushed into the cave and churned over sharp, shallow rocks to places unknown. The cavern was a huge lava tube consisting of jet-black volcanic rock that swallowed all available light.

Conrad cautiously swam into it, allowing ample time for his pupils to adjust. McStarley was likely hiding in here planning an ambush. There was no reason to doubt that he still had the machete, since Conrad had managed to hang on to his own knife. He stayed low, keeping his eyes just above water level like an alligator. A submerged lava rock lacerated his chest but his adrenaline suppressed the pain.

As the cave grew darker, the roar of the waterfall gave way to the peaceful sound of a flowing stream. The calm before the storm, thought the Texan. His pupils had fully dilated, but he could make out only vague shapes at best.

He saw a pair of eyes in his peripheral vision. Conrad bolted from the surface and slashed with his knife as they came at him.

A shrill cry echoed inside the cave. *Hundreds* of

them. His eruption from the water triggered a domino effect as a colony of vampire bats exploded off the walls and ceiling. The creatures filled the cavern with their flapping black wings and a cacophony of high-pitched shrieks.

He went underwater again and swam forward, allowing the bats to settle. Conrad brought his head up like a periscope and swam on.

The river took a turn and light twinkled off its surface from a source up ahead. He kept a careful watch as he continued onward. There was still no sign of his foe.

The illumination began to brighten. All he could see was an overexposed flare of brilliant sunlight at the other end of the cave. Again, Conrad took his time and let his pupils contract. McStarley would likely be planning a surprise attack as soon as he emerged from this cavern.

When his vision had fully adjusted he could see a massive canyon up ahead with a million places to hide. Hesitating at the cave's mouth, he sprang out looking left, right, and up.

McStarley wasn't there. No sign of him at all.

Conrad revisited the notion that his enemy may not have survived the jump but again discarded it. There had been no sign of a body, no blood or torn clothes on the rocks, no time for him to sink if he'd been knocked unconscious. Moreover, McStarley was Special Forces. Military men like him didn't die easily. The real puzzler was why the Englishman hadn't ambushed him in the cave or right outside of it, which would have presented his best opportunity. Then again, McStarley had chosen to run rather than fight when he'd leaped off that ledge. But was he really willing to give up and die at the thirty-hour mark rather than face his final obstacle to victory? Winning meant life, as well as freedom—how could he let that opportunity pass without a fight? McStarley was a coward, but he wasn't stupid.

Something wasn't adding up.

He pressed on, the rock canyon fully materializing. There were a series of stairstep waterfalls leading down into a massive rock arena. It was like a coliseum made of natural stone, constructed by Mother Nature herself. The view was breathtaking, but Conrad didn't allow himself time to appreciate it. McStarley was down in this canyon somewhere, planning something.

He descended the stairsteps as water rushed over his legs. Looking up again, he spotted a camera mounted on a boulder as it electronically panned down on him. He gazed at it hatefully at first, then softened. Breckel and his minions were certainly watching, but someone else might be, too—Sarah. It gave him yet another reason not to die, knowing it would tear her apart actually to witness it.

Conrad didn't know it, but there were forty cameras positioned around this arena. Breckel had insisted on it after the first location scout. He knew it would make a spectacular setting for any and all battles.

"Found him," said Goldman, bringing the shot of Conrad onto the main screen. "He's in the rock canyon. We got angles, lots of angles."

Breckel sighed with relief. Maybe McStarley wasn't stupid after all, jumping off that ledge. Whatever the case, he'd made it to the canyon and they were back on track.

"Get a live unit down there. Where's my boy McStarley?"

Eddie used the GPS to pinpoint his coordinates in the canyon. Breckel moved to Baxter and said something at a volume too low for Goldman to hear. Baxter nodded and quickly left.

Julie was also in the room and saw the exchange. Like Goldman, she didn't have a good feeling about how this was going to end. Talking to Ian about what he was up to was pointless. She had become invisible to him during these final hours of the competition. As hard as it was to stomach, Julie had been forcing herself to watch the show to remain informed. The escalating violence continued to have a numbing effect on her, which disturbed her as much as anything else. She was becoming desensitized, just like Eddie, Bella, and the public at large. Furthermore, the strange turn of events that now pitted Conrad against McStarley was impossible to ignore. The only good thing that could possibly come out of this was to have Jack Conrad triumph.

The Blue Boot contingent felt the exact same way.

"There he is!" bellowed Farland when Jack's face splashed back on the screen outside the cavern. "He's all right!"

"That's my boy!" yelled Burdick as he high-fived Lyle, Jack's old classmate.

Sarah's heart skipped again as the boulder-mounted camera pushed into a close-up on him. He turned and looked into the lens with a cold stare at first, but then his expression changed, almost as if he was looking at her and no one else. She saw the Jack who had kissed her good-bye and walked out the door, never to come back. Sarah wouldn't let herself cry. He was alive. Somehow he was going to survive this.

At this same moment, Breckel's chopper was lifting off and heading for the rock arena.

Conrad heard the thud of its blades as it descended into the canyon. A bag was shoved out the door with a miniparachute attached. It dropped about a hundred yards away from him, leaving an unmistakable trail of yellow-green smoke. As it drifted down, it all began to make sense to him. The deck had been stacked against him—against *all* of them—right from the get-go.

He sprinted toward the smoke as fast as he could, though in all likelihood McStarley was closer and would arrive first. They had his GPS signal, after all, and he'd been given an advantage all along. What was in the bag was anybody's guess, though Conrad wagered it was something lethal.

The bag landed behind a huge boulder as the colored smoke continued to billow out, surrounding the area in a thick blanket of yellow-green.

Seconds later, McStarley appeared from the unnatural haze like an apparition. He was wet and glistening, just like Conrad, and still had his machete. The bag, as always, brought a big grin. He set his machete down and proceeded to unzip his final gift from the producer.

His eyes smiled as wide as his mouth at what he saw. McStarley glanced at a camera mounted about twenty feet away and winked back his appreciation.

There would be no need for the machete from this point on, not with a sawed-off 12-gauge shotgun and a full box of shells having just been dropped into his lap.

30

DIA agent Wade Meranto returned to Washington, DC, wondering if he would still have a job. Assistant Director Gerald Rupert, his superior, had most likely caught wind of the unauthorized flyover by now.

The Defense Intelligence Agency employed approximately eight thousand men and women under three primary directorates—agency subdivisions, with a multitude of branches under each umbrella. Meranto was even more expendable than Jack Conrad. Rupert, who possessed the humor of a stone, headed up the Strategic Support Branch of the Directorate for Human Intelligence. The SSB was another appropriately vague label for a division that deployed field analysts, technical specialists, interrogation experts, Special Forces, and black ops to quietly clean up problems all over the world. Former Defense Secretary Donald Rumsfeld created the SSB in the wake of 9/11 to bypass the limitations of the Central Intelligence Agency. For years, nobody knew it even existed.

After leaving the CCCTF in New Haven, Meranto had flipped open his phone twice, only to close it both times. Calling Rupert and arguing the point would be a waste of time. If he was serious about saving one of their best men, he had to act quickly. Meranto also received a message from his office that Special Agent Wilkins had called three times. He didn't want the overzealous young agent lighting more fires until the current one was extinguished, so he didn't call back.

The next time he opened his phone, he called the navy directly and gave them the coordinates, authorizing the recon on his own. No one questioned it, such was the muscle of the DIA. An F/A-18C Hornet was dispatched from the *USS Nimitz*, which had originated out of San Diego and was currently in the South Pacific. The plane would begin its search at roughly the same time Meranto walked into his office at the Pentagon.

Assistant Director Rupert was waiting for him when he arrived.

"What the hell do you think you're doing authorizing a flyover without clearing it with me first?"

Meranto paled. He started to explain but was cut off.

"I told you to clean this mess up, not stir it up," said the military man with a severe crew cut.

Meranto barely nodded to himself. He should've known that his boss would have his finger in every pie at all times. Rupert had probably learned of the dispatch within minutes of the plane's departure.

"Conrad transmitted partial coordinates to the CCCTF—he's no longer under the jurisdiction of El Salvador," Meranto began, simplifying Sarah Cavanaugh out of his explanation. "I made two attempts to reach you, and seeing as how time was of the essence, I phoned in the requisition on my own."

He hadn't lied exactly—he *had* made two attempts to call but couldn't bring himself actually to dial.

"You could lose your job for pulling a stunt like this," his superior jabbered on, the veins in his face filling with blood.

"I know, sir, but I was willing to take that chance. Conrad is a good man. If we bring him back alive, it will bode well for the SSB."

"And if we don't?"

"At least we made the effort. Either way, since I authorized the mission without your approval, I shoulder all responsibility."

Although Meranto maintained his stoic face, he smiled inwardly. All anyone cared about at any government agency was CYA—cover your ass—and he had just covered his boss's. It was a no-lose proposition: if they saved Conrad, Rupert would get the credit. If the mission failed, Meranto would take the fall.

Assistant Director Rupert stared back for several seconds and then marched out the door, hesitating in the threshold.

"We didn't have this conversation."

"Yes, sir."

Meranto exhaled as his superior exited. A big part of him felt great for the first time in many years. But another equally large part thought that he had just done the stupidest thing in his entire career. It all came down to whether Jack Conrad lived or died.

* * *

"This is bullshit!"

Farland pulled off his Texas Rangers baseball cap and threw it on the ground as if he were pissed at a ref's call.

He was not alone in his anger—the entire bar was in an uproar.

Up on the screen, McStarley was thumbing shotgun shells into the chamber of his brand-new pump-action 12-gauge. Jack didn't stand a chance.

Sarah was the only one not shouting at the screen. She was too white-hot with anger right now even to scream. She knew firsthand that life wasn't fair, but this . . . this was the work of someone egotistical enough to play God for the purpose of entertainment. Whoever was making this show deserved his just deserts as much as the creep holding the shotgun.

The coverage on the big screen changed to a shot of Conrad jogging between boulders, getting closer to McStarley as the latter went on loading cartridges.

"He's got a gun, Jack!" somebody shouted, as if Conrad could hear him.

At this exact same moment in the canyon, Conrad heard nothing but his own footfalls. He was zigzagging between the rocks as a precaution since there was no telling what his competition had received.

The closer he came, the more he sensed that food, knives, and more Molotov cocktails were not part of this new care package. That asshole Breckel had this whole thing planned—that was perfectly clear now. The audience would not want to see both of them go up in smoke at the end of thirty hours. They'd want a bloody battle in the remaining minutes of his fun little show.

He was nearing the source of the dissipating smoke when intuition told him not to go any farther.

"Hey, Yank! You looking for me, you piece of shit?"

McStarley materialized as he climbed on top of a boulder with his sawed-off.

"You dance, Yank? Let's dance!"

Conrad dove as a blast of buckshot flew over his head. He scrambled behind a rock as another shot clipped his leg, the taped-on iron bars saving him from serious injury.

McStarley was beaming with delight as he hopped off the rock and strutted toward him, pumping a fresh round into his chamber.

Meanwhile in the control room, Goldman was on autopilot as he cut among all the camera angles, trying to distance himself emotionally. It didn't help when Breckel began to applaud.

"THIS IS ENTERTAINMENT!" he bellowed. "Now we need the big finish!"

Goldman closed his eyes, willing himself to continue, but he couldn't. The sleep deprivation and lack of food, along with his tremendous guilt, were sinking him in mental quicksand. He eyed Breckel, as well as Baxter, hovering in the corner. The two had conspired to rig the contest in favor of the one person who deserved punishment more than any other. Goldman shook his head and found himself standing.

That's it, he told himself. *No more.*

JJ automatically took over as he paced up to Breckel.

"You've helped this maniac the entire time, manipulated the whole thing," he said with utter disgust.

"He put on a good show, I threw him a bone," dismissed Breckel as he grinned at the main monitor.

Conrad was scrambling for cover as McStarley continued to pop off rounds.

Bella was also watching the big plasma, though her usual glee was dampened. Maybe it was because she'd been up for thirty-six hours straight, but what she was seeing didn't seem right.

"Wouldn't a fair fight have been better?" she let slip.

"Fair fight? Hell no," Breckel shot back, surprised that Bella, of all people, had uttered the words. "A Texan up against insurmountable odds, that's international entertainment. The French. The Germans. The Arabs. They love seeing an American get his ass beat. Flips the tables. Fulfills their fantasies," he preached.

Goldman just gazed. It was obvious that Conrad and all the rest of them had never been human to Breckel. They were characters in a fictional story he had written, no more. McStarley had been the predetermined winner from page one.

The technical director stopped and wondered what he had gotten himself into. He hated Breckel for what he had created, but he hated himself more. Goldman knew he should walk away from it all, but he couldn't.

Julie watched. It seemed that Goldy was going to walk, and then he didn't. She was disgusted with him, and herself. Julie wondered if she too had lost her soul. She stared at the monster before her.

Breckel didn't even bother looking at her. He eyed Bella again, who was also starting to weaken. It didn't really matter at this point. They were in the home stretch.

"Eddie, numbers?"

"We're on fire." His resident internet junkie beamed. "Almost there."

Breckel smiled at him. Thank God for the Eddies of this world.

"Tell me when we hit forty."

He turned his attention back to the screen. Making a deal with McStarley had been a smart move, no question about it. Now it was time for the curtain to drop and his star to take a bow.

Ewan McStarley was of the exact same mind-set.

"LET'S FINISH THIS MAN TO MAN," he shouted as he confidently stalked Conrad down. McStarley couldn't see him hiding between the rocks, but there was only one way out for him now. And that was straight to hell on the 12-gauge express.

He practically salivated thinking about how he would do it. Wing him in the leg and let him crawl for a bit, and then take out the other leg. Roll him over and blow out his groin. Leave him alive long enough for him to see, feel, and taste the barrel shoved into his mouth. And then let 'er rip and blow off the top of his fucking head from inside out.

Best of all, the whole extravaganza was being captured on video, so he'd be able to replay it over and over after he won. Breckel was sending him off with a pile of cash per their deal, so he'd buy one of those big fancy plasma screens and watch it on that. It didn't get any better.

Conrad had different thoughts, which didn't include how he planned to torture and kill McStarley. He was currently in survival mode. A knife was no competition for a shotgun. He had to even the odds again.

Not unlike Saiga's strategy, Conrad crisscrossed through the canyon to draw fire. He wasn't sure how much ammo the maniac had, but it needed to get used up.

McStarley cooperated and blasted his gun like there was no tomorrow—because there *wouldn't* be a tomorrow if he didn't kill the American in the next forty-four minutes, and ticking.

Conrad dashed by a bush that didn't seem right— its shape and colors were slightly off—though there was no time to contemplate it as another shot rang out. He felt a few pellets sting his back as he tumbled. Conrad strained to touch the wound. Blood came back on his fingertips but not enough to slow him down.

McStarley, meanwhile, was cramming more shells into his chamber. He had a pocketful and wasn't going to be running out anytime soon. The Yank was leading him on a foxhunt, which was good sporting fun but was taking too much time. He needed to pick up the pace, fully aware that the military-trained Yank knew how to throw that knife he was carrying. McStarley ran in a crouched position, rushing past the same bush Conrad had noticed.

As soon as he was gone, the bush moved.

Donaldson, the Australian cameraman who had videotaped the Russian's audition, had been wearing the camouflage for nearly thirty hours now. He was beat physically as well as emotionally. Videotaping Petr Raudsep's brutal fight in Belarus had been disturbing, but this assignment would require years of therapy to overcome. The viewfinder had long ago ceased to shield him from what he was capturing. He was filming murder as entertainment—that was the cold, harsh reality. As he now crept forward to videotape yet another gruesome murder, Donaldson thought of his wife Darcy and their baby daughter. All Darcy knew was that he was shooting a reality show on a tropical island—another *Survivor* spin-off, he'd told her, only "edgier." When Donaldson and his armed protection, who was camouflaged a few bushes away, had been dispatched to the canyon, they'd been told about the ratings and worldwide press the show was receiving. Darcy probably knew what he was involved in by now, which brought on a rush of guilt. Although he'd taken the job to support his family, he now felt disgusted with himself. He pictured a future where his daughter got dirty looks because of what her dad did for a living. He was no better than a guy who shot porn. Worse, actually.

"Move," whispered his backup.

Donaldson hesitated. Right now he wanted to quit

and fly home so badly that he almost walked right out of the canyon, but his fear of being blackballed in the industry, combined with the payday he would lose, stopped him. The ship had already sailed, anyway—he was more than twenty-nine hours into this with less than one to go. He was a young man, he told himself. He had his whole life to put this behind him, plenty of time to redeem himself with legitimate and even meaningful work.

He leveled his lens on McStarley as the criminal circled around a rock and fired his gun again.

Conrad felt the bolo knife torn from his grasp and the sting of pellets on his forearm. He could hear the pump action of the 12-gauge behind him and knew that the next blast could be the last thing he ever heard if he didn't disappear fast. Twenty yards away sat a large natural rock pool. Conrad sprinted for it and dived in.

Buckshot peppered the surface as he went under.

McStarley marched to the edge and reloaded his gun, circling the pool.

There was no sign of the American.

"Show your bald head, you chickenshit mother-fucker!" he shouted, his voice echoing back with a delay.

Conrad still didn't surface.

McStarley was pretty sure he'd missed him. It was going on a minute now; the Yank couldn't hold his breath much longer.

There was movement in the foliage about twenty feet away from the pool.

McStarley figured that Conrad had somehow slipped out of the pool and was taking off. He hopped over the rocks and darted through the reeds at full speed. Now that the redneck was weaponless, it was just a matter of catching up.

He spotted a bush move and leveled his sawed-off.

"Game over, Yank!"

He took a closer look at the bush and saw a lens poking out of it.

Donaldson slowly revealed his face from behind his viewfinder. The grainy pixels that had separated the cameraman from reality were of no help now as he looked into the killer's eyes. What he saw turned every muscle in his body rigid.

A tense, awkward moment passed between the two before McStarley spoke. "What do you think this is, a fancy fuckin' costume party?"

Another bush moved in McStarley's peripheral vision.

Donaldson's backup was aiming his machine gun. He had been instructed not to shoot the competitors unless it was absolutely necessary, so he hesitated.

It cost him his life.

McStarley turned in a blur and blasted a hole in his gut. Donaldson's backup was blown onto his back, dead before he hit the ground.

The killer turned back to Donaldson and took point-blank aim.

"I'm just a cameraman," the young Australian uttered.

"Film this."

Donaldson heard a loud roar, saw his wife's and daughter's innocent faces smiling at him, and then left the world.

At this same instant, JJ had a shot of Conrad up on the screen, who had just surfaced in the pond. She'd missed the live unit's double murder.

"Where did those shots come from? Where's the live unit?" Breckel yelled with frustration.

"Live unit's down," said Eddie, checking his grid.

JJ brought up Donaldson's camera as fast as she could. It was lying sideways on the ground in a static shot. Donaldson's armed backup was in view, crumpled on the ground beside his machine gun.

They all knew what this meant. McStarley had just killed two of their own.

"That's fuckin' great," Breckel moaned.

He didn't know the fallen men and wouldn't have cared if he did, but the loss of their coverage had just put another hurdle in front of his fabulous ending.

McStarley's boots appeared in the fallen camera's crooked angle. His hands dipped into view and picked up the machine gun.

JJ cut back to Conrad just as he disappeared from view.

The Texan had avoided death by mere moments. He'd remained underwater for as long as he could, and when his breath ran out, he surfaced in a thicket of reeds just as McStarley dashed past him. Conrad heard him talking to somebody and then a shot rang out. He silently crawled from the pool and heard a voice say, "I'm just a cameraman," followed by another blast.

As he crept closer, he saw McStarley through the reeds as he reached down and retrieved the machine gun.

Conrad realized that his chances had plummeted even further. Running was no longer an option. He had to strike first, and fast.

McStarley glanced around. The Yankee was out here somewhere, most likely over by the pond. He paced back the way he had just come.

Conrad lunged.

The machine gun barrel was swinging toward him, spraying bullets, but he knocked it away before it completed its arc and sawed him in half. As the MP5 flew into the air, McStarley brought up his sawed-off. Conrad kicked it away as it blasted.

The two men faced off. There were no cheeky words, no game playing, no goodie bags being dropped from the sky. It had finally come down to survival of the fittest.

31

Nearly forty million people across the globe were riveted to their screens as the fight began.

McStarley made the first move. He connected with a fist-foot combo that showed off his martial arts training, though it was far from a knockout. Conrad countered with a series of street-fighting moves that were all power with very little flash: swift, hard punches to the face, kidneys, and stomach. McStarley toughly fielded them and then lit into Conrad again, connecting less solidly the second time around. The Texan was dialing him in, now able to block most of his blows. He retaliated with a barrage of heavyweight champion–style jabs, hooks, and roundhouses that sent the limey staggering.

"Go, baby, go!"

It was Sarah. Up until now, she had remained quiet at the Blue Boot, on the edge of her seat. The wave of emotions had threatened to drown her—there had been depression, followed by hope, and now exultation as her man took charge. Sarah didn't watch prizefighting. Didn't care for football much either. Would not allow her boys to watch violent movies. Yet here she was, cheering Jack on in a fight that would almost certainly see him kill with his bare hands. She had taken him for dead at least once already, but now, as she watched him beat this evil murderer to a pulp, it felt *good*.

Wilkins and his team had much the same reaction as they watched in the Computer Crime Task Force's conference room. His boss Moyer was also viewing it from the privacy of his corner office, his brow furrowed with worry. The assistant director secretly wished he'd had Wilkins's chutzpah to stand up to that DIA agent Meranto. Now that Conrad was kicking this asshole's butt on the Internet and a navy jet was on its way to rescue him, Wilkins was going to get a big promotion. Maybe even take his job.

But the fight was far from over.

Inside the last duffel that had been dropped was a little insurance to go along with the shotgun—a leather-sheathed combat knife. That knife was now strapped to McStarley's ankle, hidden under his right pant leg.

He was taking a beating to be sure, but McStarley was playing it worse than his actual condition. Conrad slugged him onto a rocky ledge and he flopped into a fetal curl, giving the impression he was a beaten man. It allowed him to discreetly unsheathe the knife.

When Conrad leaned down to finish him off, the Englishman slashed out.

Conrad fell back with a gash across his chest. He dropped as the pain registered in his brain and sent a shock to his system. His shirt began to bloom with red.

Rather than stab him again, McStarley resheathed his blade. He still had a vision, one that involved the shotgun and plenty of carnage. He now intended to fulfill it.

Conrad was too incapacitated to stand, much less run. He saw McStarley hunting for his 12-gauge and knew what was coming. He looked over the rocky ledge where their battle had just ended and saw an incline leading to another series of pools. Tumbling down the slope would surely do more damage, but he was a dead man if he remained where he was.

He rolled himself off the ledge as McStarley picked up his shotgun. The rocks felt like hammers against his flesh as he careened down the slope. There was a loud crack and buckshot caught him in the back like a thousand needles. Conrad kept rolling and felt a blowtorch across his arm as another blast went off. The buckshot ripped what was left of the rebar from his arm and shredded off a layer of flesh. He forced himself to keep rolling, which hurt almost as much as the gunshots, and made it to a rocky wet stairstep with a waterfall that filled the lower pools.

McStarley moved to the ledge and continued to empty his chamber as Conrad tumbled down the stony steps.

As he descended, Conrad didn't think about Sarah, the boys, his dad, or anything. Pain obliterated all thought. He'd been told that a body shut down like a circuit breaker during extreme trauma, but that had never been true in his case. No matter how bad it ever hurt, his nervous system wasn't kind enough to let him pass out. He'd been trained by the military to suppress pain, which he tried to do now.

Another peppering of lead stung his entire body as he rolled into the water facedown. There was a murkiness, and then silence.

That was the last thing his brain recorded.

McStarley peered down at him from the ledge. Conrad was in a dead man's float. He fired, pumped, and fired once more for good measure. The lead splashed into the water around Conrad's body like a hailstorm. Conrad remained facedown and motionless. McStarley still wanted to blow his balls and head off, but it was a long walk down and he was out of shells regardless. Despite the minor letdown, he sighed with satisfaction and glanced around for a camera to capture his triumph.

Sarah gasped, went pale, and then cried. Jack was floating upside down, his draining blood turning the water pink around him. The camera lingered quite a while, dissolving between McStarley's gloating grin and Jack's body.

The rest of the bar went pin-drop silent. Nobody could believe his eyes. Jack had been winning, was *supposed* to win if there was anything right in this world. If someone needed to be reminded that life wasn't fair, this tragedy had proved it in spades.

For the second time that day, the room began to mourn Jack.

At the island compound, Ian Breckel digested it with a mixture of relief and supreme satisfaction. The finale had been good. Very good. All this despite no live unit. He would have preferred a graphic close-up of McStarley mutilating his final victim, but the other side of the coin was the possibility of having McStarley lose, which had looked likely at one point. The world wanted to see the bald, racist, child-killing Texan die rather than triumph—or so he thought—and Conrad certainly hadn't put on the show McStarley had. And still was.

Breckel watched as JJ pushed into a screaming close-up of his star, the "hero" shot. Sensing it, McStarley faced the lens and flashed a toothy grin for his worldwide audience, along with a wink. As he mugged for the masses, Bella played a triumphant music cue that Breckel had selected specifically for this moment, an unapologetic rip-off of the *Rocky* theme.

The moment was a proud one, indeed, especially when he looked over Eddie's shoulder at the subscription number his underling had just brought up.

"Forty million," Breckel said reverentially.

He had achieved his dream.

There in the rock canyon, the mad Englishman had as well. He was prancing for the cameras like a peacock showing off his feathers. McStarley had spotted at least three lenses and played to every one of them. This was his moment in the spotlight. He was ruthless. A supreme stud. Feared by man and beast. And most important of all, a free man thanks to Ian Breckel, with expendable income as a parting gift.

McStarley heard a low roar and glanced up. A navy jet was passing over the island.

Security head Baxter heard it two seconds later and

rushed out of the control room to see it. A dark glower shadowed his face. Trouble was on the way.

Thousands of miles away, Brad Wilkins was beyond depressed. The fight had given him false hope; it was obvious that Conrad had been meant to lose from the start. Ian Breckel had committed felonious acts and would eventually be charged, but that didn't do Jack Riley-Conrad any good right now as he floated upside down in his own blood.

His coworkers shook their heads, a pall cast on the entire department. Moyer entered, oblivious of the group mood. He had been called away to his own boss's office when the tide had turned against Conrad and didn't know he was dead.

"You'll be pleased to know they found the island," Moyer said almost reluctantly. "Navy SEALs are on their way."

Wilkins slowly faced him, all but spent. "Too late."

Moyer looked at the screen behind him and saw Conrad's floating body, followed by McStarley's big grinning close-up. It ended with the *Hollywood Squares* shot as a big red X went over Conrad's mug shot and McStarley's box began to flash.

"That's too bad," Moyer said quietly, though half of him was relieved. Wilkins wouldn't be taking his job after all.

Wilkins could read his expression. He gave his boss an appalled look and walked out.

Simultaneously, Ian Breckel remained fixated on his big plasma, basking in his own glory.

"Bella, you have the highlights reel cut together?" he asked without looking away.

"Done," she answered alertly. She was trying to regain some ground with her boss after inadvertently questioning his ethics. In her heart, she knew it wasn't fair that the contest had been rigged, but the crowd-pleaser ending had proved that Breck knew best.

"Run that until we bring our winner back and do a closing ceremony," he said in a drained, satisfied voice that sounded like he'd just had an orgasm.

She nodded back with a smile. "We did it, Breck, we did it."

He looked at her and returned the smile. She wasn't a bad kid and she'd come through in the end. Bella would get to work for him again.

He glanced around for Julie. Surely she would see the light now, having witnessed his genius.

Julie was gone.

Before he could let this irritation get to him, Baxter appeared in his line of sight. He motioned Breckel over, his expression grimmer than usual.

"What is it?" the producer asked, annoyed to have anyone raining on his parade.

Baxter guided him out of earshot of the others.

"We've been spotted. U.S. Navy, looked like an F/A-18."

The news hit Breckel like an atomic bomb. He had taken every precaution to keep their location a secret, paid off every pilot, crossed every *t* and dotted every *i*. Then it hit him. Conrad had done this. He'd been in the weather tower for some reason, and now he knew why. He had gotten their coordinates out. If Conrad wasn't already dead, he would've gone and shot him himself.

"How do you want to play it?" Baxter asked quietly as he glanced at Bella, Eddie, and the others.

Breckel followed his glimpse. Getting his entire crew off the island quickly was never part of the plan, but several could be protected depending on their status in the food chain.

"Big choppers here?"

"No, just yours," answered the security head. "They took the setup crew back to the mainland."

The Bell JetRanger would hold only four of them plus the pilot. That meant himself, Baxter, Julie, and one more. He peered around the control room and saw Goldy looking back at him suspiciously. Goldman had been a good friend and solid worker for many years.

He then looked at Eddie and Bella. Both had worked hard and were very loyal, but both had also made mistakes. It was a toss-up; he was unable to choose between the two.

Breckel didn't have time for this dilemma. He decided it would just be the three of them.

"I'm going to gather my things," he whispered as Goldman started to walk over. "Meet me at the jeep in ten minutes."

"And the crew?"

"If the military's coming, they're coming for me, not them. It's my ass that will fry."

This was mostly a lie and they both knew it. Many

on the crew would likely be prosecuted for their part in this, not to mention not get paid.

"Hi. What's up?" a suspicious Goldman asked.

Baxter said nothing and left. Goldman watched him go, not trusting the security chief for a second. This wasn't the first show they'd worked together. Baxter was deceptive, unethical, and dangerous. If half the stories about his history on the police force were to be believed, he was also capable of brutality and murder. Goldman had tried to persuade Breck to hire someone different for *The Condemned*, but he'd been overruled. *He's a good man*, Breck had said. *He gets the job done*.

Goldman knew about the navy jet flyover. He knew something was up.

"Not now, Goldy," said Breckel, walking toward his private tent at a quick clip.

Goldman followed right on his heels. "Going somewhere, Breck?"

He didn't reply, continuing on.

"Where the hell are you going? C'mon, I saw the plane that just flew over—are we being busted or something?"

Baxter was still within earshot and stopped in his tracks. Goldman was about to become a big problem.

Breckel was of a different mind as he appraised Goldy. His friend had folded under pressure, which had never happened before. Still, they had a lot of history between them. As they entered his private tent, he decided to give Goldy the benefit of the doubt and level with him.

"The navy's comin'?" Goldman erupted. "You can't just leave everyone here!"

"Keep your voice down, Goldy."

"You *promised* everyone," he said louder. "You'd pay us, protect us, take us with you . . ."

"Things have changed," he said as he hastily packed.

"Fuck that. I'll tell everyone. Bella, Eddie, Julie, everyone . . ."

Breckel immediately thought of Julie. Where was she? He had expected her to be in his tent.

"We're coming, or you've got a big fuckin' riot on your hands," Goldman jabbered on.

Breckel saw Baxter standing quietly in the doorway. The look in Baxter's eyes foreshadowed Goldman's future. Breckel was in a position to change Goldy's fate and he gave him one last chance.

"We have room for one more. I'll take you. Give you a million in cash."

Goldman was offended on many levels. He cared about all the others, but he also cared about what he was getting out of it. He'd sold his soul to do this show. They had a deal that included profit participation. Fair was fair. He was owed.

"A million? We talked about five percent of the gross. You owe me *millions*, not a million."

Goldy had just officially ceased to be worth caring about.

"You're a technician," the producer said coldly. "Below the line. Your memory must be hazy, because you don't get back end. Never did."

"You motherfucking son of a—"

Goldman moved on him, but Baxter was there in a flash. He ripped Goldman off the producer and punched him hard in the gut. Goldman doubled over, gasping for air.

Breckel and Baxter met eyes. No words were exchanged, the necessary task implicit. Breckel took one last look at the crumpled man on the floor, who at one time had served him well, but like all of his subordinates was just a tool in his shed. This one had not only gone dull but threatened to cause damage. It needed to go.

He gave Baxter a nod to confirm what had to be done, then returned to packing.

Baxter dragged Goldman out the rear of the tent, where no one could see. Goldman was just beginning to find his wind when he saw Baxter's military knife come out.

"Please," he managed to gasp.

Baxter put the knife against Goldman's throat as he struggled. The security chief had been watching people commit murder for the last thirty hours and had felt a pang of jealousy. As a cop in Florida, he'd rarely been able to treat suspects as they deserved, much less kill them on the spot. The private security business was a slight improvement, but still not at the satisfaction level of what he was about to do to Goldman.

Baxter's lust for murder had been compounded by not being able to personally kill Conrad. The Texan's elbow jab to his face had turned his cheek a nice shade of purple and he had longed to return the favor, and then some. Goldman didn't know it, but he was the unfortunate scapegoat for much of Baxter's frustrations.

More important, the sniveling technical director was about to blow the whistle on them. Goldman was tantamount to a government traitor. Traitors received the death penalty.

He shoved his knee into Goldman's diaphragm to cut off his wind and whining, and sliced open his throat. Baxter stood there and watched until his body went limp and his eyes glazed over. He felt a sense of satisfaction as well as a craving. It felt good . . . very good. But he wanted more.

32

When McStarley finished preening for the cameras, he decided it was high time to collect the fruits of his labor. He tossed his empty shotgun and retrieved the MP5. He was going to pay Breckel a visit and get the bomb off his leg, for starters. The timer was still ticking down, with fewer than twenty minutes till boom time.

Five minutes later he had climbed from the canyon to find a welcoming party of six guards, all armed with machine guns just like his.

"Drop your weapon!" one of them yelled.

McStarley paused, trying to calculate if he could take them all. It was an innate reflex, his desire to kill them purely instinctual. Some of them he recognized from the hangar. They were all in their twenties and looked inexperienced. Hell, even their leader had taken an elbow to the face.

"I said drop it!"

They surrounded him. The odds against him were too great. He set down his gun.

"You won. It's over," the guard told him.

McStarley was now glad he didn't shoot them,

which might have put a crimp in his deal with the producer. He'd already counted up the explosions and done the math but decided to play dumb. He wanted them to think he was stupid and underestimate him just in case the deal soured for some reason.

"It's over? Shit, boys, I was just beginning to enjoy myself."

"Breckel wants you back at the compound. Let's go."

They took his machine gun and patted him down, removing the knife strapped to his leg.

"Hope you got some cigars and brandy for me, boys." He grinned, fully cooperating. There was no reason not to now.

They arrived at the compound one minute after Baxter slit Goldman's throat. Breckel was coming out of his tent with a suitcase as the transport truck pulled up with his star. Two armed guards remained with their MP5s trained on the prisoner.

"Congratulations," Breckel said with no fanfare. "You won. You're free."

"How about taking this bomb off my leg, mate?" McStarley asked, still not fully trusting him. The timer had eight minutes left on it.

Breckel removed a silver chain from around his neck. A slender silver key dangled from it. He slid it into McStarley's ankle bracelet. The timer and LED lights all extinguished as the locking mechanism unlatched.

"Enjoy your life."

What the producer didn't tell him was that the navy

was on its way and he would most likely be reappre-
hended, but that didn't concern Breckel at the moment. He had a girlfriend to find and a helicopter to
catch.

McStarley pried the device off his leg, keeping a
careful eye on him.

"Don't take the piss so fast. Where's my fucking
money?"

Breckel reluctantly turned back. "Be happy with
what I'm giving you. You're a free man."

The limey's eyes narrowed. "Me and you had an
arrangement. I give you a good show. I win it. You
make me a free man. But a free man needs a big
bankroll, my friend. Me and you, we had a deal."

"The deal's whatever I want it to be," he said impatiently. "You won because I let you win." Breckel turned
to his guards. "Keep him here. I'll be right back."

He walked away, having no intention of ever
returning.

McStarley was seething but did an admirable job of
concealing it. He winked at the guards and shrugged
as if he was graciously conceding defeat.

"Hell, I'm a lucky man."

He watched Breckel go with a smile, raging inter-
nally. The psychopath wasn't about to let him get away
with it.

33

Conrad floated facedown in the lagoon as the cameras continued to record his demise.

He remained that way for nearly two minutes, slowly drifting into swampy, shallow water. By then the lenses had gotten their fill of him. The attention was now focused on McStarley on the ledge above.

Conrad had stopped breathing. His body was covered in blood and slime. There was a gash across his chest, buckshot embedded in his flesh, and an eyebrow split open from tumbling over the rocks. He was dead for all intents and purposes.

Out of the blackness came a dreamlike vision. He saw his father, but not on the beach at South Padre Island or at their old home in Granville. He was in full military uniform, floating in suspended animation with soft blues and greens glowing around his body. It was a tranquil, pleasing image. Maybe this was heaven. Maybe he was about to join his dad, whom he missed so much. Then the image came into better focus. His father was floating facedown in some kind of pool. The colors behind him were distorted reflections of the sky and jungle foliage.

His dad frowned and shook his head, as if to say *no*.

Suddenly his father's face became his own. Conrad was looking at himself.

He coughed underwater, rolled himself over, and expelled more liquid. Oxygen rushed into his lungs and revived his basic senses. It hurt to breathe, to move.

His blood started to flow again, much of it oozing from his battered body, but enough was pumping into his brain for him to realize he was still alive. He glanced around and it all came back. He was on an island. He was fighting for his life. He had a bomb on his ankle.

Conrad lifted his leg from the water. The dreaded timer read *00:15:26*. He had fifteen minutes left in a life that had already ended. Somehow he had come back from the other side, though it seemed pointless in his present condition.

And then he thought of Sarah.

Like a phoenix rising from its own ashes, Conrad pulled himself from the water and leaned against a tree, suppressing his agony. He saw McStarley in the distance, climbing out of the canyon.

Conrad's will to kill became even stronger than his will to live.

34

Julie had left the control room right after witnessing Conrad's death. To her, it signified the end of hope.

The last thirty hours had stripped away what little innocence she possessed about the state of the world in which she lived. She'd prayed Ian was wrong—wrong about everything—but in the end, he'd been right. Forty million people had paid to witness this horrible event, most of them no doubt cheering at Conrad's demise. It was like everything else that was wrong with society: news was twisted to heighten the entertainment value, wars were shaped to garner public support, and people were painted in strict shades of black and white to honor or vilify them. A handful of powerful people controlled the world's perception of global events, reducing the message to the lowest common denominator. Ian Breckel was one of these people. With power came a moral obligation to use it wisely, a fact he had blatantly ignored.

Unlike Goldman, she hadn't fully realized what she'd gotten herself into. Julie had been sold a bill of goods, seduced by a master. Death had been camouflaged in saturated colors and flashy graphics, the morality manipulated to justify the content. She didn't blame Ian completely, however. Her naïveté was to blame, along with a set of values that would forever be questioned in the wake of these events. Julie had once been a strong believer in capital punishment, but the last thirty hours had forced her to reconsider that conviction. She knew, unequivocally, that the unspeakable deaths she'd witnessed, along with her culpability, would haunt her for the rest of her life.

After the red X had appeared over Conrad's face, she wandered around the compound alternating between numbness and tears. Julie felt like a prisoner inside the razor-wired complex who had to escape, but the guards wouldn't let her "for her own safety." As far as she was concerned, it was no safer on the inside.

Gathering herself, she returned to the control room in search of Ian, who could authorize her departure. He was gone, busily packing for his own quick escape and allowing his best friend Goldman to be murdered, though she had no way of knowing this.

As she entered, the highlight reel played on the main monitor—a flashy spectacle of action and death that rivaled Hollywood's big-budget flicks. It seemed even more fictional out of context, like it had never really happened. These were actors and stunt doubles putting on sensational performances, with a dose of visual and sound effects to heighten the drama, not live human beings actually dying.

No one knew where Ian had gone, but Bella assured her that he would be back for the big wrap-up with Mc-Starley. Julie thanked Ian's young protégée and waited patiently by his chair. She just wanted to go home now. She was happy to leave by helicopter or boat or swim if she had to, just as long as it wasn't with him. The thought of even looking at him made her sick right now, but Ian called all the shots. He was her only ticket out of this place.

Breckel strode in a few minutes later with a suitcase in one hand and McStarley's ankle bracelet in the other. He'd just finished telling the criminal he was free but wasn't receiving any money for his troubles.

Bella saw him first. "What's goin' on?"

"Sit tight," Breckel replied, spotting Julie standing in the corner.

He walked past his leather lounge chair, which had functioned as his throne for the last day and a half, and set the deactivated bracelet on it.

Breckel moved to Julie and grabbed her arm, speaking in a hushed tone. "Come with me."

She pulled her arm away. "Don't touch me."

It had been a knee-jerk reaction. There was no way for her to suppress the disgust and repulsion she had for him. She'd wanted to calmly ask him to get her off this wretched island, but too much was bottled up— the deaths he had made her watch, the physical and emotional abuse, his arrogance in thinking he could order her to do anything he wanted . . . the combination of these transgressions was impossible to hold back.

Breckel saw everything in her face. Another outburst from her was imminent, one he didn't have time for.

He also noticed that his entire crew, including Bella and Eddie, was looking at him with confusion. They were supposed to do a big wrap-up. Where was Mc-Starley? Why did their boss have his suitcase?

He took one last look at Julie and headed for the back door without her. Julie—all of them—could be replaced.

"I'll be right back," he lied to everyone.

Breckel walked out and never returned.

Meanwhile, McStarley remained just outside, flanked by the armed guards. His infuriation at being screwed by Breckel was reaching its peak. He'd glimpsed the double-crossing asshole entering the control room but hadn't seen him leave.

The killer casually eyed the guards. One of them had a knife attached to his belt. The other was puffing on a cigarette.

He smiled genially at both of them.

"Got a spare smoke? You'd think I deserve one after the day I've had, lads." He chuckled.

The guard reached for his pack of smokes.

That was all the distraction the Special Forces killer needed. McStarley popped him in the face and snatched the other's knife in one seamless motion, stabbing him before he could fire. He spun and slashed the other's throat a split second later.

He reached down and grabbed one of the machine guns as another guard came around the corner. This guard received the gun stock directly in his face and went down in a heap.

McStarley eyed the control room tent with his

mind on retribution. He strolled inside and glanced around for Breckel, completely low-key. The producer was not in his immediate view.

Bella, closest to the entrance, noticed him with a moment of disorientation. The man she'd been watching on the plasma for hours upon hours was standing there in the flesh. Ironically enough, his face was currently plastered across multiple monitors as part of the highlights reel she had edited. It was like meeting a movie star. The fact that he was unescorted and holding a machine gun didn't register for several seconds.

He put a finger to his mouth, motioning for her to be quiet as he looked around for Breckel. Bella was too stunned to do anything but nod back.

JJ turned around and saw him. She screamed.

"SHUT UP, YOU UGLY BITCH—SHUT YOUR FUCKING MOUTH!" he howled. "One of you fucking twitches and I'll BLOW YOU AWAY."

The room froze in terror. The man killing people up on the screen was not an actor. He was real. And he was in the room.

McStarley paced through the tent interior, making sure that Breckel wasn't hiding somewhere like the yellow belly he was. It was easy for the big shot to hide behind his screens and make people die, mused the Brit. He was itching to give him a genuine sample of what it was like on the other side of that barbed wire.

He returned to Bella, pointing his barrel at her chest. "I'll start with you, four-eyes. Where is he?"

She was too shocked even to speak, his real-life presence having finally gelled in her consciousness.

"It's an easy question, princess. WHERE IS HE?"

"I d . . . d . . . don't know," she stuttered.

He opened fire and shot holes in her chest with no warning whatsoever. Bella was blown backward out of her chair, killed instantly.

Everyone screamed.

"NO!" shouted Eddie, rushing to her on the ground. He cradled her lifeless head and started to sob. The computer genius had never seen real violence before, had never witnessed death up close. Eddie was too young to have lost his parents or anyone close, so he didn't know anything about grief. He gazed at Bella's open, lifeless eyes and felt an invisible fist reach in and squeeze his heart. He and Bella had been close. They'd joined Breckel's team within weeks of each other and had worked on a half dozen shows together, both moving up the ladder with a good-natured rivalry. *The Condemned* had moved them both into key positions. As he held her, he thought of the show's send-off party where they drank champagne and toasted each other's success. She had even kissed him that night, though they were more like brother and sister and laughed it off the next day.

And now here she was, dead in his arms. His whole body shivered with an ache . . . and fear. Eddie gazed at the armed madman, who couldn't be deleted or shut down or reset to a different character.

"You want reality? THERE'S SOME FUCKING REALITY!" McStarley shouted at him, and everyone.

He moved to JJ, who had her hands in the air and was shaking.

"You! Where is he?"

"He left." She quivered.

"You're fuckin' pathetic."

He pulled his trigger and blew her into a bank of monitors.

As the others cried out, he opened fire on the entire room, blowing out monitors, equipment, and several other young technicians.

"HAVE I GOT YOUR FUCKING ATTENTION NOW?"

An intern ran for the door.

"Where're you going?"

McStarley maniacally grinned as he shot him down.

He gazed around the room at his carnage. It was just like those villages in Africa. An extermination free-for-all. It felt good to let loose with no fear of retaliation. He had no qualms about killing innocent people, much less these droids. They had all exploited him, had put him through some bloody hell to pad their pockets and beef up their résumés. Every one of them deserved it.

"What's your name, love?" he said to a tech cowering on the floor.

She cried out unintelligibly.

He shot her, too.

Two guards burst through the front entrance. McStarley mowed them down like dogs before they could even take aim.

Eddie was still cradling Bella's body as McStarley marched over to him.

"Get up."

Eddie couldn't move. His brain had crashed just like his computer systems did. He wanted to reboot, reformat his mind, erase everything that had just happened and reinstall a bug-free program. This wasn't supposed to happen. Characters didn't pop off the screen and kill their programmers.

"GET UP! BE A FUCKING MAN AND GET UP!" McStarley shrieked, pointing his barrel at Eddie's head.

Eddie let Bella slip from his arms. He staggered to his feet. He was crying hard and couldn't look at the killer.

"Look me in the eyes." McStarley seethed.

Eddie slowly tilted his head upward and came face-to-face with McStarley's grimy, sweaty, evil countenance. There was nothing in his gray pupils—no compassion, remorse, or sadness. Not even anger. It was something more primal, not of this earth. He was like an alien Eddie had done battle with in one of his virtual reality games. Its eyes had been dead, too.

The monster gestured with his barrel at the highlights reel still playing on the big monitor.

"You enjoy watching all this?"

Eddie reluctantly looked at the screen. McStarley was slashing Rosa, the murder having been vividly captured by a cameraman who was now deceased. To think he had enjoyed watching this earlier . . . how could he have become so detached? It took all of his self-control not to vomit.

He then looked around the control room. All of his

coworkers were dead. And Bella . . . Bella was gone, lying in a huge pool of her own blood.

Eddie began to heave with great sobs.

"Do you?" the killer goaded. "Enjoy watching death?"

"I'm sorry," Eddie finally managed.

"Too late for that, lad."

He gunned down Eddie with a flurry of bullets, just like the others. The young computer genius crumpled beside Bella, his own blood pooling into hers.

35

Conrad followed McStarley's route up through the canyon, every step an exercise in overcoming pain. His body was a bloody mess, but fortunately enough determination remained to propel him forward.

When he arrived on the plateau, he could see the top of the weather tower less than a mile away. There was little doubt that McStarley had been taken there. Conrad figured it would take him ten minutes to get to the compound in his present condition; any faster and too much blood would leak from his wounds. He looked at his timer. Exactly twelve minutes remained before it exploded. That gave him two minutes to find McStarley and kill him after he arrived, which wasn't enough.

Conrad alternated between a brisk stride and a jog as he made his way through the jungle. He lost some blood in the process, but when he arrived at Breckel's compound, he had five minutes and nine seconds left until detonation.

A burst of machine gun fire broke loose inside one of the tents. The two guards manning the entrance gate ran off. Conrad slipped in as more shots rang out.

He could hear screaming coming from inside the big tent.

It had to be McStarley.

Conrad ignored his condition and sprinted for the tent. He arrived just in time to see a technician appear in the doorway trying to escape. The kid was gunned down right in front of him. Two young guards ran into the tent a few moments later. They, too, were murdered in a flurry of bullets.

Conrad could easily hear McStarley from this distance as he ranted obscenities and shot more people.

He quickly looked around and spotted the pair of guards McStarley had stabbed by the transport truck. One of the guards had been relieved of his machine gun, which explained McStarley's weapon, but the other still had his MP5.

As Conrad reached down to grab it, a boot came out of nowhere and caught his chin, knocking him on his back.

It was Baxter. He pointed the barrel of his 9-mm semiautomatic pistol right between Conrad's eyes. "Don't move, redneck."

Baxter had glimpsed him entering the compound. He couldn't believe the Texan was still alive after what he'd seen on the screen, but here he was, coming back for more. Although Baxter couldn't wait to blow his face off, he was smart enough to know that his gunfire would draw McStarley's attention. He didn't want to battle the English madman any more than the next guy would, especially when the maniac was armed with a submachine gun.

One second later, Breckel came around the corner. It had crossed his mind to take off without Baxter after he'd heard the gunshots and screaming, but he was too afraid to leave without his muscle. He'd pissed off McStarley in a big way. As soon as the psychopath realized he wasn't in the control room, he would be coming after him. Breckel needed protection now more than ever.

He saw Conrad on the ground at the end of Baxter's barrel and was visibly surprised. This man simply refused to die.

"Thank you for the show," he said glibly.

"Show ain't over yet," Conrad replied as blood dripped from his chest.

There was another cry from inside the tent, followed by gunfire. The men hovering over him were going to do nothing about it.

"Let's go," Breckel said urgently. "McStarley will take care of him."

Baxter kept his barrel trained on Conrad. His desire to kill him was too great.

"Wait at the jeep. I'll be right there," he told Breckel.

Conrad craned his neck at Breckel as he started to leave. "I'm going to kill you."

The producer disregarded him and continued on.

Conrad then looked up at Baxter. "I'm going to kill you too, sweetheart."

Baxter almost laughed. "Yeah, whatever, asshole."

He'd barely finished the sentence when Conrad knocked aside his barrel and snapped Baxter's knee with his boot. The bearded man collapsed in agony, fumbling to regain control of his machine gun as Conrad overpowered him and wrestled the weapon away.

He shot the security chief with an efficient three-bullet burst in the chest, killing him instantly.

Breckel heard the shots and glanced back. He jumped into the jeep and raced away in a panic.

Conrad rose just in time to see him speeding off.

More shots rang out inside the tent.

Breckel would have to wait.

Inside the tent, McStarley gazed down at the body of Eddie, whom he had just murdered. He heard a short burst of gunfire outside and started to investigate it when movement in the back of the tent caught his eye.

Julie was standing there, the only one left.

The tall, lithe blonde was terrified down to her marrow knowing she was about to die like the others. Although her eyes were welling, she maintained her dignity, refusing to break down and beg for her life. At this point she felt tremendous guilt for being a part of this slaughter-for-entertainment. If this was her fate, she was willing to accept it.

McStarley knew who she was and smiled. If anybody knew where Breckel had gone, the boss's concubine would. He'd get the information out of her, all right, and have a ripping good time doing it. McStarley paced to her with a widening grin.

He saw a flicker in her eyes, like she had just seen a ghost behind him.

331

Suddenly he knew they were not alone, but it was too late. The barrel was already pressing against his spine.

McStarley held perfectly still. It was probably another guard, or maybe that flunky Baxter. He would bide his time and then spring on him. They were all so fucking stupid it would be easy.

Conrad reached around and took the MP5 away from him, tossing it.

"Sit."

He shoved McStarley into Breckel's leather lounge chair as the highlights played on the monitor opposite him.

When McStarley saw it was Conrad, he went sheet white. The American was back from the grave.

"Take it easy, Yank," he fumbled out. McStarley nervously eyed his butchery on the screen. "I didn't volunteer for this. No one got nothing they didn't deserve. I certainly didn't want to fight you."

"Bullshit," the Texan replied matter-of-factly, keeping Baxter's pistol carefully trained.

"No. It's not bullshit . . ."

Conrad could see he was starting to sweat. McStarley's eyes were no longer dead, either. They were very alive. With fear.

"The military sent me to every hellhole on this earth to do their killing," he anxiously rattled in a high-pitched tone. "And then they disown me. Four years in an African prison, I take it up the ass twice a day by the fucking natives. THAT'S BULLSHIT."

His eyes were starting to water.

Conrad appraised him. "Sounds like you've had a hard life."

McStarley nodded. He knew the American had a soft spot.

"Yeah . . ."

"Good thing it's over."

Conrad emptied the entire clip of Baxter's 9-mm semiautomatic into McStarley's body.

36

They stared at each other for several seconds as the pistol smoke drifted up over McStarley's perforated corpse. Julie still didn't know all the details of Conrad's life, but his actions had spoken volumes. He was almost superhuman in her eyes, having somehow risen from the dead to make it back here and save her life. While Jack Conrad was a man capable of killing if the situation warranted it, he was also selfless and compassionate.

As she searched for the right words to thank him, the distant thud of Breckel's chopper starting up broke the silence.

Both were thinking the same thing when they heard it: *He's getting away.*

Besides the convicts who'd been slaughtered for his pocketbook and ego, Breckel had abandoned his loyal staff in their greatest time of need. He'd delivered McStarley to the compound and given him the impetus to kill, then turned tail without the slightest regard for anyone's life but his own. It was the same as if he had pulled the trigger himself.

Conrad grabbed McStarley's machine gun and ran

out the door, collecting another from a fallen guard along the way.

Julie stood there watching him go, realizing she had been passive for too long. All the bodies strewn around her were dead because of Ian; he'd left her to be murdered as well. She couldn't let him get away with this either. It was time to act.

Meanwhile, Conrad's intense desire for vengeance and justice fueled him as he sprinted out the compound gate. The overgrown trail was all uphill, but he willed himself on. He could hear the chopper blades revving up. It hadn't taken off yet.

The jungle road ended at the sheer edge of a bluff that fell nearly two hundred feet to the rocky coastline below. The last time he'd seen this side of the island was from the air when he'd been delivered here.

Breckel's jeep had been ditched at the end of the trail. A hundred yards farther up the ridge, his JetRanger was perched at the bluff precipice, waiting to lift off. The producer was hiking on a steep, narrow path toward it with his suitcase.

Conrad ran for all he was worth.

Breckel glanced over his shoulder, expecting to see Baxter. His eyes expanded when he saw Conrad sprinting after him. Breckel ran as fast as he could and quickly climbed in the helicopter. He frantically gestured for the pilot to lift off with the door open. As Breckel buckled up, the helicopter blades rotated faster and the aircraft slowly rose.

Every wound on his body was oozing blood as

Conrad raced on. Refusing to give up, he opened fire on the metal bird with both machine guns blazing.

The chopper was already thirty meters off the ground when the bullets pelted its underbelly. A side window shattered, spraying Breckel with Plexiglas. A second later the front windscreen and console were perforated with lead.

The pilot started to lose control. The chopper dropped altitude and rotated counterclockwise as Conrad emptied both magazines of his MP5s into it. Bullets sparked off the fuselage and shattered the remaining side windows, using up the last of his ammo. He wanted to shoot out the tail rotor and force a crash, but the angle was wrong.

The battered Bell was now hovering over the jagged coastline at eye level with Conrad. He could see Breckel clearly as the pilot tried to stabilize his craft. The producer was in a sheer panic as the chopper rocked back and forth.

All Conrad could do now was wait to see if it crashed.

Out of the corner of his eye he saw Julie running up the trail. She was holding something.

He looked back at the helicopter, which had stopped bouncing and was beginning to stabilize.

The pilot, like everyone else who'd signed on to this job, had never expected to be shot at. A retired marine, the pilot had served in Vietnam but hadn't seen combat since the late sixties. His blood pressure was rising with concern, but also excitement. The war vet wished he was piloting his old HU-IA Huey, in which case he'd mow that bald bastard down with a pair of 30-caliber guns and then blow him off the bluff with a 2.75-inch rocket, neither of which this civilian bird came equipped with. For now he put aside his war flashbacks and focused on keeping them airborne. The JetRanger had suffered some damage but nothing fatal. Fuel was leaking, communications were down, and the altimeter had been shot out, but the rotors were A-okay. He could probably limp them back to Papua New Guinea using visual references, just like the old days in 'Nam.

Breckel squeezed the pilot's shoulder, still panicked. "We good?"

"Good enough to get us back to the mainland," he shouted over the rotor noise, which was extraloud with the windscreen gone.

Breckel sighed with huge relief. He composed himself, looking out his open door at Conrad just as Julie ran up and joined him.

Now that he was safe, his expression reverted to that of the arrogant megalomaniac. Breckel met their gazes as the chopper began to regain altitude, offering them a smug smile and a little wave good-bye. *Fuck you, assholes*, his expression said. *I won. I always win.*

Julie stared back icily. Running up here, she hadn't known if she could go through with this, but now there was no doubt in her mind.

She handed Conrad what she had brought: McStarley's security bracelet.

The silver pin was still in it. Julie reached over and pulled it. The timer instantly reactivated, ticking down from *00:2:41*.

Conrad looked at her. He understood what it took for her to do this and his face told her as much.

He pulled the red activation tab. The clock disappeared, replaced by the timer ticking down from ten seconds.

Conrad waited five seconds and then heaved it into the air with every ounce of his remaining strength.

Breckel's sick device sailed through the open door of the cockpit and landed behind his seat.

The telltale beeps told the producer exactly what it was. Sheer terror flooded his face as he scrambled to unclasp his seat belt and get to the device. His mouth and eyes were agape in horror as his fingers caressed the bomb, but it was just out of reach.

The last thing he saw was the timer turning from one to zero.

The Bell exploded in a massive fireball, its remains careening into the treacherous face of the bluff. Flaming shrapnel rained down over the craggy rocks into the crashing sea below, sending thick black smoke into the onshore wind.

Conrad and Julie watched the spectacular death of Ian Breckel almost numbly. Her emotions had already been used up and he was half dead himself.

Julie took a long, hard look at the man who had saved her life. Now it was her turn to save his. She handed Conrad the silver key and found her eyes beginning to well.

Conrad took it from her wordlessly. He reached down and slid in the pin. The timer and lights went out on his bracelet and the locking mechanism snapped open.

They both looked at each other for several long moments.

He found himself nodding.

Julie drifted back down the path.

Conrad watched her go and then looked back at the smoldering wreckage below.

He was bloody, beaten, and exhausted, but he was a free man.

Epilogue

Nobody at the Blue Boot Bar & Grill knew that Jack was alive. They thought they'd seen him die in the bunker explosion, only to inexplicably resurrect himself to take on Go Saiga, the Japanese convict, as well as the sadistic Englishman McStarley. When Jack had jumped into the gorge, there was silent speculation that he hadn't survived this either, but his reappearance in the rock canyon made him seem invincible once again.

Seeing him floating facedown with his body soaked in blood after repeated blasts from McStarley's shotgun removed all of their hope. There was no room for speculation about trapdoor escapes or jumping into pools. They had seen him die, live and in vivid color. They all watched the red X go over his picture. Jack Riley was gone.

The highlights reel played for a few minutes before Farland shut off the TV. If he had left it on, they would've seen the webcast turn to snow when McStarley's machine gun tirade in the control room blew apart the satellite transmission feed. Forty million viewers out there were pissed they didn't get a final interview with McStarley or some type of closure to help justify the fifty bucks they'd shelled out.

Sarah wasn't a drinker, but Mike insisted she have a glass of whiskey at the end. She found herself drinking it, though it might as well have been water. No amount of alcohol would ever dull her grief.

An hour later she hugged Mike and several others good-bye and drove home, tearful the entire way. She had no idea that at this exact same moment, thousands of miles away, Navy SEALs were arriving via helicopter to rescue Jack, who was battered but very much alive.

Special Agent Wilkins had also watched the black ops hero be murdered at the hands of Ewan McStarley, as well as when the webcast inexplicably turned to static thanks to McStarley's control room murder spree. Like the rest of the world, Wilkins assumed Conrad was dead and spent the next hour commiserating with fellow staffers while halfheartedly keeping tabs on the SEALs' operation. His only satisfaction at this point would be to bust Ian Breckel for being an accessory to murder and any Internet content crimes he could drum up against the man.

His jaw dropped when he heard the news.

"He's alive?"

The SEALs captain confirmed it over the satellite phone. Conrad was being treated by a medic but would pull through. Wilkins was also told that the former military hero had killed McStarley in self-defense according to a female eyewitness and that Ian Breckel's helicopter had crashed shortly after he'd made an attempt to escape.

The eyewitness had been Julie, of course, though Wilkins wouldn't meet her face-to-face for another day when his office and the Justice Department questioned her.

Wilkins hung up elated. He started to tell the others and then stopped himself. There was someone who deserved to know first.

When the phone rang at the Blue Boot, Brad Burdick picked it up. Burdick told the man on the other end that Sarah had gone home. Wilkins almost told him the incredible news but decided to wait until he spoke with Sarah personally. It was rare in his job to be able to deliver a message as amazing as this, and he didn't want Sarah to hear it thirdhand.

When he called Sarah's house, her voice mail picked up. He left her a message to call him, saying only that it was extremely important.

Brad Wilkins was beaming when he hung up. He couldn't wait for her to call back, though it would take longer than he expected.

When Sarah pulled into her gravel driveway, her boys were playing on a rope swing that dangled from an old oak in the field. She waved at them, hiding her face. Her lids were almost swollen shut from crying. The last time Michael and Scotty had seen their mother in this kind of shape was when Jack had left them. Back then they'd also started to cry, and she didn't want to trigger any of those old feelings. At some point she would have to tell them what happened to him, but that time wasn't now.

She walked up the wooden stairs onto the porch as Karen came out, who took one look at her daughter and knew it hadn't turned out good.

They were hugging each other with tears flowing as the phone rang. Neither bothered to answer it.

Special Agent Wilkins's voice came out of the tinny answering machine, urgently asking her to call him. Sarah couldn't hear all of it from the porch and didn't want to. The last thing she needed right now was to be questioned by the FBI. She went inside, unplugged the phone, and collapsed on the couch.

Twelve hours passed before she woke up. In the daze between sleep and consciousness, everything was okay. And then it hit her again. Jack was dead. She started to cry. Pulled herself together. *Stop it*, she told herself. She needed to get on with her life, for the sake of her kids if nothing else.

Sarah sent her mother home and spent the next day with her sons. They played tag, tended to farm chores, did some homework. The phone remained unplugged.

Dinnertime came around and Sarah decided to make navy beans and ham hocks. It had been one of Jack's favorite dishes. It was her way of mourning him.

"Why are you crying, Mommy?" probed Scotty.

"I'm just happy that I got you two," she said, blotting her eyes with the tea towel.

That was good enough for Scotty, who then tackled his big brother. Normally she would've put an end to the roughhousing, but not tonight. If Jack had been here, he would've been in the middle of it.

She heard a car engine pulling up her drive, its tires

crunching on the gravel. She wasn't in the mood for visitors and kept on cooking. The vehicle kept idling for fifteen seconds or so, and then it sounded like it was driving off again.

Sarah moved to a window and glimpsed an army Humvee turning back onto Farm Road and heading toward Granville. Maybe they had dropped off a package, possibly personal effects belonging to Jack that he had wanted her to have. Why didn't they at least knock? Something wasn't right. She opened the screen door, stepping onto the porch.

Sarah practically fainted.

Jack was standing there holding the same duffel he had left with a year earlier. He was wearing a clean white T-shirt, jeans, and work boots. There were stitches above his left eye and bandages on his arms.

When he saw her, he began to feel again. His wounds all ached, but not like his insides. He had been hurting for a long time. Ever since he left here.

Michael and Scotty came onto the porch and saw him.

"Jack! Jack's home!" they screamed.

Sarah continued to stare at him. She thought she was all cried out. She was wrong.

Jack met her eyes, telling her everything she needed to know in his faint, weary smile.

He was finally home.

Rob Hedden is an award-winning writer, producer, and director of numerous movies and television shows. Among his credits are *Clockstoppers*, for which he also wrote the novelization; *Friday the 13th Part VIII: Jason Takes Manhattan*; *Star Trek: Enterprise*; *The Twilight Zone* and *Alfred Hitchcock Presents* revivals; *The Commish*; *MacGyver*; and *Boxboarders!*